S0-BAT-243

I HAD TO FIND A HIDING PLACE . . .

I rolled under a round table and stuffed a fist into my mouth. I heard the footsteps coming closer . . . then stop. A tense silence told me my assailant was listening.

Please go on . . . please go on . . . But this time my prayer wasn't answered. I saw the tablecloth twitch . . . then it was jerked up. As I scrambled out from under the table, a knife blade sliced across my arm.

No place to run now. I was trapped. My strength was running out. I had to do something before I fainted.

I don't remember how I made it to the front door. I only know that I could hear the heavy breathing behind me, almost feel it on my neck. I only had a few more yards to go when the door swung open. Daniel stared at me as I stumbled forward into his outstretched arms.

"Darling, what . . . ?" He stopped when he saw the blood. "Dear God."

I opened my mouth but a wave of weakness like a black fog invaded my body and I floated away like a speck on a gray horizon . . .

SUSPENSE IS A HEARTBEAT AWAY —
Curl up with these Gothic gems.

THE PRECIOUS PEARLS OF CABOT HALL   (3754, $3.99/$4.99)
by Peggy Darty

Recently orphaned Kathleen O'Malley is overjoyed to discover her long-lost relatives. Uncertain of their reception, she poses as a writer's assistant and returns to her ancestral home. Her harmless masquerade hurls Kathleen into a web of danger and intrigue. Something sinister is invading Cabot Hall, and even her handsome cousin Luke can't protect her from its deadly pull. Kathleen must discover its source, even if it means losing her love . . . and her life.

BLACKMADDIE   (3805, $3.99/$4.99)
by Jean Innes

Summoned to Scotland by her ailing grandfather, Charlotte Brodie is surprised to find a family filled with resentment and spite. Dismissing her drugged drink and shredded dresses as petty pranks, she soon discovers that these malicious acts are just the first links in a chain of evil. Midnight chanting echoes through the halls of her family estate, and a curse cast centuries ago threatens to rob Charlotte of her sanity and her birth right.

DARK CRIES OF GRAY OAKS   (3759, $3.99/$4.99)
by Lee Karr

Brianna Anderson was grateful for her position as companion to Cassie Danzel, a mentally ill seventeen year old. Cassie seemed to be the model patient: quiet, passive, obedient. But Dr. Gavin Rodere knew that Cassie's tormented mind held a shocking secret — one that her family would silence at any cost. As Brianna tries to unlock the terrors that have gripped Cassie's soul, will she fall victim to its spell?

**THE HAUNTED HEIRESS OF WYNDCLIFFE
MANOR**   (3911, $3.99/$4.99)
by Beverly C. Warren

Orphaned in a train wreck, "Jane" is raised by a family of poor coal miners. She is haunted, however, by fleeting memories and shadowy images. After escaping the mines and traveling across England with a band of gypsies, she meets the man who reveals her true identity. She is Jennifer Hardwicke, heiress of Wyndcliffe Manor, but danger and doom await before she can reclaim her inheritance.

WHITE ROSES OF BRAMBLEDENE   (3700, $3.99/$4.99)
by Joyce C. Ware

Delicate Violet Grayson is hesitant about the weekend house party. Two years earlier, her dearest friend mysteriously died during a similar gathering. Despite the high spirits of old companions and the flattering attention of charismatic Rafael Taliaferro, her apprehension grows. Tension throbs in the air, and the housekeeper's whispered warnings fuel Violet's mounting terror. Violet is not imagining things . . . she is in deadly peril.

Available wherever paperbacks are sold, or order direct from the Publisher. Send cover price plus 50¢ per copy for mailing and handling to Zebra Books, Dept. 4164, 475 Park Avenue South, New York, N.Y. 10016. Residents of New York and Tennessee must include sales tax. DO NOT SEND CASH. For a free Zebra/Pinnacle catalog please write to the above address.

LEE KARR

THE DARK SECRET OF HUNTERS HALL

ZEBRA BOOKS
KENSINGTON PUBLISHING CORP.

ZEBRA BOOKS

are published by

Kensington Publishing Corp.
475 Park Avenue South
New York, NY 10016

Copyright © 1993 by Lee Karr

All rights reserved. No part of this book may be reproduced
in any form or by any means without the prior written
consent of the Publisher, excepting brief quotes used in
reviews.

Zebra and the Z logo are trademarks of Kensington Publishing Corp.

If you purchased this book without a cover you should be
aware that this book is stolen property. It was reported as
"unsold and destroyed" to the Publisher and neither the
Author nor the Publisher has received any payment for this
"stripped book."

First Printing: May, 1993

Printed in the United States of America

Chapter One

The minute I saw the jeweled brooch, I knew I was going to steal it. The woman sitting beside me in the swaying narrow-gauge train had made it so easy. All I did was wait until the warmth of the passenger car caused her to fling back the short summer cape she wore over her high-necked traveling dress. Pinned to the lapel of the black lace cape, the exquisite gold brooch hung casually to one side, almost rubbing against me in the narrow seat.

If she had been more perceptive, the fashionably dressed woman might have noticed my gaze fastened upon her jewels, but she had shown little interest in me upon my entering the train at the Colorado Springs depot. Her irritated glance as I took the only seat left, which happened to be the aisle seat beside her, was the only acknowledgment she had made of my presence. Graying raven hair showed from under a felt hat turned up high in front and trimmed with blue feathers and black satin ribbons. Tiny wrinkles radiated from narrow black eyes; the woman's forehead was furrowed with permanent lines. She sat erect, her feet placed properly together, her waist tightly laced to a modest span. Her gray dress was of

China crepe trimmed with gold embroidery and cutwork on the bodice and sleeves. She wore pearl-gray gloves and had a matching parasol at her side. Her opulent attire was a sharp contrast to my serviceable traveling dress of blue striped faille and modest straw bonnet.

"What kind of town is this Brimstone, Colorado?" she had demanded of the porter as he swung my portmanteau on the rack above our seats. My trunk had been deposited at the front of the train. "It must be no more than a wide spot in the road."

"You might say that, ma'am," the gray-haired man agreed. "All kinds of little towns have sprung up in these foothills, some growing out of the gold camps of a few years back. Nowadays, people are turning to ranching and other things since the prospecting fever is over. Brimstone's lucky enough to have a half dozen mineral springs that are supposed to be good for what ails ya. Becoming quite the summer resort, it is. The Saratoga of the West, some call it."

The woman snorted. "Well, I can't believe my sister has chosen to reside in such an uncivilized part of the country. Kansas City was bad enough, but now this. Brimstone . . ." She wrinkled up her imperious slender nose. "Even the name is distasteful."

Her derision made my stomach muscles tighten. I had been born and raised in Brimstone, Colorado, at the foot of the Rockies. Until five years ago I had never known anything else. A hasty glance around the crowded car upon my entrance had assured me that no one recognized me after my five-year absence. I took a deep breath and tried to relax. I was not ready for raised eyebrows, gaping mouths, or wagging tongues. Every mile of clacking iron wheels and

6

belching smoke brought me closer to a past I had tried to leave behind. The voices in my head started up again in rhythm with the laboring engine of the train as we pulled out of Colorado Springs. *The Banning girl? A peculiar family—one of them murdered, I believe. Strange the way she ran away.* My mouth went dry; I moved my tongue in an effort to moisten it. My hands clutched the chain of my beaded bag tightly as I gazed unseeing out the train windows.

"Disgusting, really." The woman's voice intruded upon my troubling thoughts. "Nothing but craggy cliffs and barren terrain fit for wild beasts." Her scathing eyes darted to two men dressed in buckskins who were sitting across the aisle. One of them had a chaw of tobacco bulging his cheek. Her nostrils quivered. "I don't know how I will endure a whole summer in this Godforsaken place. Brimstone must be the end of the line."

I shook my head. "The train runs up the canyon to Deadman Gulch, about forty miles farther into the mountains."

"Deadman Gulch," she echoed. "How apt. Is that where you're going?"

"No. I'm going to Brimstone."

The woman eyed me with sudden interest. "Do you know my sister, Nina Milburne, and her son, Brian? Her husband owned the bank before his death."

"Yes, I know the family," I answered evenly, though my heart began to beat rapidly in my chest upon hearing the Milburne name. Unwittingly, my eyes fell upon the woman's lovely brooch, a gold basket filled with flowers of rubies, pearls, opals. I was mesmerized by its beauty, and the warmth and contentment its possession promised.

Driven by a need that I didn't understand and couldn't control, I directed the woman's attention out the window. "See the dramatic outcroppings of red sandstone? The ponderosa pines look like green velvet against the cliffs, don't they? And high up, there's a cluster of summer cabins built along the ridge. Can you see them?" I leaned into her, gesturing with one hand while deftly loosening the clasp on her lapel pin with the other. "And down there at the bottom of the ravine . . . Can you see the narrow stream that follows the tracks? Devil's Creek runs right through the center of Brimstone. The air is cool in the mountain canyons even on the Fourth of July . . . unlike the sultry summers of the East Coast."

"Well, I certainly hope so," she responded, and then firmly pushed me back. "No use sitting on top of each other." She fanned herself. "It's frightfully warm in this miserable train. How much longer must we endure this appalling discomfort?"

"We're over halfway there," I said.

"Thank heavens." The woman took out a small leatherbound book from a crocheted bag and began reading, not about to encourage any more of my tourist-guide ramblings.

I drew back, smiling contentedly as I opened and shut my beaded reticule. With a deep sigh of satisfaction, I looped its chain over my arm and let my head lean back against the seat. For the moment, all emptiness inside me was gone. An aching need had been appeased.

I didn't need to look out the window to see the landscape sweeping by. I knew well the intense blue skies, jagged snow-capped peaks that sent banks of cool air down wooded slopes into emerald green mountain valleys. Eagles and hawks swooped down grandly from rocky precipices. Like a migratory bird, I was returning to the place I belonged. I had been twenty years old when I fled, and had grown older in my five-year absence . . . much older! With a bitter sense of defiance I made a silent vow: "Deanna Banning has come home again. To stay."

Chapter Two

The shrill whistle of the train and billows of steam rising up into the blue sky heralded our arrival at the Brimstone depot. The flow of departing passengers carried me out of the crowded car, and as I descended the steps, I was almost blinded by the bright sunlight.

Through the bustle of the crowd, I heard a familiar voice call my name. "Deanna!"

When I shaded my eyes and saw my brother waving to me, I hurried through the crowd and into his open arms. "Steven," was all I said and my voice was barely more than a sob. He hugged me close and then held me away from him. Tears were running down my cheeks; embarrassed at my sudden display of emotion, I murmured something about the bright sunlight.

"Still as pretty as a picture," he said smilingly.

I dabbed at my eyes with my gloved hand and studied him. There were hardly any physical signs to confirm I'd been away at all. His eyes were the same, still warm, still gentle. His angular frame was still slender, and his hands felt the same in mine as they had in childhood. Steven and I were fraternal twins. We shared fair hair that had been almost white in

11

childhood, and blue eyes tinged with green.

Our half-brother, Walter, had inherited our father's robust stature and strong features, features that were as bold as his behavior. Eight years older than Steven and me, Walter had done as he pleased. We had learned not to interfere with his pleasure while we were growing up. Strong, willful, able to command men and women alike, my half-brother hadn't been the kind of man one would have expected to end up with a knife in his back.

"How wonderful to see you," I said happily. "How are Elizabeth and the children?"

"Fine. Wait until you see the two little ones. You're going to love Patty and Nicky. They're absolutely the smartest, most beautiful little girl and boy in the whole world." He grinned. "My unbiased opinion, of course."

"Of course," I agreed, laughing.

"It's good to have you home again, Dee."

"Yes," I breathed. Satisfaction welled up from deep within me. In the bright sunlight of the June day, all my fears seemed to have fled. No specters remained to haunt me, no shadows to cover me, no loneliness threatened. A warmth within me penetrated the cold chambers of my soul. I'd made the right decision, after all. Why had I ever doubted it?

"Come on. I'll send someone to collect your trunk later," Steven said. "I brought the buggy. Thought you might want to take a quick tour of town before we head home." With this last statement he frowned. "I guess I ought to warn you. Elizabeth is having some kind of to-do this afternoon for a new minister. I hate to take you into a gathering like that right off, but Elizabeth had this all planned before . . ." His voice trailed off.

"I understand," I said in an unconvincing tone. "I have to face them all sometime. Might as well get it over with." I hoped my outward manner would compensate for the sick feeling developing in the pit of my stomach. We took a few steps down the platform; I was attempting to quell this new flood of anxiety when I felt a hand on my arm.

"Deanna! Is it really you?"

I turned to face Brian Milburne and the woman who had sat beside me on the train. I should have expected that Brian might be meeting his aunt.

"Hello, Brian." I hoped my smile came off as genuine. I had known that this moment would come—but I had hoped I'd have time to prepare for it!

"I must be dreaming. I can't believe it." Once there had been a shyness about his crooked grin, but now his lips curved boldly without hesitation. His shoulders had broadened and the gray business suit he wore matched the derby that topped his dark head. His manner was polished and less spontaneous than I remembered, but then he must find me changed too, I thought under his gaze.

His voice was still warm and deep. "Steven didn't tell me you were coming."

"I didn't send him a telegram until the last moment."

"I can't believe you've come back. Welcome home." He seemed to mentally take himself in tow. "Have you met my aunt, Della Danvers?"

"Not formally," I said.

His aunt gave a perfunctory nod to me and Steven as Brian introduced us, and then she said impatiently, "I do think we'd best be seeing about my luggage, Brian."

"Yes, of course," he said, continuing to stare at me.

13

"I just can't believe it, but it must be you . . . no one else can match those blue-green eyes and that cornsilk hair."

"You haven't lost your command of pretty speeches, I see." I felt slightly dizzy. A reaction to seeing Brian again? Or did the giddiness arise out of a flood of relief? Perhaps my return wasn't going to be the nightmare I had anticipated. I might be safe and secure, after all. I smiled into his handsome face. "Are you at the bank?"

"Yes. My father passed away last year, so Milburne Bank and Land Office is my responsibility now."

"I'm so sorry about your loss."

"And what about you? Are you still governess for that New York family? The Lowensteins, wasn't it?"

"Not anymore. The children are old enough for boarding school. I've come home—to stay." I hoped the words didn't sound too defiant.

"I'm so glad. Some of us are planning an outing at Hunters Glen. It will be great fun, a wagon ride and plenty of baskets loaded with food and lemonade. You'll have to come."

I was grateful for his exuberance, but fully cognizant of the time and distance between us. "Thanks for the invitation, but I'm planning on staying close to home." I slipped my arm through Steven's. "Have to catch up on the time I've missed."

"We really should be going," Steven said. "Elizabeth will be expecting us."

"My mother is having tea at Hunters Hall this afternoon," said Brian. "Some folderol for the new minister. That's why I'm in charge of getting Aunt Della settled."

"And I suggest we cease this dawdling and be on our way," the woman responded curtly, twirling her parasol impatiently. "I assume you have a carriage

14

waiting, Brian?" With these words she took her leave; Brian shrugged and smiled.

"I'm glad you're back, Deanna," he said, squeezing my arm before turning to follow his aunt.

I smoothed my dress with the palms of my hands. How well I knew that confident gait of his. I remembered how when we'd go out walking together I had always felt proud that he preferred my company to a dozen other young ladies vying for his attention.

"Sorry about that, sis," Steven said as he helped me into a black buggy. He took the seat beside me and directed a sleek sorrel mare into a quick trot down Shoshone Avenue.

I let my body slump back into the tufted leather seat. "It had to happen sooner or later," I replied, taking a deep breath. "He hasn't married?"

"No. Been engaged since last Christmas, though." Steven shot an anxious glance at me. "Heading for an August wedding, I hear."

"Who?"

"Carolyn Lareau, daughter of a Denver businessman. Investments of some kind. Plenty of money, I guess. Carolyn and her mother have been spending the last few summers at the Miramonte Hotel, taking the waters and enjoying the social whirl. Seems like a nice young woman." Steven again glanced at me worriedly. "She'll be at the house, too. I'm sorry, Dee . . . I really am."

I felt the color drain from my face, but I gave him a reassuring smile. "Don't you worry about me. Now, tell me all about yourself."

"Nothing much to tell. The same old thing. Nothing changes, really. A few more buildings have gone up in Brimstone. The same horde of visitors take the waters in the summer. More saloons and gambling houses are prospering across the tracks."

I glanced from one side of the street to the other as the buggy rolled down Shoshone Avenue. The small buildings crowded together along the street looked the same to me, except for the addition of a high false front on the livery stable and some new paint on the saddle shop. A few new attractions reminded me of the boardwalk in Atlantic City—there were tawdry souvenirs for sale, penny arcades, and taffy shops. At one time I'd thought the sprawling Miramonte Hotel must be the biggest building in the whole world: four stories tall, pretentious towers on the east and west wings, and a wide porch offering an excellent view of the health seekers and visitors promenading along the main avenue. Now that I'd seen the mammoth structures of New York City, the Miramonte didn't seem so very formidable.

"The Miramonte has hot and cold water in the bath houses on each floor now. Joe and Sabrina have redecorated the dining room and hired a chef straight from Kansas City," Steven said proudly.

I smothered a smile. In my duties as governess to the Lowenstein children, I had taken electricity, hot water, and delectable meals for granted. I'd forgotten how provincial the small town of Brimstone really was. The park across the street from the hotel was dwarfed in comparison with the one of my childhood memory of green lawns and tall cottonwood trees that seemed to stretch for miles along the river. Several mineral springs in the city park had been covered with stone gazebos in my absence, and some new gardens had been laid out along familiar walks. Red sandstone hills cupping the town were dotted with more summer cottages. But Brimstone was the same as ever aside from these things—it

16

was I who was different.

"Well, there's the store," said Steven with a nod of his head.

Our family name was spread across a four-window expanse, THE BANNING DEPARTMENT STORE. I had always been proud of my father's business. I carried a memory of Banning's as a huge mercantile store offering only the best in stylish clothes, delicate china, cut glassware, and fashionable merchandise matching that sold in city stores. When Papa had been alive, he had made trips to New York every year to order merchandise, and had prided himself on serving a discriminating public for miles around. I had always thought the store offered the finest and most fashionable items around. Had I been mistaken—or had the store changed?

Steven slowed the horse to a walk and looked at me anxiously, waiting for my reaction. "Well, what do you think?"

In every case, the window displays were overcrowded, lacking aesthetic balance. I couldn't see that any effort had been made to offer a pleasing arrangement. As many items were displayed in the windows as space would allow. Stiff mannequins wore colorless gowns and bonnets far behind the fashion trends. Bolts of material fought for space with items like dishes and pans, while tools, boots, and tobacco tins were as arbitrarily arranged.

I sighed deeply, and Steven translated this as my approval. "I can't take the credit for it," he said. "Millie runs the store. I've given her a free hand to do what she wants."

I remembered Mildred Dillworthy as a sturdy, colorless young girl whom Papa had hired as a clerk before he died. She was orphaned at sixteen; her parents had kept a store in one of the mining camps

17

and had not survived a particularly harsh winter. Walter had kept Millie on after Papa died and moved her into the office. My half-brother had said that Millie had more business sense than any man. Apparently Steven had given her even more responsibility after Walter was killed. She must be close to thirty now, I thought. I wondered if she was still the hardy, plain-faced woman she'd been when I left.

"Millie wanted to be at the house today to greet you, but someone had to stay and keep the store open," Steven said, frowning. "I think Millie's about to marry Harold Haines. He's a bookkeeper and a lot older than she is but they've been going to church together for nearly a year. He's a deacon at the Methodist church. I don't know what I'll do without her." The look on his face was almost apologetic. "You know how I've always hated the store."

"Yes, I know," I said. I remembered Papa's broad face flushed with fury and his agitated movements as he railed at young Steven. *Built that store from nothing. Nothing!* Papa had yelled. *Put my life into it and you don't give a damn! Not a goddamn! Oh, you like money to spend . . . expensive clothes, violins, newfangled stuff. But work? Hell, no. Good honest sweat makes you sick. Well, thank God for Walter. Thank God for one son to keep a man's life from going down the drain. . . .*

I raised my hand and pressed my fingers against my temples to drown out the voice.

"I've always hated the store," Steven repeated defensively.

"I know. I know. Then why didn't you sell it, Steven, after—after Walter's death? I would have gladly given up my share. I mean, I ran out—why did you stay?"

"Elizabeth."

18

Of course that would be the reason. Elizabeth wouldn't let him sell. She had married Steven when he was eighteen and was nine years his senior. She'd been raised on a ranch a few miles out of town and her marriage had brought her the one thing she wanted most—a social position in the town.

"After things blew up the way they did, I should have thought she'd want to leave," I said.

"Not Elizabeth." Steven's laugh was hollow, mirthless. "Even murder can be forgotten, given enough time," he said.

We rode in silence. Papa would have been horrified that the family name had been shamed by his eldest son. Papa's first wife had died from diphtheria when Walter was only a toddler and Papa had remained a bachelor for nearly six years before marrying our mother. Sadly, Mother survived Steven's and my birth by only a year before she passed away from influenza. Papa was left to raise three children . . . and Walter had always been his favorite. Steven and I grew up in the shadow of our elder half-brother, and through the years I had come to know why—Papa and Walter had been alike in both looks and manner. After Papa's death seven years ago, it was Walter who had seemed for months as if some part of himself had died. Not only had Walter worked side by side with Papa in the store, he had gone hunting, fishing, and riding with him. I remembered the two of them coming home dirty, unshaven, having packed into the high country to hunt elk or grizzly bears. They sat the saddle the same, threw a fishing line with the same skill, and in appearance their strong features and build were nearly identical. Walter took over the store after Papa's death, until five years ago, when he was murdered. I didn't think Steven was right about people forgetting. Not when

Walter's killer had never been found. There was a dark shadow clouding the Banning name.

I glanced at Steven's finely molded features and fair coloring, his well-groomed mustache only adding to the air of delicacy surrounding him. Suddenly I was angry that he had been forced into a mold he didn't fit. My heart ached as I remembered a slender child of the past, now a man, who had looked on, lonely, alienated, while his father and brother shared a robust companionship.

If only our mother hadn't died when we were babies, I thought, and then pushed the thought away. What did I really know about our mother? Her portrait over the mantel in the parlor was the only memory of her that I had. Perhaps if the ethereal young woman in the painting had lived, things would have been different.

I straightened up in the seat and said firmly, "Steven, I think you ought to sell the store if you feel that way about it—no matter what kind of fuss Elizabeth puts up." Impulsively, I touched his arm. "I'll be around to back you up, you know. Remember how we could take on half the kids in town when our supply of green apples held up?"

And suddenly we were laughing together. But my laughter faded when we reached the western edge of town and we turned into the driveway of the house I had left five years ago. Hunters Hall was built of stone and covered with heavy, dark green vines. The structure bore all the signs of what the place had been originally—a hunting lodge. Papa had bought it from a German immigrant who had come to Colorado with the first influx of prospectors and early settlers. When Brimstone was still in its infancy, Papa had purchased the lodge and forty acres stretching along the mountain valley. He had

20

added a wing when he married the second time, keeping the austere rock exterior, unrelieved bargeboards, and tall narrow windows that were recessed into the thick walls. Mammoth evergreens hugged the driveway and the front of the house, casting shadows over the structure even on the sunniest days. Several stone buildings including a stable and carriage house rose in the trees beyond a small clearing at the back of the house.

Everything about the place defied the word *home,* I thought as we circled the building. Homes were special kinds of enclosures that ensured the people inside were protected and safe. The size of the house didn't matter. Some could be as big as all outdoors, I thought, and still supply a warmth and security to those that lived within. Hunters Hall was never like that. Something had always been missing. But I had come back to it, for all that it lacked, for all that it had withheld, it was the only home I'd ever known—and I had rejected it for too long.

"I thought you'd probably want to slip in the back door," Steven said, nodding to the line of buggies and carriages lined up along the circular drive. "Maybe you'd like to freshen up a bit before you meet half the town."

The thought of confronting a house full of company was less than reassuring. I wondered if there was some way I could disappear into my upstairs room until everyone had left. I summoned my courage. *Get the first challenge over with.* After all, I had seen Brian and hadn't been devastated. He could have been any old friend—not one I had once dreamed of marrying. I was relieved that everything had gone so well. I took a deep breath as we circled the back corner of the house, and then gasped aloud.

Steven laughed. "Do you like it?"

Instead of the barren clearing that I remembered between the house and outbuildings, a beautiful flower garden stretched before us. Pastel roses, white and yellow daisies, stately lavender and white delphiniums, masses of saffron poppies, and variegated snapdragons blended together in a riot of color. There was an over-all harmony of design that saw low-blooming pansies with tall hollyhocks whose weighted stems were laden with dancing lady's blossoms. Masses of carnations of every hue covered the ground, which sloped to the edges of a thick band of trees edging the property.

"I've never seen anything lovelier," I breathed. "Beautiful."

Steven's face was luminous with a delight that had not been evident when he sought my assessment of the store. "I have a small greenhouse behind the stable," he confessed. "I'll give you a personal tour and show you some experiments that I'm doing with cross pollination." His voice had lowered to a conspirator's whisper. "I think I may have developed a new strain of carnation."

"Steven, that's wonderful!" I exclaimed. "I didn't know you had an interest in horticulture."

He put his finger up to his mouth. "Don't say anything to Elizabeth. She thinks I waste too much time puttering with such nonsense." He smiled sheepishly. "I'm afraid I do neglect other things." He swung down from the buggy and reined the horse, then helped me down.

"I'm glad you're home, Dee. Everything's going to be fine," he said as if to equip me with some kind of armor for whatever trials lay ahead. His arms encircled me. "I've missed your fiery spirit. Together we were a match for everything." As Steven released me he eyed me seriously. "It isn't like you to run away from anything. Why did you go, sis?"

"Just got restless, I guess," I lied. "Wanted to see a little of the world."

"But you came back."

"Yes." I prayed Steven would never know the truth. I had gambled, coming back, but five years had elapsed. Surely by now it was safe to return.

Chapter Three

The back door of Hunters Hall led into a scullery where fresh game was gutted, skinned, and butchered. The floor was stone and the table tops marble. Several ducks lay with their heads dangling from a sink board. In a large basin of fresh water, a half-dozen glassy-eyed trout floated belly up, already gutted and ready for the frying pan. Two limp rabbits with bloody fur waited to be skinned. The scene took me back to my childhood; I almost expected to hear Papa's booming voice relating the details of a successful shoot or catch. The house had always been full of his cronies—several rooms on the first floor had been given over to their drinking and gambling. After Papa's death, Walter had kept up the tradition, filling the house with sportsmen. I was surprised to learn that the custom was still being honored.

Steven must have read my mind. "Walter's friend, Jon Duval, brings them by. Remember him? He can't forget the old days, when he and Walter were out hunting at dawn. You remember how inseparable those two were?"

I nodded. The burly Frenchman had been Walter's

shadow; they drank and caroused together. Duval had always leered at me with glistening black eyes and a mouth that curved lasciviously. He would never have dared touch me, because of Walter, but I remember how I had avoided being alone with him.

"Duval comes by with his kill and spends a lot of time in the kitchen, visiting with Maude. I heard him telling her that Papa must be turning over in his grave to see his son smelling petunias instead of bringing down a five-point elk like a man." Steven smiled sadly. "I never could bring myself to shoot anything. Walter and Papa tried hard enough to change me, but—" He shrugged. "I guess I turned out to be a disappointment to everyone."

"Not to me," I said quickly. "I think courage and virility are defined differently for every man. Sometimes it takes a lot more strength of character to stand alone." I gave a soft laugh. "I think Shakespeare said it better. To thine own self be true."

"You said it just fine. Thanks, sis."

We went into the large kitchen and I was immediately enveloped in thick soft arms that had cuddled me as an infant, comforted me as a youngster, and lectured me as a young lady.

"My baby. My baby," crooned Maude. "Let me look at you. It's really true, Deedee. You've come back. I ought to paddle your backside for staying away so long," she scolded.

I blinked furiously, trying to hold back the tears welling up in my eyes as I looked into her dear, weathered face. "You look just the same, Maude. Not a day older," I said. Her hair was grayer, pink neck skin looser, but she did look the same, quite ageless as I had remembered.

"Just passed my sixty-fifth birthday, my girl. Now

26

don't tell me that isn't climbing up there toward St. Peter."

"Now, you know St. Peter isn't going to have anything to do with a renegade Methodist like you," teased Steven, winking at me.

Maude shook a chubby finger at him. "Renegade, is it? Now look who you're calling names. Your old Nanny, that's who. Should have taken a switch to you, that's what. Then you'd have grown up with more respect for your elders."

I laughed outright at the old familiar banter. The same Maude. Bellowing, threatening, and all the time holding out warm arms where one could run with a hurt.

"You look peaked to me," Maude said, studying me. Her gaze traveled down to my buttoned shoes and back again. "Don't they feed governesses in them rich families? I'm going to fix you some vittles that'll put color back in those cheeks, and some meat on them bones. Your room's all fixed up for you, too, just the way you always liked it—I saw to that!" The belligerent tone of her voice as she said this last made me think that there might have been some question about it.

"I think I'll go and freshen up a bit then," I said.

Maude nodded, but before I could take a step toward the hall, Steven's wife, Elizabeth, came sweeping into the kitchen with her starched petticoats rustling and a pink silk gown flowing about her like rippling rose petals. She was a large woman, tightly corseted, who always held herself very erect, the way an actress might in the presence of an audience. Although she did not lack poise and dressed in the manner befitting a great lady, there was something about her that indicated a past familiarity with hard work—and perhaps a secret liking for it.

I had always thought Elizabeth's most attractive feature was her naturally curly hair, which was deep brown and styled in a high coiffure that added height to her already imposing stature. A frown lingered on her face just long enough for me to take note of it before her mouth eased into a welcoming smile.

"Deanna! How wonderful to see you. Everyone has been talking about your homecoming. You must come right in and say hello. Just a small gathering." Without waiting for my response, Elizabeth gestured to Maude. "Please bring in more hot water for tea and another platter of currant puffs," she said, then turned back to me. "Brian's mother is pouring. You remember Mrs. Milburne, of course. And then there's our new minister. A fine man. The Methodist church has the biggest congregation in town. We used to be behind the Baptists in numbers, but not anymore. Steven, are you coming in?" A sharp glance took in her husband's rumpled brown suit.

"Count me out," said Steven wanly, a statement that did not seem to cause Elizabeth any vexation at all.

My brother's eyes caught mine. "See you later, Dee. After you've bearded the lions." He quickly made his escape out the back door.

Elizabeth frowned. "Now what did he mean by that silly remark?"

"I really would like to freshen up a bit, Elizabeth."

"Nonsense. You look fine," she said unconvincingly, resting her eyes on my simple straw bonnet.

I decided to take off the hat, and left it with my gloves and beaded bag on a hall table. The center corridor of the long house was as dark and dreary as I remembered. Heavy beams ran the length of the hall and dark black walnut wainscoting gave the passageway the illusion of a long dark tunnel even on the sunniest of days.

Straightening the lace collar at my modest neckline and smoothing the folds of my striped dress, I followed Elizabeth down the hall, consciously stiffening my back and moistening my lips with a dry tongue.

My steps faltered when we reached the dining room doorway, and I resisted the pressure Elizabeth put on my arm as she turned and looked at me with some impatience. If she had an ounce of compassion, she would have taken heed of the beads of sweat forming along my forehead and the nervous quivering of my lower lip.

"You'll want a cup of tea, I'm sure," she said briskly, pulling me along like a truculent child.

For a moment I thought the dining room was empty, and was relieved that my entrance into the gathering had been momentarily delayed. Elizabeth's guests were obviously milling about in the large room beyond the dining room, a huge foyer that resembled the grand banquet hall of a castle. The German who had built the lodge had made the large hall the center of the house. Papa had added other rooms when he bought it, but he had used the center hall for gatherings; I remembered the raucous merriment of hunting parties enjoying all-night celebrations, drinking, carousing, the hall filled with male bravado.

Two wide doorways opened into the hall from the dining room, one on each side of a mammoth stone fireplace. A steady hum of voices, clinking cups, and spurts of laughter floated into the dining room.

"Look who I found in the kitchen, Nina," said Elizabeth, addressing a woman sitting alone at one end of a long heavily laden table.

Nina Milburne set a silver teapot down rather forcibly and clumsily as she caught sight of me.

Elizabeth ushered me to the table. "Deanna, you remember Brian's mother, Mrs. Milburne. Of course, you do." Her laugh was forced. "How foolish of me."

While Elizabeth relished my discomfort, I stared into the woman's face, as always unsmiling and impenetrable. Her arched nostrils quivered, and she looked at me with gray eyes as cold as pewter. Now I could see the family resemblance to her sister, Della Danvers, the woman I had met on the train. Their common air of condescension was unmistakable.

"Of course, you must have some tea, Deanna," commanded Elizabeth. "And then you must meet Reverend Norris. I must attend to our other guests. Nina, you'll see that Deanna has some refreshment? Then both of you must join us in the hall." Without waiting for a response, she hurried away as if more pressing matters awaited her attention.

Nina Milburne poured the tea and then handed the cup and saucer to me, deliberately locking her eyes with my own.

I was amazed to find my hand steady—steadier than the older woman's as she set the silver teapot back down.

Yes, I'm back. I refused to lower my gaze.

"A mint, perhaps, Deanna?"

"Thank you." I nibbled on the sweet. "Delicious." *See, I'm not afraid.*

"And how did you find the East? Less demanding than our western society, perhaps? Less strictures? More privacy?" Her jeweled hands moved between the china and silver purposefully, almost with the air of someone dispensing justice. Then she lifted a cup to her lips, allowing a smile to curve the edges of her thin mouth as her cold eyes glared into mine.

30

I tightened my grip upon the cup's handle, determined to keep my hand steady, but I lowered my eyes against her piercing gaze. *I can't hide my emotions the way she can. She can read me.*

"I was surprised to hear of your return," she said coldly.

"Mrs. Milburne—" I began, wondering how I could preempt the cat-and-mouse game that could destroy me. I remembered our last meeting, and I knew the consequences of my return to Brimstone. Nina Milburne had not changed; five years had only strengthened her dislike for me. I was a fool to think it would be different. I moistened my dry lips. "Mrs. Milburne," I repeated, but before I could continue, Elizabeth returned to the dining room with a guest in hand, a pretty young woman wearing a white tulle afternoon gown, and a bonnet covered with blue silk roses. Lovely dark hair hung in long curls along her petal-white cheeks and her blue eyes were openly curious as she surveyed me.

"Well, Deanna," said Elizabeth in a tone of reprimand. "If you're not going to join us, we'll join you. I want you to meet Carolyn Lareau, Brian's fiancée. My sister-in-law, Deanna Banning."

"My pleasure," the young woman said with a hesitant smile.

She was quite young, as much as ten years Brian's junior, I guessed, and there was an unsophisticated, genuine air about her. I found myself returning her smile. "I'm pleased to meet you, Carolyn."

"I understand you were governess for the Lowenstein family. A girl I know, Anita Clayborne, knows the Lowensteins quite well. Did you ever meet Anita?"

"Not that I remember."

"Anita and I don't keep in touch, I'm afraid. Just

Christmas cards. When Brian told me you were governess to the Lowenstein children, I wrote and asked if she knew the family and she said her parents had spent the summer at Newport with them. Small world, isn't it? You'll have to give her my best when you go back."

My mouth was suddenly parched. "I'm not going back. I've come home to stay," I said, feeling as if with those words I had hoisted a battle banner. My stomach gave a sickening lunge as I waited for Nina's attack but the woman's controlled expression remained fixed.

At that moment, a cluster of people migrated into the dining room. "Oh, Reverend Norris," Elizabeth said, "I want you to meet another member of our family." She pushed me forward as if I were a small child. "Deanna, this is Reverend Daniel Norris, our wonderful new minister."

The first impression I had of the honored guest was that his black attire did not suit him at all. He looked uncomfortable in such somber garb, especially since his black suit jacket was obviously too small for his rather impressive frame. My gaze settled on his youthful features, so at odds with his starched shirt and clerical collar. Freckles were spattered across his lightly tanned face; his thick brown hair, I thought fleetingly, probably looked quite red in the sun. He might have been thirty, but certainly was no older, I calculated. Instead of being warmed by his casual smile and frank brown eyes, I was uncomfortable and annoyed; he looked at me as if he knew some secret I was keeping. I bet he loves all the fuss women make over him, I thought with irritation. My smile was stiff and formal as I pointedly ignored his outstretched hand. "Pleased to meet you, Reverend Norris."

Before he could respond, Nina Milburne was suddenly at his side. "We're delighted to have the pleasure of your company, Reverend. You've stayed much too close to the parsonage the month you've been here," she scolded none too lightly. "We were beginning to despair that you were opposed to accepting any of our social invitations. But now that Elizabeth has managed to pry you loose, you must accept my dinner invitation for next Sunday."

I glanced up at him quickly to see if he dared to refuse this royal command. He must have guessed at my curiosity for I was positive he sent me an almost imperceptible wink. "Why, I do thank you, Mrs. Milburne." He smiled warmly at her. "But I really must refuse. You see, the truth is—" He chuckled—"The truth is . . . my shoes pinch! I only endure them at Sunday services and on other rare occasions."

Mrs. Milburne's nostrils flared. "Really! I should think the adequate salary the board decided upon would cover a suitable pair of shoes."

"Oh, the trouble is not with the shoes. It's my unwilling feet. How they fuss at being confined. Only my devotion to the Lord could make me give up the delight of touching this good earth with my bare toes."

I put my hand against my mouth in an effort to suppress the laughter bubbling up in my throat. I couldn't believe it! Mrs. Milburne trying to get a bare-footed minister to accept a dinner invitation. Mirth threatened to break forth despite my tight control.

The young minister must have sensed my struggle because he tossed me a quick grin and said, "I believe Miss Banning understands." With feigned solemnity, his glance traveled down to my high-buttoned

33

shoes. "I will never understand how you ladies endure those narrow, pointed monstrosities." His eyes twinkled with a challenge.

"They are torture," I responsed just as solemnly. "I always get rid of them . . . *second thing*." I started to say "first thing" and then changed my mind.

"What's the first?" His grin held a challenge.

The pause was barely discernible. "My lacings."

Elizabeth gasped audibly. Mrs. Milburne's eyes sparked like flint. The other female guests simply clamped their mouths shut, their eyes bulging as if they were unable to breathe.

"Very sensible," he responded, obviously trying to control his own amusement. "I'm glad men aren't expected to go around all squeezed up like that. Don't know why women put up with such things myself. Do you, Miss Banning?"

I'm game, my eyes said. I knew I should stop the conversation before disaster descended upon us, but I couldn't. This grinning preacher wasn't going to prove me a coward. "From the bathing suits I saw in Atlantic City," I said, returning his smile, "women are beginning to rebel. Only one layer of clothing and plenty of bare ankles in view . . . I wouldn't be surprised—"

"Deanna!" Elizabeth gasped. Her expression was one of utter horror.

"Never have I been witness to a conversation of such despicable taste," exploded Nina. "I certainly hope it will never be repeated, especially in the presence of respectable church members." Her glare held a warning as she looked at him. "We will excuse today's impropriety, Reverend, because Deanna Banning has apparently used her absence to broaden her education in some very unfortunate ways. But then I am not surprised. Reverend Norris, you are at a

34

disadvantage. You don't know the family's history."

So we had arrived so soon at the moment of truth. I kept my head up. *No more running. Not any more.* I hoped that I kept any trembling out of my voice as I said, "Go ahead and tell him, Mrs. Milburne. I'm sure that Reverend Norris would find our family scandals very interesting."

"Please, Deanna." Elizabeth's round face had gone quite pale.

I ignored her plea. I couldn't hold back the words. A dam had been thrown open. Dark forces swirled within me, sweeping me on. "You see, Reverend, we've had, among other things, a murder in the family."

"My brother-in-law," said Elizabeth quickly, as if trying to settle the matter and salvage from the conversation some measure of respectability.

"After what has happened today," said Mrs. Milburne acridly, "perhaps it's best that Reverend Norris know *everything*—so that his judgment will be better in the future."

"Get everything out on the table, is that it, Mrs. Milburne?" I demanded bitterly. How I hated this vulture of a woman. She could destroy me and my family with the knowledge that she possessed. Five years ago, I had given in to her blackmail and fled to buy her silence. But now I was back . . . I refused to pay any more.

All amusement had fled Reverend Norris's eyes as he looked at me, obviously aware that the waters had suddenly deepened. "Skeletons have a way of disappearing once they are gotten from closets and exposed to the light. And fear leaves with them."

He probably meant the words to be reassuring, but I knew that he would be the worst judge of all. I'd had dealings with men of the cloth before. Unrelenting, dogmatic, unwavering in their convictions. I didn't need his interference. My sensibilities were alive to the threatening woman before me. This was the foe. Every word she spoke could impale me.

"Yes, my half-brother was murdered, wasn't he, Mrs. Milburne. But that's not the ugliness that you're interested in passing along. Not *that* he was murdered, but the circumstances surrounding it. You see, Reverend, what this dear lady wants you to know is that Walter Banning was murdered in a whorehouse!"

I was on the verge of tears. I knew that after the initial silence following my admission, Mrs. Milburne would open the closet again, and none of my secrets would be safe. I would stand before them all, stripped naked. But there were no words of protest rising in my throat. I would face the inevitable head on.

"Let the dead bury the dead," said the minister hollowly. "We must not stand in judgment of each other."

I wanted to laugh. What a fool he was. As if such a sordid tale could be forgotten.

Mrs. Milburne glared at me and walked out of the dining room as if by remaining in my presence she risked contamination. The rest of the guests seemed grateful to follow her. Elizabeth took the preacher in tow. "Come, Reverend. Some of our guests are leaving. I think you should bid them goodbye." Her warning glance made me mumble some polite words about the pleasure of meeting him.

"You'll be coming to services?" he inquired with the same level of politeness.

"Yes, of course," I lied.

Elizabeth was eager to lead him out of the room. It was obvious that she didn't relish the idea that I would be inflicting my presence upon society even at Sunday services.

I stood in the empty dining room, wondering if I had the courage to brave the hurricane that could level everything Papa had fought so hard to protect. And Steven? Would I destroy his life and marriage by staying?

My eyes drifted to Mrs. Milburne's empty chair. I saw then that she had forgotten her velvet purse, which lay open on the table. The glow of a tiny gold pencil captured my eyes. How pretty it was, how perfectly sweet. A warmth invaded me. All sense of loneliness eased away.

A moment later, turning away from the table, I left the dining room and sought the back stairs. They squeaked in the places I remembered, and a cold draft bathed my face as I climbed the narrow passage and pushed through the door that opened onto the second floor.

I paused. My ears strained for any movement or sound. I wondered where the children were. From below, I could hear voices floating up the main staircase as Elizabeth's guests took their leave. The preacher's resonant laughter filled the house. I wondered why on earth I'd let him make a fool out of me.

I walked quietly down the carpeted hall to the last door in the west wing, my old room. The familiarity of my brass bed and skirted dressing table was comforting. I shut the door quickly and leaned back against it, suddenly breathing heavily as if I'd unconsciously been in flight since I'd left the dining room. My head throbbed. A bone-deep fatigue that I had held in abeyance swept over me all at once.

I walked across the room and looked out at Steven's garden, as lovely as a rainbow in the late afternoon sunshine. I remembered the light in his eyes when he talked about his greenhouse and plants. It was no surprise that Elizabeth didn't share his enthusiasm. For his sake I was glad I was back.

A biting pressure in the palm of my hand brought my eyes to my clenched fist. I slowly eased back each finger. Light made of the metal little golden stars, flickering and quivering in the palm of my hand. For a long moment my eyes remained riveted upon the tiny pencil's loveliness. Then, with a sharp cry, I flung it away from me. It bounced across the floor and disappeared under my dressing table.

Sobbing, I threw myself across the bed and prayed that sleep would overtake me.

Chapter Four

I pleaded fatigue and stayed in my room the rest of the afternoon and evening. Maude brought me a dinner tray.

"Lordy, Lordy," she fussed. "You look as peaked as a bleached dish rag. Now you eat every bit of this," she ordered as she lifted the cover from the plate and handed me a napkin. "Crisp chicken, just the way you like it—and your favorite piece, too. I remember how you and Steven used to fight over the wishbone. And here's some fresh garden peas in my special butter sauce, and carrots swimming in honey and brown sugar, some soft oatmeal bread, and for dessert—" She brandished a piece of chocolate cake that was five inches high.

"Maude, I can't possibly eat all of this."

She raised a tufted gray eyebrow. "And what are you aiming to do, then? Pick at a bite or two? You know I don't put up with that kind of nonsense. Clean your plate. You're home now and I'm determined to get some color back in them cheeks."

It had been a long time since anyone fussed over me. During my five years with the Lowenstein family, I had been treated well, and I had been paid adequate wages, but only the children expressed any kind of affection for me. My relationships with the other hired staff had been merely professional.

"I'll unpack your satchel and we'll tackle your trunk tomorrow."

"Thanks, Maude," I said gratefully. "You're an angel."

"Angel, is it? You always were one to spread the honey on thick." Her eyes twinkled. "'Course, I can still see through your pretty speeches. Could always tell when you been up to some mischief."

"Me?" I echoed with mock innocence.

"Yes, you." She waggled a fat finger at me. "And from what I hear, you set everyone at the tea party on their ears with some scandalous exchange with the new preacher."

"He started it."

"So you had to finish it. Lordy, Miss Elizabeth is fit to be tied. She's set herself up as the great lady, don't you know? Your sister-in-law don't take kindly to reminders that her folks were lowly ranchers and that she can muck out a stall with the best of 'em. No, siree, Miss Elizabeth is one queen bee, let me tell you. She hobnobs with all the important folk who come to Brimstone to take the waters. Between her and Mrs. Milburne, nothing of consequence goes on in this town without their fingers in the pie." She eyed me and nodded. "You two will be locking horns, if I don't miss my guess."

"I'm sorry if I upset Elizabeth. I really am. Sometimes my tongue just runs away with me. Especially when I feel I'm being challenged— especially by a man. But I'll try to behave myself, I promise."

She chuckled. "That will be the day, Deedee. Now you get yourself into bed, hear? I don't aim to have you wandering around like some dry dandelion the wind can blow apart."

After she left, I sat in front of the window, curled up in my favorite cushioned chair and thought about Elizabeth. Steven had been so young when he married her. I tried to talk him out of it at the time, but Papa was delighted to have her in the family, and pushed the marriage. "Just the kind of woman Steven needs," he told everyone. Maybe Papa knew that Elizabeth would make certain that Steven stayed the course that he had set for the family. Of course, things didn't turn out the way my father had expected. He died of a stroke the same year Steven and Elizabeth were married, and two years later his favorite son was knifed to death outside a house of ill repute.

I rose up from my chair, wandered restlessly around the room, pulling back a window curtain and pressing my hot cheek against the cool pane. Clouds moving across the moon created swift shadows that flitted over sandstone walks and under the slightly swaying trees. The scene below my window was a foreign one. Papa had never cleared away any of the natural growth of evergreens, scrub oak, and wild grass that hugged the house; I had expected everything to look the same. But most of the familiar trees I knew as a child had been cut down and Steven's garden seemed alien in the moonlight. As I stood there in the house of my birth, I felt as displaced as I had when traveling with the Lowenstein family, always living in strange places and in impersonal quarters. The need to anchor myself in time and space had brought me back to Hunters Hall even though I knew I could set a dangerous tide in motion. I felt a shiver run up my back as I thought about the implications of my actions.

41

* * *

I spent a restless night and was awakened early the next morning. I opened my eyes to behold a blond, blue-eyed cherub peering over the covers at me. The child's full lips parted in a smile, made no less perfect by a smear of strawberry jam at the corners.

"Hi. You're Aunt Dee," she informed me. And without waiting for an invitation, clambered up on the pillow beside me. "I knew you were coming," she said wisely.

"Did you now?" I smiled as I eased into a sitting position.

She nodded solemnly. "I even saw the boy who brought the telegram."

"Then you must be Patty Banning," I said with matched solemnity.

She nodded, jumped from the bed and stretched her chubby arms above her head. "See how tall I am."

"My goodness, what a big girl."

She held out four fingers. "I'm that old. Lots bigger than Nicky. He's only one," she said disparagingly. "He's my baby brother. I had another one, but he went to heaven just after Mommie brought him home."

Chagrined that I had forgotten about the baby who would have been three if he'd lived, I said, "It's nice that God sent you another brother."

Instead of returning my smile, the little girl leaned closer and said in a conspirator's whisper, "I don't think God is very smart."

Thoroughly charmed, I responded in the same secretive tone, "You don't?"

Patty shook her blond head and without blinking whispered, "No, daddy and I ordered a girl and he sent Nicky." She wrinkled up her nose. "You'd think

42

he could tell the difference. Nicky has a peewee and I don't."

I laughed outright as she plopped back onto the bed. "I'm the only girl," she said proudly.

"Well, I'm glad he sent you." I reached out and gave her a hug and a tickle under the ribs. She squealed and bounced like a playful puppy. We were laughing loudly when a tall, plain girl in servant dress peeked in the bedroom door.

"So there you are, Miss Patty. I've been looking all over for you." The maid was obviously embarrassed and barely met my eyes as she said, "I'm Sarah, and I'm sorry, miss. I was bathing young Nicholas when she left the nursery. It won't happen again, I promise you."

"Oh, but it must—I mean, I like having Patty's company. I'm looking forward to spending time with both the children. Are you their nanny?"

She looked slightly bewildered. "No, just the upstairs maid. Mrs. Banning looks after the children mostly, but sometimes she needs a helping hand. Especially in the morning." She hastily wiped the jam off Patty's face, and then firmly took the little girl's hand. "I left the baby in his crib and he'll be howling like a banshee if I don't get back."

"Please let the children come and see me any time. I'm going to be lost without something to do. For five years I've been in charge of two active children. Now that I'm home I'd like to spend a lot of my time with Patty and Nicky."

"That'll be up to Mrs. Banning," the girl said with an apologetic frown. "She doesn't like disruptions in the daily routine. She's very busy and the children's schedule has to fit hers. Come on, Patty. Your mother won't be pleased to find your breakfast half eaten."

Patty protested loudly as Sarah hurried her from

the room and down the hall.

I was disappointed that Elizabeth kept such a tight rein on the children. I chuckled over Patty's bright remarks and her playful exuberance. Romping with her on my bed had made me feel young and happy again. My life would be brightened considerably if Elizabeth would delegate some responsibility for the children's care to me, but Sarah's remarks had not been encouraging.

I got out of bed and took my toiletries down to the center bathroom. I wondered if the staff had heard Elizabeth voicing her displeasure over my part in the incident at the tea party. Maybe she had already deemed me unsuitable company for her children. Blast that preacher, anyway. He'd deliberately goaded me into making a fool of myself and then offered platitudes when the going got rough.

I dressed quickly in a floral summer frock of pale yellow linen. Cool and comfortable, the dress was fashioned with a square neckline, bell sleeves, and an overskirt that was a darker daffodil yellow. I secured my hair in a smooth twist, impulsively weaving in a narrow gold ribbon to hold it firmly at the nape of my neck.

The encounter with Patty had brightened my spirits considerably and my steps were light as I descended the center stairs, gathering my full skirts with one hand and grasping the banister with the other. With a smile on my face I entered the small breakfast room just off the kitchen. "Good morning," I said brightly.

Steven and Elizabeth sat at the large oak table. My brother gave me a welcoming smile as he rose from his chair. "Good morning, yourself. You look rested, Dee." He held a chair out for me.

Elizabeth smiled tightly, but the curve of her lips

44

didn't match the censorious coldness in her eyes. Several letters had been placed beside her plate and she immediately turned her attention to them, discouraging any attempt I might have made at conversation.

"Here you go." Steven presented me with a plate of scrambled eggs and sausage patties.

I protested that tea and toast were my usual fare.

"I have orders from Maude to fatten you up."

"That's right," Maude echoed as she bustled into the room through a swinging door, carrying a covered dish. "Nobody in this house is going around looking like they haven't had a square meal."

She watched me like a mother bird until I took a steaming biscuit and ate several bites of the golden eggs. She gave me a nod of satisfaction and ambled back to the kitchen.

I grinned at Steven. I had enough food on my plate for two meals, but I doggedly attacked the feast. Surprisingly enough, my plate was almost empty before I finally pushed it away. "I can't eat another bite."

"Another cup of tea?" Steven asked.

I nodded.

He seemed content to ignore his wife's silence. I suspected that most of their meals were conducted in a like fashion. Steven seemed to be content with his own thoughts, and I made a few casual attempts at conversation, but words were not necessary between us. I enjoyed the familiar ease and comfort of our relationship. When Elizabeth suddenly put her letters aside and addressed me, I almost jumped.

"I'm heading a committee to raise money for an opera house," she said. "It's time that we brought some culture to Brimstone. Even miserable mining towns like Cripple Creek and Central City have spacious buildings that attract all kinds of theatrical companies." Then her nostrils narrowed. "Of course, I don't suppose you would be impressed, Deanna. I'm sure that anything we'd offer would seem provincial to you. You must have enjoyed productions at the Winter Garden in New York. I've read that Edwin Booth was perfectly marvelous in his Shakespearean roles."

She made it sound as if my five years of servitude was nothing more than a glittering pastime, spent going to plays and the opera.

"I never had the plesure of attending the Winter Garden, although my employers went many times," I said evenly. "I think it would be wonderful for Brimstone to have an opera house, but raising that kind of money seems an enormous challenge."

Elizabeth was apparently mollified enough to explain that she had been able to secure some large donations, and had hopes of more contributions being raised through organized events. "That's why the carnival is such a good idea. A Fourth of July celebration and fundraiser, all in one. All kinds of games, races, a fishing contest, and an ice cream and cake social. We'll have a band concert and dance in the park pavilion in the evening. I'm sure it will be most successful."

"Sounds like a lot of work for one person," I said honestly.

She gestured dismissively. "All the churches and women's clubs have agreed to help. I'm just in charge of organizing everything."

And you'll enjoy every minute of it, I thought. Elizabeth's upbringing had not been privileged. She was used to physical labor. As Maude had said, Elizabeth had been raised on a ranch and she had worked as hard as any hired hand while growing up.

46

Now that she was mistress of a less demanding household, she had plenty of pent-up energy to channel into her social endeavors. Obviously, Elizabeth was proud of the stature she had in the community. The knowledge gave me a sinking feeling. I hated the thought that I might be the one to tarnish that image forever.

She gathered her letters and stood up. "Well, I must spend some time with the children and then take care of this correspondence."

"Can I help in any way?" I asked. I had thought to ask about the children but her expression silenced me. It was clear that the previous day's events had not been forgotten.

She pursed her full lips. "Thank you, Deanna, no." With that she sailed out of the room, a ruffled morning cap sitting high on her curls and the flounce of a brown twilled silk morning gown drawn into a stylish bustle at her ample derriere.

Steven's lassitude disappeared with his wife's departure from the room and I sensed a rise of excitement in him. He leaned over the table toward me. "I've thought about what you said yesterday, sis, about the store. I know a man in Denver who's interested in it. He's been in Brimstone several times trying to get me to name a price. He told me if I ever decided to sell it to let him know." Steven lowered his voice. "I'm going to write him and tell him to come. He could look over the stock and books and make me an offer."

"Have you told Elizabeth?"

He nodded. "Last night. I told her I was seriously considering selling, but she told me to quit talking nonsense."

"What would you do—if you *were* free of the store?"

He swallowed hard, as if by even thinking of his plans he was committing some sort of criminal act. "I've been thinking hard about it. There's a piece of land up the valley, the old Williams' place. That spread would be perfect for growing nursery stock and putting up some greenhouses. It's close enough to town for selling trees, shrubs, and flowers. A lot of people are putting in fancy Victorian gardens, with fountains and statues, and rose gardens. I'd never make a fortune, but I think I could turn the investment into a paying enterprise—"

"And you would love it," I concluded for him with a smile.

He looked sheepish. "Yes, I would."

These days Americans had become passionate about their lawns. Even modest homes often had charming gazebos and grape arbors. The wealthy planted romantic glades around their mansions and hired dozens of gardeners to care for elaborate flower beds and sweeps of impeccably groomed lawns. I shared with Steven some of the landscaping ideas I had seen back East. "Most of the large hotels displayed windows full of ferns, lemon and lime trees, and other plants that are now considered fashionable indoor decor. I think you could be very successful," I said.

"I wish I could finance it without selling the store. That would make everybody happy."

"Well, I'd be willing to invest my share of the store in your new venture. As far as I'm concerned, I think you should go ahead and find your buyer. I'll back up your decision with Elizabeth," I promised, wondering if Steven and I would be left standing in a showdown with her. Being the wife of a nursery man who smelled of dirt and manure would not do much for her social image.

48

He frowned. "What are your plans, Dee? The profits from the store have been going down every year. I don't know how much we can expect to make on the sale of it. Bannings isn't what it used to be."

"Don't worry about me. I'm going to look around for a teaching position for this fall. I have some savings, and whatever the sale brings will be enough for me to get along." I touched his hand. "The important thing is for you to be happy."

"Thanks, sis. I'm going to need your support."

"You have it."

He took a deep breath. "Well, I'd best get to work," he said reluctantly. "I've got to give Millie a hand in the office. Would you like to come along? I know she'd love to see you."

I shook my head. "Not today, thanks." I wasn't ready to go to Bannings and meet Papa's ghost just yet. Strange as it might seem, I knew I hadn't freed myself from his domination—even from beyond the grave. The store would stir up old memories and emotions. I gave Steven an apologetic smile. "I'm still a little weary from my journey."

"Of course you are." He bent and kissed my forehead. "There's no hurry. Enjoy yourself, sis. When I get back this afternoon, I'll show you the greenhouse."

I sipped my tea after he had gone, wondering what I ought to do with myself. My days had always been filled with duties from morning until night. Mrs. Lowenstein made certain that I had tasks to complete even when the children were engaged elsewhere. In truth, I had been a combination governess, seamstress, and lady's secretary, but I didn't mind. I was grateful to fall exhausted into bed every night. The demanding position left little time for thinking, but now I was back at Hunters Hall—and unfortunately there was plenty of time to be introspective.

I rose from my chair and walked down the hall to the small family parlor. The room had been a refuge for Steven and me when we were growing up. When Papa and Walter were home, they preferred the library or the trophy room, with its mounted animal heads and sprawling bear rugs. Boisterous parties were given in the center hall, but the small front parlor had become Steven's and my retreat.

But as I entered the room and looked about, once more I felt displaced. Elizabeth had redecorated the parlor to her liking. Nothing remained that would offer me the comfort of the past. Tassled velvet love seats and a new horsehair sofa replaced old rustic furniture that had been hewed from pine and oak. High-backed chairs slung with doilies offered a formal setting in front of the fireplace. Porcelain kerosene lamps with oyster-shell shades and an assortment of figurines, snuffboxes, and other bric-a-brac cluttered lace-covered tables and ornate shelves. Heavy paintings in gilded frames competed with a wallpaper of pink cabbage roses that gave the room a claustrophobic air.

For one wild moment, I had an impulse to pull away the heavy brocade drapes and let the sun in. I felt that the busy walls were closing in upon me, and it was difficult to breathe. There was too much color, too much clutter. *Things! Things! Things!* I felt as if I had to fight them off. I whirled, intending to flee the room. Then my eyes caught sight of the portrait hanging over the fireplace. Panic swept away. The constriction in my breast began to ease.

In the entire room, only this one thing remained the same—an oil painting of my mother. Slowly I walked across the room until I stood beneath it. I felt as if I were looking at the portrait for the very first time. With a shock, I realized that I could have been looking into a mirror. The same golden hair, green-flecked eyes, and finely molded face as myself, but my mother's expression was soft and wistful, almost like a child's. She had died young, only twenty-two years old, a year after Steven and I were born. Her formal pose didn't obscure the tenderness of her features nor the fragility of her slender hands—but I rejected the appeal of the lovely woman. *Your mother was weak,* Papa had told me repeatedly. *And I've had enough of weak women, do you understand?*

For a moment I couldn't define the emotion that swept over me, and then I recognized it as anger. *Yes, I understood.* For many years I had hated my mother for making me unworthy in my father's eyes. I had been indoctrinated to accept Papa's rejection of me and Steven as valid. But no more. I jerked my eyes away from the portrait and blinked back hot tears forming at the corners of my eyes.

Like someone driven by a hidden fury, I hurried up to my room and collected my straw bonnet, gloves, and parasol. Childish laughter and Elizabeth's voice emanated from the nursery; I paused in the hall. My heart cried out to join them, but I knew I wouldn't be welcome. Elizabeth would suffer my presence in the house because of Steven. She would not share her children with me.

Quickly tying the streamers of my bonnet, I descended the main staircase and left by a side door that opened into Steven's garden. The morning air was still crisp but a bright sun promised a clear, pleasant day. After a moment of collecting myself and subduing my tumultuous emotions, I acquired a pair of shears from the shed and impulsively began cutting a bouquet of long-stemmed snapdragons, daisies, and purple phlox.

My mood was steadily improving when a gruff voice assaulted me from behind. "What do you think you're doing?"

I reeled around to face a wiry man tensed like a bulldog ready to attack. His black eyes were daggers; his hand closed over the handle of a hoe as if it were a lethal weapon. His unkempt black hair fell around craggy features. He looked at me as if I had not flowers in my hands but the family jewels. Obviously, he was the gardener Steven had hired.

"I'm cutting a bouquet of flowers," I answered evenly. "And who might you be?" I was sure to employ an aggressive tone that matched his. The man was hired staff, after all. He had no right to address me in such a way.

He muttered an oath and then spat a sentiment that reached my ears as "fancy bitch."

"I'm Mr. Banning's sister," I flared. "And I'm certain that he would have no objection to my enjoying his garden in any way I choose!"

The man eyed me suspiciously. "This ain't no ordinary garden," he said, his pugnacious tone softening a bit. "We got some brand new flower mixes planted here. When they seed, we'll have something that ain't been grown before."

I was instantly contrite. I should have been more careful with Steven's flowers. "Of course, I'm so sorry," I said. "I didn't realize." I held out my cuttings feebly.

"Those ain't nothing special. Just plain old daisies and phlox." He gave me a disdainful glare. "But you'd just as likely cut down a carnation that's taken three years to develop, wouldn't you? I ain't going to stand back while some fool female throws all Mr. Banning's hard work into the trash heap . . . sister, or no."

"Of course not. You were right to stop me." I smiled apologetically. "I won't cut anything else."

He shook his head scornfully and turned on his heel, but not before giving me a look that said he'd wring my fool female neck if I so much as showed my face in the garden again.

Amply chagrined and clutching the ill-gotten flowers, I left by a back gate and walked along a path that led high up a foothill, toward a mesa where Brimstone buried its dead. The sun had grown warm and I was thankful for my parasol and cool summer dress. The walk was beginning to fatigue me; I felt a bit breathless and realized that I had not yet adjusted to the high altitude. Several times, I stopped to rest under the shade of a cottonwood tree or upon a flat, cool rock.

Devil's Creek threaded its way along the bottom of the canyon, bounding over shiny rocks and spewing glistening water and foam. The pungent perfume of pine needles made the air clean, fresh, and invigorating.

I continued at a leisurely pace until finally I stood at the edge of the cemetery. No attempt had been made to fence in the area. Weathered wooden crosses, granite tombstones, and other markers that were little more than smooth rocks dotted the expanse of wild grass. Drifts of wild scrubs and mountain flowers grew freely amid clusters of pinyon pines and deciduous trees. Not at all like the manicured cemeteries of the East, I thought as I walked slowly along a dirt path, but the legion of graves were perhaps better served by this natural setting. The Banning plot was banked on three sides by a hedge of wild roses. My father's tombstone was impressive, and taller than the one marking Walter's mother's grave. My mother's headstone was small and unadorned and her grave was not in the same line as Papa's, but to one side and slightly behind his.

My hands were trembling slightly as I knelt beside her stone and spread the flowers upon the dry ground. I read the plain inscription and felt my chest tighten. CHRISTINE LOUISE BANNING. WIFE. My mother's birth and death dates followed.

That was all. Not beloved wife. Not beloved mother. Just "Wife."

Tears stung my eyes. I had come hoping to establish a feeling of belonging, but a deeper sense of loneliness overtook me. "Mother," I whispered, but the word was empty. There were no memories attached to it, only my father's derision, which continued to pain me now, when both my parents were dead.

I was so preoccupied with my own inner anguish that I did not hear the sound at first. But as the clang of a pick against hard dirt continued, I was gradually brought to an awareness of it. I stood up and wiped my eyes quickly. The disturbance came from behind a nearby stand of cedar and pine trees beyond a row of graves.

I slowly walked toward the noise. As I came through the trees, I saw him before he was able to straighten his back and take notice of me. He blinked against the sun, as if I in my yellow dress were some kind of apparition.

For a moment we just looked at each other. Then he tossed down his shovel and walked toward me. He wiped his forehead with his sleeve. "Miss Banning. How nice to see you again. What brings you to such a desolate place?"

Chapter Five

The Reverend Daniel Norris was dressed in stained work pants and a light blue cotton shirt with the sleeves rolled up to his elbows—no clerical collar. His thick hair fell across his forehead and he brushed it back as he grinned at me. "You gave me a bit of a start. For a moment I thought I was seeing things. In that summer dress you looked like a golden nymph flitting through the trees. I was afraid to blink for fear you would disappear."

"I didn't mean to interrupt you," I said, taking in the area behind him. "You're digging a grave?" I asked, surprised.

"Yes, but not for anyone in the church. A Mexican family lost a young boy in a gun accident. They didn't have any money for a proper burial, so I'm doing it."

"Does the church board approve of this kind of thing? I would think the membership would be jealous of such noble diversions as this."

"They don't know about it—yet. And what brings you here—a pilgrimage?"

"You might say that," I acknowledged, stiffening. I wasn't about to reveal my inner turmoil to this unconventional man of the cloth. "Well, I'll take my leave and let you get on with your work."

"As it happens, I was ready for a break. Come on, there's a nice cool spot under that old tree and a smooth rock perfect for sitting."

"Thank you, but I must get back—"

"Nonsense!" He took my arm and firmly guided me to the shaded spot.

Dappled sunlight flitted over a shelf of red sandstone sheltered by a tall cottonwood tree. A glass jar and paper sack rested on the ground nearby. He took a tin cup out of the sack, poured me a cup of lemonade, then sat down on the ground near me, Indian style, and took a deep drink out of the jar. "Hummm," he said with a smack of his lips.

I had to agree. The lemonade was cool and refreshing.

I began to relax, suddenly grateful for the company. "I'm disappointed," I chided, smilingly. "You're wearing shoes."

He chuckled. "I guess I did stretch the truth a wee bit."

"You mean you told a white lie, Reverend?" I teased.

"I just wanted to see if Nina Milburne would really invite a barefoot preacher to dinner."

Mention of the woman's name sent a chill up my spine. The preacher must have sensed this.

"I'm sorry about the entire incident," he said hurriedly.

"Don't be. I rather enjoyed shocking the good ladies of Brimstone."

He chuckled. "Now how did I know you were some kind of renegade?"

"Perhaps it takes one to know one," I quipped. "You started the whole thing, after all."

"I know. And I'm sorry it got so out of hand." He wrapped his arms around his drawn-up legs and studied me with a frankness I found disturbing.

I leaned back and let the sun warm my face. The chatter of blue jays and rustling of the leaves and the busy hum of bees dipping into some nearby sunflowers was soothing.

"Nice, isn't it?" he said as if reading my thoughts. His brown eyes traveled over me. "Why are you so reluctant to enjoy yourself, Miss Banning?"

I avoided his gaze. "The creek looks like a pretty blue ribbon twisting through the trees," I said.

"Why did they name it Devil's Creek?"

"Mineral springs feed into it. The natural effervescence causes the water to bubble. I guess someone thought it resembed a boiling cauldron from the underworld."

"I would have named it differently," he said. "Something musical, like Angel's Fountain." He smiled at me.

"What part of the country are you from, Reverend—"

"Daniel, please," he insisted. "I haven't gotten accustomed to the 'Reverend' yet. I was born in Louisiana, in a little town on the Mississippi, but I went to college up north."

"I thought a hint of the South was in your voice. How'd you find your way to this lost corner of the West?"

"Just lucky, I guess."

"Lucky? I didn't think preachers believed in luck."

"Just a figure of speech, Miss Banning. Aren't preachers entitled to that?"

I looked at him seriously. "What made you decide to become a minister? You—you don't exactly look the type," I said.

"I'll take that as a compliment. You might say the Good Lord threw a halter on me when I wasn't looking. Oh, I did my share of bucking, trying to break free, but it didn't do any good. When I tried a half dozen other jobs and hated facing every new day, I knew that I might as well give in and get saddle broke." He grinned. "The Lord works in mysterious ways, his wonders to perform. Take you, for instance. I've been wondering how I could corner you for a little talk, and here you walked right into my lair."

"Another figure of speech, I hope."

He grinned. "Miss Banning. Are you doubting my good intentions?"

I had to laugh at his exaggerated expression of pain. I had been right, his hair was quite red in the sun. "I don't know what to make of you, in all honesty," I said.

"I just can't resist the opportunity to stir things up a bit now and again. People can be unbearably stuffy and judgmental. When I first saw you, I sensed I had met a kindred spirit. I was happy to join forces with you to bring a little life into that high society tea. I didn't expect things would get out of hand."

"It wasn't your fault."

He suddenly grew serious. "What's this business between you and Nina Milburne?"

"I don't know what you're talking about."

"The temperature dropped drastically when the two of you were in the same room. I thought I was going to get frostbite just being in close proximity."

Well put, I thought. "You're imagining things."

"It might help if you talked it out, Deanna. I guarantee complete confidentiality."

I laughed hollowly. "Please, Reverend, I'm not one of your parishioners."

"Wrong. I checked the church roles. You and your

58

brother were baptized a few weeks after your birth—that makes you a member of my church. And even if it didn't, I'd want to help you."

"What makes you think I need help?" I answered scornfully. His interest in my personal affairs began to irritate me. I resented his presumptuousness. The man knew nothing about me. "Why don't you spend your energies on good church folk like Elizabeth and Mrs. Milburne. I can handle my own affairs just fine, thank you."

"Can you? Is that why you have the look of someone haunted, and your mouth quivers like a frightened child's when you talk about the past?"

"That's not true!"

His brown eyes darkened. "What are you afraid of, Deanna?"

I put down the cup. "Thank you for the lemonade," I said with some finality.

"Please, won't you let me help? I have a feeling that you're hounded by the past. You're too young to live that way." He searched my face anxiously. "Life must be understood backwards but . . . it must be lived forwards."

"Where do you get your theology, Reverend? That happens to be Kierkegaard, not the Bible."

"Not all the world's truths come from the Bible," he said archly. "Maybe your view of the world is too narrow, Deanna."

"And maybe yours is too invasive," I snapped. "Please stay out of my affairs."

"You're very much afraid," he said flatly. "And running away from something."

"I'm a coward. Is that what you're trying to tell me in your sanctimonious way?"

"Not at all. I believe you have a lot of courage, Deanna. Maybe too much. I suspect that you know who murdered your brother."

He was so far off the mark I had to laugh. "You couldn't be more wrong. Walter was a gambler and a ladies' man and any number of people could have decided he deserved a knife in his ribs. It could have been an impassioned act of jealousy or vengeance . . . Walter Banning was not discriminating in his choice of women."

"And he was killed in a whorehouse?"

"Just outside," I said, "but none of the girls admitted to seeing him that night. He'd been playing poker in the saloon, but left before the game broke up. He told the other players that he was going to visit one of the trollops that lived in the shacks behind the saloon. Jon Duval, his companion, came to the house and told us he'd been found in the alley with a knife in his back." I shivered, remembering the horror of that night.

"I'm sorry." Daniel touched my hand. "Deanna, there's no reason to keep torturing yourself about this. You don't have to endure a life sentence of pain because of it."

I decided that it was in my best interests to let him go on believing it was my brother's murder that was responsibile for the burden I bore.

"Why don't you tell me about it?" he asked softly.

"All right." I took a deep breath of relief. His self-satisfied expression was absurd. How superior I felt to him at that moment.

He moved to sit beside me on the smooth rock shelf. His presence was slightly disconcerting; I stared straight ahead as I began to talk. I felt as if I was in a trance. It had been so long since I had relived the events of that night.

"Walter didn't say anything at supper that night about where he was going," I began. "Steven and

60

Elizabeth were married by then and I remembered that things had been tense at dinner. Elizabeth had it in her head that she was going to redecorate the whole house and Steven had promptly said no. His wife made some remark about not needing his permission, since Walter controlled all the money. Walter was the one working to keep Bannings—the department store—in business." I moistened my lips and firmed my chin. "Elizabeth was always throwing this up to Steven, complaining that Papa had only settled a small income on Steven and me and left all the property to Walter. Steven could only take so much of this; eventually he threw down his napkin and left the table.

"Walter finished his dinner quickly and then rode off on his horse. He didn't say where he was going— he never was one to let Steven and me in on his business. My older brother always kept his own counsel, maybe because he was eight years older than us. Papa was the only one Walter really confided in, and after Papa's death, my half-brother seemed to draw away from the rest of us even more. Steven and I tried to ease his grief, but Walter wasn't the kind to let anyone see what went on underneath. He didn't seem any different that night.

"I remember Elizabeth leaving the table soon afterward, telling me that she was going to drive out to see her folks. She was extremely agitated."

"So both Steven and Elizabeth were out that evening?"

"Yes. I settled down with a book, and I must have dozed off in a chair in the parlor, because I was startled awake at the sound of someone knocking frantically on the front door. I realized then that it was almost midnight. Later I learned that Elizabeth had stayed at her parents' house for the night and

61

Steven had slipped up the backstairs to bed. I opened the door to Jon Duval, Walter's best friend. I knew immediately something was wrong.

"I should have known it was Walter, but my first thought was that something had happened to Steven. My twin brother is the dearest person in my life. We had been thrown together in the same heap when we were babies and had always relied on each other. Besides, Walter was the kind who could take care of himself. Never for a second did I think that something had happened to him. I couldn't believe it when Duval said there had been an unfortunate accident. That's what he called it at first, an accident. But then he told me that Walter had been killed outside some prostitute's crib."

"Did you know Walter was spending his time with ladies of the night across the river?"

"I told you. He liked women—all kinds. But he never was serious about any of them. He and Duval were always bragging about their amorous exploits. They're the kind of men that could make a seventy-year-old woman blush and wish she were young enough to compete for their favor. There're plenty of men who could have wished them both dead."

"And your brother, Steven, inherited the store after Walter's death?"

"We both did. Papa left Bannings to Walter, but upon his death it fell to us. Some people suspected Steven might have killed Walter to get the store, but they didn't know how much he hates it."

"And you left Brimstone right after the murder?"

"Not long after."

"But weren't you and Brian Milburne courting at the time? Surely his mother didn't blame you for your brother's indiscretions." He looked puzzled. "She doesn't seem to hold it against the rest of the family now, being that she moves in the same social circle as Elizabeth."

I was silent and stared at a small wild primrose trailing between two rocks, valiantly defying the barren ground. Even though the sun was high overhead, shadows stretched over the tiny plant that still raised a fragile blossom upward. Its tenacity shamed me.

"What drove you away from Brimstone, Deanna?"

My defenses locked into place. Maybe I hadn't fooled him after all. "Walter's murder."

He looked skeptical. "You weren't in any danger, were you? Did you think the murderer suspected you knew who had killed your brother?"

I side-stepped the question. "A position was offered me by the Lowenstein family, who were vacationing in Brimstone at the time. When Mrs. Lowenstein offered me a governess position, I accepted. I wanted to get away and see a little of the world, that's all."

"There's more to it than that. I don't know what specters you're trying to keep hidden." He gave me a warm smile. "I suspect that most individuals would have been crushed under the pressures you've endured. I'd like to ease the torment, if you'd let me."

I wanted to laugh at his simplicity. As if he could change anything! I was growing impatient with his meddlesome ways. "I told you that I've come to terms with Walter's murder."

"But there's something else you're not telling me. What is it, Deanna?"

"Why don't you mind your own business?" I snapped. I rose to my feet. "Thank you for the refreshment."

Some people just don't know when to quit.

Lifting my skirts, I marched away defiantly. I was

afraid he would follow, but he remained sitting and did not call after me. I felt him watching me as I descended the hill, stumbling upon loose sandstone in my haste to flee. I attempted to catch my breath. Damn him, anyway! I had enjoyed his company until he began to pry. I could see why the women in his congregation sought his company at their dinner parties and social functions. He was attractive and charming when he wanted to be. There were moments in his company when I had felt an almost girlish excitement, but of course that was ridiculous.

I vowed to keep my distance from the persuasive Reverend Norris. The conversation about Walter had brought back some feelings which I had kept buried deep within me for too long. The preacher's speculations had disturbed me. Was there some truth to them? Could it be that my brother's killer was only waiting for me to make a threatening move? Maybe an instinctive need for self-preservation had made me deny the knowledge that lurked in my subconscious. Daniel had asked me if I was afraid. I had lied when I said I wasn't.

The next few days were uneventful. I settled into a languid routine, eating, sleeping, and sneaking time in the nursery when Elizabeth was away attending to her numerous civic duties. The maid, Sarah, was happy to have some time free and became my conspirator. Almost every morning Patty bounded into bed with me. We giggled and snuggled until Sarah was finished bathing Nicky. Sometimes Sarah left the baby with me and when he gave me his lopsided grins, my maternal instincts reared; little Nicky was like a bellows fanning a flame. The boy was a happy one-year-old, crawling everywhere, exploring the land under tables and chairs. Patty and I squealed with delight when he tried his first steps from my dresser stool to my bed.

Steven eagerly kept me informed about his greenhouse and experimental projects. He laughed when I related to him one afternoon my confrontation with the bellicose gardener. "That's Jericho. He's an old misanthrope, but his hands can turn a wasteland into paradise. Don't know what I'd do without him. He's as rough and uncouth as they come, but he tends every flower as if it were one of his children. Very possessive."

"Indeed!" I agreed. "His glare was so menacing I thought he was going to hang me from the nearest tree for cutting a bouquet. I was in the wrong and I admitted it." I didn't tell Steven the extent of the man's unpleasantness. I didn't want to cause any trouble.

"You'd better check with Jericho first if you want some flowers . . . better yet, ask him to cut them for you. Elizabeth has had her own run-ins with him. He nearly stabbed her with a pair of shears when he caught her bringing one of my experimental plants inside. She was furious and ordered me to get rid of him, but I couldn't manage without Jericho. Come on, let me show you my new vermilion rose."

I had to laugh at his parental pride. He strutted like a new father, when showing me his garden.

Maude interrupted us a few minutes later, saying "There's some folks in the parlor waiting to see you, Deedee."

My stomach lunged. "Who?"

"A couple of ladies . . . and a man. Miss Elizabeth says you're to come right away."

I looked at Steven questioningly. He gave a

puzzled shrug. "I guess you'd better run along and see."

Before I reached the door of the family parlor, I heard Elizabeth talking animatedly and stopped short when I recognized the voice that responded to her. Moistening my dry lips, I entered the room briskly, attempting to appear collected.

"There you are, Deanna." Elizabeth's sharp glance of disapproval at my dusty day dress made me shudder. Perhaps I should have freshened up before greeting her guests.

Nina Milburne's glare was as censorious. Della Danvers, Brian's aunt, gave me a formal nod of her head. The look she gave me was as contemptuous as the ones she had given me on the train. A middle-aged gentleman rose to his feet and peered at me through round gold-framed glasses. He was short, stocky, dressed in a dark suit and brocade vest that stretched over an undefinable waistline. He looked like a banker. I had a feeling this was not to be a social call.

Elizabeth hurriedly made the introductions. "This is Nina's sister, Della Danvers. She just arrived from the East . . ." Then she stopped, flustered. "But of course, you know that, Deanna, since she was on the same train with you. And this is Mr. Beckner, an investigator for . . . what insurance company, Mr. Beckner?"

"National Trust and Life."

"Have a seat, Deanna," ordered Elizabeth. "These people want to speak with you."

I took the closest high-back chair and tried to appear placid as I folded my hands in my lap. I hoped no one could detect from my outward appearance the devastation that lay within. I forced myself to observe the social formalities. "It's nice to see you again, Miss

Danvers. I hope you're rested from your journey and enjoying your stay in Brimstone."

She gave a rather rude snort. "This visit has been rather less than enjoyable from the moment I arrived—and even before that. That horrible train ride. My lovely brooch lost." She touched her forehead with her lace hankie. "One aggravation after another."

"We're here, Deanna," said Mrs. Milburne with her steel-gray eyes fastened on me, "because we know you sat next to Della on the train from Colorado Springs to Brimstone."

I nodded, hoping that my expression would not give me away.

Mr. Beckner cleared his throat with a gesture that set his double chin jiggling. "You see, Miss Danvers isn't quite certain when or where she lost the brooch. We hoped you might have noticed whether or not she was wearing it on the train."

I stared over his head. "A brooch? I really can't say."

"But you must have noticed it," protested Della Danvers impatiently. "It was a jeweled basket with diamonds, opals, rubies and pearls. I designed it myself and had it made in New York. Unfortunately I didn't insure it for its full value." She sent Mr. Beckner a look that suggested it was somehow his fault. "And now it's gone, and there's a lot of nonsense about proving that it's really lost so I can collect the insurance."

"Maybe it wasn't lost," said Mrs. Milburne. "Maybe someone stole it."

Della leaned toward me. "You must have noticed it. I'm positive it was on my lapel when I boarded the train. Of course, there were a lot of questionable people aboard, and they rudely shoved against me getting on and off. I suppose any one of them could have slipped it off my cape without me knowing it."

"What about it, Miss Banning?" demanded the investigator. His forehead was furrowed as he rested his eyes on me. "Did you see anyone looking at Miss Danvers as if they might be interested in her jewelry? Anyone suspicious?"

"No."

"Nobody at all?"

"No."

"And you never noticed the brooch at any time on the train?"

"No."

"But I'm positive it was on my cape when I left Colorado Springs," protested the woman. "I remember seeing it in a mirror at the depot."

"Perhaps Deanna's memory isn't as good as it might be," suggested Mrs. Milburne acridly.

There is no way that she can know, I thought. My dire compulsion to take things had not begun until I had been away nearly a year.

"Try to remember, Deanna," Elizabeth ordered impatiently as if her own reputation were somehow at stake.

"I'm sure I would have remembered a lovely brooch like the one Miss Danvers described," I said smoothly, and found myself smiling confidentially into all their faces. At the moment, the act of taking the brooch was far removed from me; the memory was like a shadowy dream. It had no reality.

"We will, of course, attempt in every possible way to recover the lost article," said Mr. Beckner. "There will be a sketch of it in the paper—and a reward."

"I'm sorry I can't be of help," I said.

"Speaking of lost articles," said Mrs. Milburne. "I've been unable to locate my gold pencil. The last time I remember seeing it was during that unpleasant scene here at Hunters Hall. I momentarily left my bag in the dining room."

"Oh, my," said Elizabeth. "I'm sure it wasn't left on the table. I was there when Maude and Sarah cleared. Are you sure—?"

"Of course I'm sure," snapped Nina Milburne.

I was about to rise and excuse myself when a pair of blue eyes peeked around the corner of the hall doorway.

"I know where the pencil is," piped Patty, tossing her yellow curls.

Her mother gasped.

"Well, I do." She pushed her little lip out defiantly.

"Come in here and explain yourself. Did you take Mrs. Milburne's pencil?" Elizabeth demanded in horror.

Patty's mouth curled pugnaciously. Elizabeth flushed with embarrassment. "I can't believe Patty would so such a thing."

"I didn't, Momma." The child was frightened now. Her eyes widened as she saw anger mounting in her mother's red face. The attention Patty had brought upon herself was not the kind she had sought. I wondered what I ought to do.

"Elizabeth, give the child a chance to speak," Nina Milburne said.

"Yes . . . yes, of course." Elizabeth attempted to compose herself. "Tell us about the pencil, Patty."

I could imagine the little girl's mind working—the best way out of this was to keep her mouth shut. She glanced in my direction and I felt the floor shifting under me. *The pencil! I'd forgotten all about it.*

"Tell us, honey," coaxed Elizabeth.

"I forgot."

"Of course, you didn't forget." Her mother's voice rose. "You said you knew where the pencil was."

"I didn't take it!" She scooted over to my chair, crowding up against me. "I didn't take it," she cried as I put a protective arm around her tiny shoulders.

Nina Milburne's gaze moved from the child's tearful face to mine. For a moment I thought the woman was going to tell everyone that she knew I had taken her gold pencil, but the fear was only a product of my guilty conscience. *She didn't know.*

Elizabeth reached over and pulled the child away from my side. She gave Patty a shake. "Where is Mrs. Milburne's pencil?"

I couldn't let Patty take the blame for my uncontrollable weakness. "It's all right, sweetheart," I said to Patty in a soothing tone.

Her large eyes blinked. She held out a sweaty hand and there was the miniature gold pencil.

My mind whirled. Where had Patty gotten it? I couldn't quite remember what had happened to it. That was the way it always was. Like someone coming out of hypnosis, I had lost the ability to bring these events sharply into focus.

"You took Mrs. Milburne's pencil, Patty?" Elizabeth gasped in horror.

"No, no. I didn't! It was Nicky." The little girl's face scrunched up in a well of tears. "He was playing with it . . . and he's too little . . . so I took it. He's too little."

"Of course, he is," said Elizabeth with relief. She pulled Patty up on her lap and smiled at Mrs. Milburne. "There you are, Nina. The mystery's solved. You must have dropped your pencil in the dining room and Nicky found it when he was crawling on the floor."

I held my breath, expecting Patty to correct her

70

mother and tell her that Nicky had found it when he was crawling around my bedroom, but the child snuggled against her mother's breast, satisfied to leave things as they were.

Elizabeth gave an embarrassed laugh. "Well, I guess that settles that mystery."

"I hope my brooch comes to light as easily," Della Danvers said.

"I wouldn't count on it," Nina Milburne replied, and her eyes burned into mine.

Chapter Six

When I went to the store with Steven, for a brief moment as we entered the front door I felt the past rush in upon me. My nostrils were filled with the scent of new leather, cloth, perfumed soaps, rose water, shoe polish, and a familiar mustiness. The same wall ladders ran on tracks in front of merchandise stacked on shelves that reached nearly to the high ceiling. The wide oak-plank floor felt the same under my feet as it had when I was a child scampering amid tables and counters, playing hide-and-seek with Steven while we waited for Papa to take us home.

The store had seemed vast then, arranged in departments with overhead carriers that ran on wires to the office on the second floor where the money was received, change was made, and then sent back to the saleslady and her customers. The same stools were mounted on the floor in front of wooden counters where ladies could sit and contemplate patterns from the new Delineater line, or try on the latest embroidered gloves and boas.

Scattered about the store, wide tables with mammoth legs displayed a variety of dry goods: pen wipers, calico aprons, cigar and comb cases, knitted mittens, boots and shoes, and sundry household items such as stenciled lampshades and embroidered tablecloths.

The ladies' department had been a popular corner of the store. There the fashion-conscious tried on hats presented to them by obsequious saleswomen, or viewed gowns that hung on padded hangers in tall wardrobes. Three tall, free-standing mirrors were still there. I remembered preening in front of them as a young girl, pretending that I was all grown up. Steven would tease me and I'd chase after him, soon forgetting my affected poise. The velvet plush chairs were gone, and racks of garments lined up in the middle of the floor had replaced the impressive displays of feminine ensembles that had graced mammoth glass-fronted wardrobes. In the same way the crowded windows had lacked any aesthetic balance, the store seemed horribly cluttered.

Perhaps my memory was faulty, but there had been an elegance about Bannings that had made the family proud that its name hung above the store. If there had ever been such a grandeur, it was gone now. The hushed voices of one clerk and her customer did nothing to lighten the heavy, oppressive atmosphere.

My mouth was suddenly dry. What was it Daniel had said. *Life must be understood backwards but . . . it must be lived forwards.* Maybe that was the problem. I didn't understand what had happened to me—and to Steven. I looked up at his profile and saw a flicker of tension in his cheek.

Wide stairs in the center of the store mounted to a loft where the business office was located, as well as Papa's private office. Outside it was a balcony where furniture was displayed. Steven guided me up the steps and I experienced a leaden sensation in the pit

74

of my stomach. I half expected Papa to rise up in front of me, his commanding voice resonating to the corners of the store. But it was Mildred Dillworthy who greeted me from the doorway of the business office. "Hello, Deanna. Welcome home."

I reached out and squeezed the woman's firm hand. "Thanks, Millie." She hadn't changed in looks, I thought. Still plain and squarely built, with nut-brown hair twisted in an efficient knot on top of her head. Sensible and hard working. There was a more confident tilt to her broad head than I remembered, but then she had only been a salesgirl in the dry goods department when I had first met her. From what Steven had said, he had been leaning heavily on her to keep the store going. She must be thirty by now, a few years older than Steven and me, but she had always seemed much older.

"I'm sorry I wasn't able to attend the reception for our new minister," she said, sending a chastising look at Steven, "but I had the end-of-month books to tally."

"And they balanced to a penny," responded Steven, smiling. "I don't know what I'd do without Millie." He gave her square shoulders a squeeze.

"Neither do I," she retorted flatly, but I thought I saw a glint of a smile touch her round brown eyes as she looked at him. "A head for figures, you do *not* have, Steven Banning," she chided. "And someone has to keep the profits from sailing out the door. You'd buy every tomfool gadget that any fast-talking salesman passed under your nose."

Steven laughed. "I'm afraid you're right. Thank God, you have a sensible head on your shoulders. Papa was damn lucky to find you. Saved my life, you have. I hate to think what the store would be without you."

I swallowed back my negative assessment of the store's state. I knew Millie was doing the best she could, obviously carrying the heaviest load since Steven didn't have any interest in the business. Probably Bannings would have closed its doors by now if it hadn't been for Millie's dogged dedication. "We both appreciate your hard work, Millie," I said, wondering how much Steven's prospective buyer would be willing to pay for the store. Not much, I thought. I suspected that Bannings' reputation had deteriorated along with the quality of its goods.

"Are you going to be with us awhile?" asked Millie, "Or are you just here for a visit?"

The same question. The same answer. "I've come home to stay."

"I'm sure Steven is glad to have you back."

"She'll not get away again," Steven vowed, smiling at me. "Now, I'll let you two ladies chat while I tend to business," he said in an officious tone, which might have convinced someone who didn't know him that he was every inch the manager. As he went in the business office, he gave a cheery wave to the cashier, an older woman, who was making proper change for the tiny carrier that had come sailing up from the floor below. Steven sat down behind her at a small desk and proceeded to sort through some mail that had been deposited there.

"Would you like a cup of tea?" Millie asked. "I keep a small burner in the office."

"Yes, thank you."

She turned away and I watched, stiffening as she entered Papa's private office. I suppose I had expected Steven to be using the room, the way Walter had after Papa's death. I followed her, and once again was assailed by a feeling of displacement. I saw that in subtle ways Millie had made the office her own, even

76

though most of the furnishings remained the same. Papa would have never chosen for his desk a kerosene lamp etched with silver flowers. A porcelain teapot, two cups and saucers, and a tin of China tea sat on a small cherrywood cupboard that once had displayed Papa's pipes and tobacco. His large English desk was loaded with invoices, orders, and stacks of folders. Of course, Millie deserved the office, since she was the one doing the work. What would Steven do if she married and left him to manage alone? Surely he had better arrange to sell the store before Millie announced her engagement.

"Please have a seat, Deanna."

I hesitated. Surely Papa had spoken those exact words to me once, sitting behind the desk, his robust figure filling the leather chair as he bent over his important papers. I could see him sitting back leisurely on the black horsehair sofa against the wall, smoking and talking business. His old coat rack made of elk antlers still stood near the door, and brown photographs taken at Hunters Hall hung in their usual places on the wall. If Papa had walked in at that moment, I don't think I would have been surprised. His presence lingered even years after his death.

"What did you think of Reverend Norris?" Millie asked pointedly as she prepared the tea.

The question caught me off guard. I knew Millie had always been a staunch church member, singing in the Methodist choir and teaching Sunday school. The minister whom Daniel Norris had replaced had been of the old cloth, administering to his flock in traditional fashion—preaching the Bible on Sundays, baptizing, marrying, and burying with the solemnity of God's anointed one. Millie had been a devoted member of his congregation. I couldn't see that the new preacher fit that pattern in any way. Still, it wasn't up to me to judge.

"He seems to be enthusiastic about his work," I said in a neutral tone, adding silently, *even when it comes to digging graves.*

"Yes, I suppose 'enthusiastic' is a good description," she replied in the same tone. "The other evening, he came to choir practice and before we knew it we were singing old camp songs that I hadn't heard since I went to meeting with my folks." She smiled, and her face lit up quite pleasantly. "I think he's going to stir things up a bit."

I certainly could vouch for that. He'd done a good job on me, and I hadn't even attended services. I wondered what Millie's intended, Herbert Haines, felt about the controversial minister. Steven had said he was a member of the board. As if reading my thoughts, Millie commented, "Herbert feels Reverend Norris is too progressive for this part of the country. He voted against hiring him. So did Nina Milburne, and the Reverend hasn't impressed her the way he must if he expects to stay. She runs things around here, you know."

I knew.

We chatted for several minutes about the changes that had come to Brimstone, and I left the store with a promise to Millie that I would drop by again.

When I left Bannings, stepping outside into the fresh clean air, I felt as if a heavy mantle had been lifted from my shoulders. *I've always hated the store.* Steven's words returned to me and I realized they were also my own. Yes, it would be better to rid ourselves of it, get out from under Papa's shadow. I had been thinking about applying for a teaching position somewhere in the area, since my experience as a governess had proven to me that I was good with children; they responded to me and I to them.

I was filled with renewed optimism as I crossed the street and took a winding path through Mineral Springs Park, delighting in the way in which sunshine filtered through a canopy of trees, onto the green lawns and pebbled paths. A large stone pagoda opened onto Mineral Spring. When I was growing up, water bubbling out of the earth from this natural spring could be sampled with the aid of a tin dipper that hung on a nearby nail. No one thought twice about quenching his thirst using a community cup, but things had changed. Now visitors sat on benches lining the walls of the pagoda while sipping the glistening water from their own containers.

Children squealed as they ran about, mothers shifted babies in their arms, young couples shared secrets, and older visitors sipped with concentration, drinking the water slowly as if in so doing they would draw every drop of healing power into their bodies. I knew that many of them frequented bathhouses. The Miramonte and other more modest hotels were always filled with summer visitors "taking the waters."

I walked toward the creek in a leisurely manner, stopping under the shade of a tree where an artist had set up his easel. I peeked curiously over the man's shoulder as he bent his gray head over an oil painting. The gentleman painter must have sensed my presence, for he swung his head to the side and eyed me in a startled manner. I quickly backed away. "Oh, I'm so sorry . . . I didn't mean to disturb you," I said.

He unwound his long legs from a camp stool, wincing slightly as if the movement caused him some pain. Then he stood to face me. I was unable to read the expression on his face; he stared at me for some moments and I sensed a rather profound sadness in him. This feeling left me as soon as he smiled. "Perfectly all right. I'm just an amateur," he said. His white teeth showed under a bushy mustache. "I'm afraid moving water is a little bit beyond me. I can't seem to get any depth." He closed one eye and squinted at the stream and then back again at his painting.

"Have you tried using a mixture of white and cobalt?"

He looked at me in surprise. "Are you an artist?"

"Heavens, no!" I laughed. "I was governess to some children who took art lessons and I picked up a smattering of this and that. I've often thought I'd try my hand, but . . ."

"You should," he said quickly as my voice trailed off. "Are you a native of Brimstone?"

I nodded.

"Wonderful place for an artist. So much natural beauty. I'd forgotten how dramatic the scenery was."

"You're a frequent visitor?"

"No, no. I was here a long time ago. I wanted to try my hand at painting then but . . . well, other things in life got in the way. So now I'm back to try my hand. There's going to be a watercolor class offered at the Miramonte on Saturdays. Maybe you'd like to try it?" Lines deepened around his eyes as he grinned. "I guess I'd like a little moral support. Most artists frighten me to death. What do you say?"

"I'll think about it." I held out my hand. "Deanna Banning."

"David Kirkland." He wiped his palms on his pants and then shook hands. "Pleased to meet you, Miss Banning. I hope I see you on Saturday."

I laughed and moved away. What a nice old man. For the first time since I had arrived, I felt as if I might be able to make a brand new start. Maybe I could let the past bury the past. I left the park and joined a group of strolling tourists as they took the air and wandered along Shoshone Avenue.

As I passed the Miramonte Hotel, I saw Sabrina Sawyer, the proprietor's wife, standing on the veranda with some guests. Sabrina DeVargas Sawyer had been one of Walter's conquests. Unwittingly, I had come upon them one day in a buggy parked deep in the wooded area about a mile from the house. Enjoying a warm May afternoon, I had been wandering contentedly through the stands of aspen and conifers, taking in the first clusters of wild columbines and iris growing in cool secluded corners. I had thought I was all alone in the mountain glen when I heard a woman's husky laughter. Through the needled foliage, I spotted the buggy and suspected that I had come upon a lovers' rendezvous.

Quietly I turned around and was attempting a furtive retreat when suddenly the woman bounded from the buggy with a playful squeal. She laughingly eluded the man's grasp as he pursued her. Her bodice was unbuttoned and she lifted her skirts high as she danced away. Her black hair hung loose around her shoulders and as it swung back from her face, I recognized her as the hotel owner's wife. The woman was younger than her dull, hard-working husband, Joe Sawyer, and full of life and enthusiasm. I was not surprised that the Spanish beauty had sought a release for her high spirits. Sabrina always had an admiring circle of men around her at the hotel. The shock came when I recognized the man who had captured Sabrina around the waist and was swinging her in the air. Walter!

She playfully broke free of his passionate embrace

81

and ran toward the clump of scrub oak where I stood gaping. I was almost successful in my attempt to keep out of sight, but luck was against me. For a moment our eyes met. Her laughter abruptly ceased, her dark eyes rounded, and then she quickly turned, leading Walter in another direction. I don't think he ever knew what had occurred between us that day. But every time Sabrina and I met since then, her daggered looks warned me to keep my silence.

As I passed the hotel's wide front steps, Sabrina turned and saw me. The smile on her face changed instantly to the threatening expression I remembered so well. For a second I thought she was going to lift the folds of her bright cranberry-colored dress and quickly descend the steps to confront me. If such was her impulse, she changed her mind when I nodded and greeted her politely. "Good morning Sabrina," I said.

She was obviously less than pleased about my return. Surely, after all this time, she trusted me to keep my silence, I thought impatiently. After all, Walter was dead, and I didn't doubt for a moment that she'd had a dozen lovers since then. Her husband was a good businessman, but a dullard. Sabrina on the other hand was bright and accomplished. She could sing and play the piano; she had even painted some impressive watercolors. I wondered if she was the one who was going to teach the painting classes Mr. Kirkland had told me about. A smile played across my lips. It might be fun to see how she would react to having me as a pupil. I had always thought I would have enjoyed her vivacious company if Walter hadn't ruined any chances of a friendship between us.

I continued my walk and imagined that I was seeing the mountain town for the first time. I was beginning to feel almost lighthearted until I reached Alpine Street, where the First Methodist Church sat on the northeast corner. It was built of white clapboard, with wide steps leading up to a double door. The church had a large cross mounted on an impressive belfry that pointed the way to heaven. A hammering sound was coming sporadically from the tower, where a large brass bell tolled on Sundays. I lifted my eyes upward to the belfry but couldn't determine the cause of the disturbance. I was just about to turn back when I heard my name called.

"Deanna! Deanna! Up here!"

There was no doubt in my mind who was flagging me from the bell tower.

I raised my hand in a lukewarm greeting. The idiot! What did he expect me to do? Partake in an embarrassing shouting exchange from the sidewalk?

"Come in!" He gestured with a wave of his arm, and then disappeared.

At least he didn't say, "Come *up*," I thought as I walked up the steps and entered the church foyer. I wouldn't have put it past him to expect me to climb to the belfry and assist him with whatever it was he was doing up there. I walked to a small door on a side wall which opened onto a narrow twisting staircase.

"Be down in a minute!" His voice echoed down the stairwell, followed by another bout of furious pounding.

I leaned against the back wall of the church and surveyed the sanctuary. A new coat of whitewash lent a pristine brightness to the interior, and the arched stained-glass windows sent splinters of rainbow light across the polished oak pews and altar railing. A new wooden cross hung on the back wall and I saw that the choir had new chairs and an impressive new organ.

My gaze fell on the pew where our family had always sat. Papa had been sporadic in his attendance, but Maude had accompanied Walter, Steven, and me almost every Sunday of our lives. My gaze slid across the aisle to the Milburne pew. The thought of Nina Milburne made my beaded bag feel heavy on my arm.

The brooch! I had to get rid of it. Find a way to return it to Della Danvers. Suddenly I conceived of a plan. Why not leave it in the church? Yes, the Reverend could return it. I dug the jeweled pin out of my reticule.

The church was suddenly quiet. The pounding had stopped. He would be down in a minute.

My frantic gaze swept over the sanctuary. Where? I had to find some place where the pin would be discovered later. I was about to despair when my eyes fell on the contribution box affixed to the side wall.

I walked to the box and furiously pushed the brooch through the slot, hearing it clang as it hit the bottom. There. I was free of the wretched thing.

I swung around and took several steps away from the box before I looked up and saw the minister standing in the doorway. For a moment we just looked at each other. I think the earth could have rumbled under us and we wouldn't have noticed. His intense gaze stabbed me, searching, prodding, filling me with fear. He seemed to be weighing factors that had not crossed his mind until that moment.

My mouth went dry.

He waited for me to speak.

I tried to identify the thoughts behind his piercing expression. Why was he looking at me like that? I had my answer when he deliberately turned his eyes from me and looked at the collection box.

He had seen me dispose of the brooch.

I backed up, trying to put as much distance between us as possible. Even now, wearing common work clothes, with waves of reddish hair falling across his forehead and freckles spattered boyishly across his nose, he represented danger. He might not look like a man of religious dedication, but his beliefs would be as rigid and condemning as any who had stood in the church's pulpit.

With a cry in my throat, I brushed past him and fled out the door.

I knew that I had earned his denunciation when he let me go without a word.

Chapter Seven

Thrashing about fitfully in my sleep that night, I dreamed that I was fleeing from Daniel Norris, climbing to the top of the belfry tower. In the enveloping nightmare, I was bounding up an endless staircase with him just steps behind me. Terror filled me as I cowered in a corner of the belfry, facing him. Dressed in black with a cape whipping ominously over his shoulders, he held out his hand showing the brooch in his palm. He walked toward me, giving a triumphant laugh as he pinned the brooch on me.

"No, no!" I struggled to get away, and when I finally got free I turned from him, only to face Nina Milburne pointing a long accusing finger at me. Her face was ugly and vicious. A crescendo of voices rose in chorus around me. "Thief! Thief!"

I put my hands up to protect my face as disembodied faces like a wild flight of birds rushed around me.

"Come, Deanna." Daniel's soothing voice beckoned me, quelling the maddening chant. I meant to go to him but suddenly the high railing gave way. I fell . . . down . . . down! Before my body hit the ground below, I sat up in bed with a cry of terror.

Sweat beaded my forehead. My hands were clammy. Fear ricocheted from one side of my skull to the other. My heart knocked loudly in my chest. *Only a dream,* I soothed myself as one would comfort a child. My eyes darted about the shadowy bedroom for reassurance. Flickers of moonlight struck the floor; their patterns were vaguely menacing.

I slipped out of bed, drew my dressing robe over my nightdress, and crossed the room to the window seat. Pressing my hot forehead against the cool pane, the nightmare receded and I attempted to compose myself. Slowly my breathing returned to normal. The nightmare had faded leaving a deep exhaustion in its wake.

I remained sitting until a pearly light diluted the somber clouds of night and spread streamers of pink across the mountain tops, heralding the beginning of another day. What would the next hours bring? The honorable Reverend Norris would perform his clerical duties. As a moral leader of his flock, he couldn't ignore my culpability, nor become an accessory to my thievery. My stupidity had involved him in this ugly affair. I had to think up something that might counter the evidence he held against me. No one would believe what I knew to be the truth. I didn't *want* the stolen things which mysteriously offered me a moment of warm contentment. I took them because . . . because . . . I bit my lip. If I knew the answer to that, I thought, I wouldn't be in this mess.

The gloom of the house invaded me. When I heard the household stirring, I wearily began to prepare myself to meet the day. I had to summon my inner strength, a strength that had helped me navigate through treacherous reefs before. Giving up had never been in my nature. That was part of my problem. Returning to Brimstone had been a defiant response to threatening forces. I knew that no matter what happened, I must face the crisis without revealing the dark secret that I was determined to keep hidden.

As my mind raced ahead to the impending crisis, I deliberately chose a dress in a partridge-plume color that flattered my fair complexion. The cashmere gown had been a cast-off of Mrs. Lowenstein, and I had managed to alter the skirt by adding a draped apron that accommodated my taller stature. A soft pouf flared the back gores in a modest bustle, and two embroidered panels rippled to the floor. Maybe a condemned man needs a full stomach to face his accusers, I thought, as I carefully swept my hair into a smooth twist, but I needed the assurance that I looked my best when trouble was nigh.

Finally satisfied that I could do nothing more to enhance the impression of outward composure and poise, I went downstairs. Steven was sitting alone at the table when I entered the morning room. "My, don't we look pretty this morning," he said, smiling over his cup of coffee. "Something special going on?"

I smiled back. "Not that I know of," I lied. *How long would it be before I was questioned about the brooch?*

"Isn't today when the outing to Sunshine Falls is scheduled? You know, the one Brian told you about. I really think you ought to go, Dee. It would do you good to be with some young people."

"You talk as if you're ten years older than I am instead of ten minutes," I chided, selecting berry muffins from the sideboard.

"I'm a settled married man with two children. And there are times when I feel fifty." He sighed. "Age is not always counted in years. I don't want to see you forfeit your youth—"

"Is that what you did, Steven?" Elizabeth interrupted him sharply from the doorway, entering the room with her skirts swishing, her eyes sparking. "Forfeit your youth by marrying me?"

Keeping my eyes lowered, I took my place at the table. *Yes, he did,* I answered silently. My brother had only been eighteen when Papa orchestrated the marriage between them. Heartsick at the announcement of their engagement, I had tried to talk Steven into rebelling, but he didn't have the courage to defy Papa. Neither of us had. Walter was the only one who went his own way.

Steven deftly deflected his wife's wrath, smiling warmly at her. "Of course not, my love, but I do think Dee should enjoy the company of other young people, don't you? Brian invited her to join a group going up to Hunters Glen today. I think she should go."

Elizabeth gave a rather crude snort. "Brian Milburne had best be attending to his fiancée. Carolyn is not the kind to . . ." She paused knowingly for a moment then continued. "To put up with his giving attention to Deanna for old times' sake."

"Good grief, Liz, how ridiculous."

"They were almost engaged," Elizabeth insisted.

"I have no designs on Brian Milburne," I told her evenly. "I think Carolyn is a very nice girl and I wish them well. Whatever was between Brian and me ended five years ago."

"I told Millie that you would love to go," Steven said.

"What?" I exclaimed.

"She's organizing the whole thing. Box lunches, a tallyho from the hotel, the works. Sabrina Sawyer is

90

going. Jon Duval, I think, and some guests of the hotel. About ten people in all. Sounds like fun. They'll pick you up about ten o'clock.''

"You . . .'' I sputtered, but my brother just laughed and looked pleased with himself.

My mind scrambled for a way out of the excursion.

Elizabeth scowled at the two of us, picked up the morning paper, and started reading. "Well, I'll be!'' she gasped suddenly, setting her cup down with such force that she spilled tea into the saucer. "They've found Della's brooch!''

I felt my stomach muscles tighten.

"Really?'' Steven said with a lift of his eyebrows. "I didn't think she'd ever see it again. Where'd they find it?''

"In the Methodist church collection box! Reverend Norris gave it to the police.'' Elizabeth's eyes moved quickly down the printed page.

"The collection box?'' Steven laughed. "Does he know who put it there?''

I gripped my fork so tightly my knuckles rose like white marbles. *Here it comes.* In the next moment Elizabeth's eyes would find mine in a stricken glare of disbelief. I set down the fork and placed my hands in my lap, gripping them so that my fingernails bit into my palms.

She shook her head. "No, but Chief Whitney is looking into it. Says here that Miss Danvers was so grateful to have her brooch back that she gave Reverend Norris a reward. The minister said he'll use the money to make needed repairs in the church.'' She lowered the paper. "Well, I'll be switched!''

I couldn't believe what I was hearing. Daniel Norris had returned the brooch, collected the reward, and played ignorant about where it came from. I wanted to laugh out loud with relief. What a scoundrel he was!

"What's so funny, sis?" asked Steven, puzzled at my expression. My twin had always had a sixth sense when it came to me. I was afraid he could read my guilty thoughts.

"Not funny . . ." I stammered. "Just peculiar . . . Della's jeweled pin showing up like that," I explained lamely.

Elizabeth scowled. "Well, I certainly hope the public doesn't think that any of our church members had anything to do with the theft."

"No one would dare think such a thing, Liz." Steven winked at me. "Everyone knows the Methodist congregation is above reproach."

"Don't be sarcastic, Steven. It wouldn't hurt you to go to church more than twice a year. Anyway, it must have been someone off the street who decided it was too dangerous to keep it."

"Yes, that must be it." I kept my eyes lowered, avoiding Steven's quizzical expression. I knew I should beat a hasty retreat before he got wise to me.

I folded my napkin and stood up. "Well, I guess I'd better get ready if I'm going on a picnic." Suddenly the prospect of spending the day away from the house appealed to me.

"Have fun," Steven said, obviously pleased I had decided to go.

"I think I will." I felt almost giddy. The outing seemed like a wonderful way to celebrate my narrow escape.

Maude insisted on sending along one of her chocolate cakes when she heard about the excursion. I was ready and waiting when the tallyho arrived. Wearing a wide-brim hat to shade me from the sun, mesh gloves to protect my hands, and carrying a silk floral parasol, I bounded down the front steps of the house amid the greetings of those sitting in the bright red carriage. Then my smile vanished.

"Good morning, Deanna," Daniel Norris said pleasantly as he leapt down from the carriage.

No. My instincts told me to flee while I had the chance. The hand he held out to me was much like the gesture in my dream. I half expected to see the brooch lying in the palm of his hand.

His eyes narrowed at my expression, but his mouth curved pleasantly. "Lovely day for an outing, isn't it?"

"Hurry, Deanna," ordered Millie. "We don't want to waste the morning."

Daniel took the cake basket from me and handed it up to Millie. Then he turned to me. "Up you go," he said, firmly guiding me to the tallyho and lifting me into the conveyance. He rounded the carriage and swung up into the seat beside me as if there had never been anything between us but a polite acquaintance.

A crack of a whip sent the two white dray horses off at a brisk clip. Laughter rose above the clatter of rolling wheels and the clop of horses' hooves. Since we were in the last seat of the huge carriage, I could easily survey the party. Millie and her fiancé, Harold Haines, were directly in front of us. Brian sat in a forward seat with Carolyn Lareau, and Sabrina Sawyer was in the front seat between Jon Duval and another man. When the man turned and smiled at me I recognized him as the old gentleman artist, David Kirkland, whom I had met in the park.

I wasn't looking forward to being in Jon Duval's company. Walter's best friend brought back too many bad memories. I had never liked him. His glossy dark hair, leathery face, and bull-like neck, his swagger, and leering white-toothed smile always set my nerves on edge. I'd seen him and Walter falling down drunk, and watched them gallop off waving hunting rifles like a couple of Comanche Indians. Still on the prowl, I thought, as Duval put his arm on the back of Sabrina's seat in a pretense of steadying her over the bumps. I wondered if he had taken Walter's place as her paramour.

With every lunge of the tallyho, I was thrown against Daniel Norris even though I gripped the side of the seat in an effort to keep as much distance between us as possible. I was dismayed by his presence. I never dreamed he would be going on the outing or I certainly would have found a way to remove myself from the party.

At least he had the decency not to try to engage me in conversation. Millie turned around from the seat in front of us, smiled at the preacher, and pointed out to him points of interest. Her plain face was shaded by a new straw bonnet and the powder blue dress she wore softened the lines of her stocky frame. Harold Haines was a thin man in his forties who worked as bookkeeper for the Spring Water Bottling Company. A black derby hat sat atop Harold's salt-and-pepper hair and he often tugged at a thin goatee which I suspected might hide a weak chin. Gold-rimmed glasses gave his face a studious look and he maintained a formal poise in the jostling carriage, but a soft smile touched his lips whenever he looked at Millie. I sighed, happy for the two of them. Millie was lucky to find someone who would provide an escape from the years of drudgery ahead. Steven could sell the store without worrying about her future.

As Reverend Norris leaned forward to hear her better, I was conscious of his handsome profile and the broad sweep of his shoulders. He was wearing gray pants, a summer jacket with frayed cuffs, a soft white shirt, and his clerical collar. His hair was properly smoothed under a summer hat. Only cowboys boots betrayed his disdain for proper attire. He was quite an enigma. He had returned the brooch and kept his silence, but I didn't fool myself for one minute that the incident was over. I turned my eyes away from him and fixed my gaze on the passing landscape.

A wagon road followed Devil's Creek. Rapid running water plunged through the narrow canyon bounded by granite walls. Wind and weather had sculpted the cliffs into dramatic shapes that were softened by a patina of yellow, green, and pink lichen. Dust rising from under the huge wooden wheels mingled with the scent of spruce, cedar, and pines. In some places the passage was so narrow that needled branches scraped the sides of the conveyance as the twisting, climbing road bent back upon itself.

I had been to Hunter's Glen and Sunshine Falls many times for summer picnics and winter ice-skating parties. My heart leapt with renewed excitement when the protected mountain valley came into view. The scene was more beautiful than I had remembered. Cupped by green velvet wooded hillside, knolls of grass sloped down to a small lake, which lapped an uneven shoreline. In a nearby canyon Sunshine Falls cascaded hundreds of feet down into a widening pool that flowed into the lake and fed the waters of Devil's Creek.

I heard Daniel's sharp intake of breath as he viewed the mountain loveliness and I felt an almost parental pride, as if somehow the beauty was mine to share. "It's beautiful!" he said in wonder.

"Yes," I said, breathing deeply to control a wild

exhilaration that suddenly overcame me. I forgot myself and smiled up at him. For a moment our eyes met and an indescribable feeling came over me, as if I was in the company of someone who shared with me a particular way of looking at the world. I had the distinct sensation of being poised on the edge of a precipice. One step forward in any direction and I would plunge off the edge.

"Sunshine Falls. Dramatic, isn't it?" Millie said, turning to point this out to him.

He tore his eyes from mine. "Very."

"When the sun hits the canyon, the water looks like liquid gold," I said.

"We'll all hike up the base after lunch," said Millie authoritatively. "But I have to warn you, Reverend Norris, that the roar is deafening and the spray is as cold as ice."

He laughed. "Wonderful! I prefer cold water baths, brisk enough to prickle the skin."

Millie blushed as if he had drawn a picture of his own glistening naked body. She turned around quickly. I smothered a smile. With his usual frankness, Daniel Norris seemed to have put both feet in it—again.

When the tallyho stopped at the edge of trees near the lake, I was surprised when Brian Milburne, after helping Carolyn onto the ground, then reached to assist me before Daniel could come around the wagon to offer his help.

"So glad you could come, Dee," he said with a warm glint in his eyes. "It will be nice to recall old times."

There was an intimacy in his tone I found inappropriate. I tried to think of some flippant response, but clever retorts never came easily to me—especially when deep emotions were involved. I didn't want Brian's attention. Not now. We'd attended several community picnics held in this very spot and he'd kissed me for the first time in one of the weathered gazebos that had offered privacy during one of our strolls.

"Remember the time we were out in a rowboat and got caught in the rain?" He chuckled. "I've never seen anyone as drenched as we were. I think you wrung a gallon of water out of your hair."

I felt Carolyn's eyes measuring the contact between us and I hoped my cheeks didn't show the embarrassed warmth that was seeping up in them. Fortunately, David Kirkland joined us at that moment and I turned away from Brian to greet him. "So nice to see you again, Mr. Kirkland."

The old gentleman gave me a warm smile. "My pleasure, Miss Banning. I confess I didn't know whether I should join the outing when Sabrina invited me . . . an old duffer like myself in the midst of all you young people."

"Nonsense. It's a pleasure to see you again." I began walking with him toward the lake. We left Millie commandeering Daniel, Brian, and Harold into carrying food baskets to nearby picnic tables. I accepted Mr. Kirkland's company with relief. "You should find plenty of things to sketch," I said, noticing the drawing pad he carried under his arm.

"Makes one feel humble, this awesome natural beauty. Awakens deep emotions, doesn't it?" He took a deep breath, moved as I was by the vista that surrounded us. We stood in silence at the lake's edge.

Canadian geese strutted along the water's edge and green-backed ducks out on the water rode the soft lapping waves as though the lake were a huge rocking chair. A deep blue Colorado sky spread like an inverted bowl over the jagged mountain tops, and a brassy sun spilled into the glen. A deep healing stirred inside me, as if nature had touched me with a magic wand.

"I love it here," I said, feeling truly at home with my feet firmly planted on mountain soil. I no longer felt displaced. In some mystic way the panorama of sky, water, and mountains gathered me close, like the arms of a protective deity.

"One can feel the human spirit expanding," he said softly, as if echoing my thoughts.

"Maybe you'd like to walk around the lake after lunch, Mr. Kirkland. There's a nice easy path and you can rest in one of the open gazebos along the way. Lots of places to enjoy the view. In the winter, ice skaters build fires there to warm their toes. I confess I spent a lot of time polishing the ice with my back side," I told him, laughing as I remembered how Steven had picked me up off the ice a hundred times when I was first learning to skate.

Kirkland smiled with me. "I bet you didn't give up, though."

I shook my head and chuckled again, remembering the first time I had victoriously skated across the lake all by myself.

"I hope you won't mind my saying so, Miss Banning, but I must tell you that you are very pretty when you smile."

"And when I don't?" I teased.

He looked flustered. "I only meant—"

I laughed. "Thank you for the compliment. Do you have any children, Mr. Kirkland?"

"Sadly, no. I'm one of those lonely old men who let the important things in life pass them by. I've made money, plenty of it in the shipping business, but at this point in my life, I'd trade it all for family."

"Belonging is important," I agreed. "But some-

98

times having a family doesn't take away the loneliness."

His response was preempted by Sabrina Sawyer. "Well, there you are, David! The food's all set out. Come along." Sabrina boldly slipped her arm through his and pouted her lovely full lips. "I absolutely forbid you to start drawing until after lunch." Her eyes found mine, and they were as dark, cold, and hard as flint. Her manner toward David Kirkland was protective, as if it were her responsibility to keep him out of dangerous company—mine.

The memory of her disheveled hair and open bodice as she playfully ran away from Walter seemed to rise like a specter between us. Was she still fearful that I would reveal her adulterous relationship with my dead brother? Or was she antagonistic toward me for some other reason which I failed to fathom?

"We were just enjoying the view," the artist said smoothly. "But I confess the smell of fried chicken is mighty tempting. Shall we join the others, Deanna, before all that delicious fare disappears?"

His use of my first name surprised me, but I was grateful for it because Sabrina was less able to dismiss me with her haughty stare.

I smiled back and he put a guiding hand under my arm and walked between Sabrina and me. I was puzzled. He was too old for Sabrina's wandering eye, a father figure if anything, but, knowing Sabrina, David Kirkland's paying attention to me was enough to spark her interest. What was she afraid of?

Two tables had been pushed together and enough food for a weekend spread from one end to the other. I filled a plate with chicken, three kinds of salad, warm biscuits, and sugared strawberries. Even though there were open spaces on the benches, I found a smooth rock nearby and took a seat.

I stiffened when Daniel Norris made a move in my direction, but he only gave me an acknowledging smile and then eased down on a bench with Millie and Harold, who were sitting across from Sabrina, David Kirkland, and Jon Duval. Brian and Carolyn chose to sit on the grassy ground just a few feet from me; the remarks between us were limited to the scenic view and the delicious food. Brian poured me more lemonade and offered me another piece of chicken.

"I couldn't," I protested after enjoying my second helping. "Besides, I want to save room for Maude's chocolate cake. I haven't forgotten the taste of that dark frosting."

"Me, either." He chuckled. "Once I ate three pieces in rapid succession before someone snatched the cake plate away."

Carolyn laughed. "Greedy urchin! I'll have to bake you one of my angel food cakes." She smiled wryly. "That's about the only thing I've mastered."

"What?" said Brian in mock horror. "Is that all we're going to have to eat—angel food cake?"

I laughed with them. Even though I wasn't entirely comfortable with Brian, our relationship had faded into the past, indistinct and unreal. I liked Carolyn and I found myself feeling protective of her in the face of Brian's teasing banter.

They wandered away, leaving me somewhat apart from the group, and much to my displeasure, Jon Duval took advantage of my solitary position and joined me. He swaggered toward me flashing a broad, white-toothed grin from his deeply tanned face. He eased down on the ground in front of me without waiting for the slightest invitation. In order to make an escape, I would have had to step over him. I was trapped. My look was anything but amicable as I glared at him.

He laughed at my scowl as if amused. "Never did like me, did you, pretty Miss Dee? But then we never had a chance to really get acquainted." His eyes were as black as his thorned eyebrows; a masculine prowess exuded from him like an animal's scent. He casually chewed on a piece of tassel grass as he gazed up at me, smiling in an infuriating, intimate way.

"I never thought about it one way or the other," I said crisply. "You were Walter's friend—not mine."

"Sure do miss that brother of yours. Life just ain't the same without Walt. Had some good times, we did." He laughed as if remembering some of their escapades. "We were a pair, all right. Always trying to best each other—in everything." He smirked. "Some of our contests weren't fit for the ears of a lady."

I felt disrobed the way his gaze followed my dress up my waist, lingered on my breasts, and then lazily smiled into my face. He always behaved as if he was going to be guilty of the most sordid impropriety at any time. I cursed myself for not staying at the table with the others. Sitting apart had invited his company. My success in avoiding Daniel Norris had backfired.

I shot a glance at Sabrina, hoping she would feel possessive about Duval's attention and interrupt us, the way she had with David Kirkland, but she was laughing at a story Daniel was telling her and I was unreasonably furious with them both. Couldn't they see how offensively Duval was behaving?

He laughed as if he enjoyed seeing me squirm. "Walter always said his little sister needed a lot of looking after. He thought Papa Banning should have married you off the way he did Steven."

"He said that?" In spite of myself I was interested in Duval's remark.

"Yep. Walter said you and Steven were about as able to take care of yourselves as a couple of suckling kittens."

"Walter was the one who got killed," I said heatedly.

Duval scowled. "By God, I wish I could get my hands on the bastard who planted that knife. If only I had kept him at the poker table for another couple of hands at the Rattlesnake Saloon, things would've been different. We would have left together. But no, Walt just had to have some female company that night. The next thing I knew someone was yelling that he'd been stabbed to death."

"Who do you think did it?" I asked bluntly.

"Hell, I don't know. He played pretty close to the edge, your brother did. Strong-willed, he was. Just like your Pa. Couldn't change him with an iron crowbar. We had a few disagreements, but none that couldn't be settled with a few swigs of a jug. We shared everything, me and Walt did. Horses . . . guns"—he smirked lewdly—"and other things."

My skin crawled. He was probably carrying on with Sabrina the same way Walter had. "You are as offensive as ever."

Duval's eyes narrowed just a moment before his toothy smile mocked my indignation. "Still flashing those greenish eyes and trying to cut a man down, eh? Well, I always thought the right man could gentle you soon enough. Maybe I'll give it a try."

Before I could protest, Millie bustled over to collect my plate.

"Did you get enough to eat, Deanna?"

I nodded. "Yes, thank you." Duval had made my stomach so tight, I wondered if I would disgrace myself by losing my meal.

"Come on. We're going to hike up to the falls," she said.

Duval hefted himself to his feet. "Good idea."

I swept past him before he could detain me any further and busied myself by repacking the picnic baskets.

Millie and Harold persuaded everyone to join the hike up to the falls. The two of them led the procession toward the small canyon, where a dramatic spill of water fell thousands of feet over a rocky cliff. Brian and Carolyn were second in line and I was relieved to see that Sabrina had collected Duval and was walking with him. Mr. Kirkland walked behind them, surveying the scene, his sketch pad in his hand.

I hurried to catch up with him, but before I could Daniel appeared at my side, boldly helping me over a pile of rocks strewn on the rough path.

"Looks like there's been a rock fall here," he said in a conversational tone.

My efforts to draw away from him were to no avail. He kept a firm hand on my elbow. Finally I stopped, determinedly faced him, and growled, "Say whatever you're going to say and be done with it." I clutched my parasol with white-knuckled fingers.

He laughed outright. "You try so hard to be formidable, Deanna. But you won't have any luck turning me into an ogre, so let's just relax and be ourselves."

How could I relax with him? I felt like a toy dangling in front of a cat, waiting for its sharp claws to reach out and swipe me. He knew I had put the brooch in the collection box. Was he going to feign ignorance? I wasn't in the mood for games. "Please, let's get this over with!"

"Get what over with?"

Ironically my respect for him diminished even as hope surfaced. I needed his protection and yet I scorned him for compromising his own integrity. I silently chided myself for being a fool, but I couldn't help myself. "The paper said that you collected a reward for returning Miss Danvers' brooch?"

"Yes. I was wondering how we were going to cover the cost of repairing the belfry. Then the brooch turned up in the collection box."

"An answer to prayer, perhaps?"

He ignored the sarcasm and gave me a patient grin. "I never pray for money . . . but I do pray for other things. Like ways to help someone who I know is unhappy. Want to tell me about it, Deanna?"

So he was going to exact his pound of flesh. I had known it all along. "About what?" I asked with mock innocence.

"About the brooch."

"What's to tell?" I parried.

"Why did you take it?"

"How do you know I did?"

"Didn't you?"

I wanted to avoid his calm, intelligent eyes but like a grappling hook, they drew my gaze to his. "Yes, I took it."

"Why?"

My throat tightened. "Why?" I echoed the word blankly. Then spiritedly, "Why? Because I wanted it. Why else do people steal things?"

"For many reasons. Desperation? Possession? Excitement? Which one is it, Deanna?" His lips curved in a soft smile. "As your accomplice, I think I have a right to know."

I shook my head. "No. You wouldn't understand."

"Wouldn't I?"

"No, because I don't understand myself."

His brown eyes deepened. "All the more reason to share the load. I promise, Deanna, that however dark and dire your secrets, they're safe with me. I want to understand. I want to help . . . as a friend."

My defenses went up. He couldn't be my friend. There were too many things in the way. "Thank you for returning the brooch," I said formally as if that were the end of the matter.

"No problem. I was able to do it without compromising you or me. Della Danvers was so happy to have it back she really didn't care how it came about. Her sister, Nina Milburne, was a little more insistent."

"I bet she was."

"Does she know about . . . ?" he hesitated.

"My penchant for thievery?" I finished for him. "No, just you."

"Can't we talk?" Without waiting for my consent, he guided me off the path to a fallen log. He brushed some dry leaves away so we could sit down. "Now tell me, Miss Banning. When did this life of crime begin?"

His warm smile assured my safety. How could I reject the haven he offered? I couldn't lie to myself. I desperately needed a friend. "All right," I said in a resigned voice. "I'll tell you the whole story." Where did I begin?

"When did it all start?" he prodded.

"The first winter I was away from home. I saw a pretty bracelet in a New York shop and for a moment when I held it in my hand, all homesickness and loneliness left me. An indescribable warmth invaded me as I touched it and in a kind of trance, I walked out of the shop without even realizing that I had it clutched in my hand. Horrified, I anonymously sent it back the next day."

"Then you didn't want to own the bracelet? You just liked the feeling it gave you when you held it?"

I nodded. "It hasn't happened very often, thank God. There's a deep ache inside me, and when I see something lovely, I reach out for it—even though I tell myself at the time that I shouldn't." I searched his face. "Why do I do it?"

"We all meet our needs as best we can. When the human spirit is starved, the mind ingeniously attempts to find ways to fill the void."

"I have a twisted mind, is that what you're saying?" I said. I should have known better than to expect him to understand. Why had I ever allowed myself to confide in the man?

"You love to put words in my mouth, don't you?" he chided amicably.

At that moment Mr. Kirkland walked down the path from the waterfall. He saw us sitting on the log and joined us. "This is a good place for sketching," he said. I had the distinct impression that he had come back to find me.

Daniel made some polite conversation with him and then turned to me. "Well, are you rested enough to continue our hike to the falls?" His almost imperceptible wink challenged me.

I nodded. Like two conspirators we excused ourselves and left the older gentleman sitting on the log with his sketching pad.

Unexpectedly Daniel turned me down the path away from the falls and the rest of the party. "Let's walk around the lake."

"We can't leave the others!" I protested.

"Why not?"

"It isn't proper. I mean, we must stay in a group."

His eyes twinkled. "I assure you, Miss Banning,

your reputation will not be compromised—I'm the chaperon."

I sputtered, but ended up laughing. How could he infuriate and delight me at the same time? He was impossible.

"That's better," he said, grinning. "I see a rowboat pulled up on the bank. How about a little trip on the lake?"

I shook my head.

"Are you afraid I'd drown you?"

"No."

"Maybe when we get to know each other better, you'll trust me."

"I think you know me all too well," I countered. I kept my chin elevated and my eyes fixed ahead on the soft lapping of water along the grassy bank as we walked back to the place where our picnic things were spread. I made a pretense of straightening up the baskets on the table.

He left me for a moment and when he came back, he startled me by holding out a small bouquet of wildflowers. The petals were silken, the yellow like spun gold. "Take them," he said.

I raised questioning eyes to his smiling face. His gaze was warm, caressing. I blinked rapidly to hold back a warm fullness in my eyes. His attention promised a relationship that could never be. I knew now that he wasn't the enemy, but he was the symbol of morality and social mores in the community. That made any continued intimacy between us extremely unlikely.

Chapter Eight

I awoke the next morning with a smile on my face. The contentment I felt was a marked contrast to my usual heavy spirits. I laughed silently. What a fool I was! A little attention from a personable, unconventional preacher and I felt as free as a bird who unexpectedly found its cage open. I looked at the bouquet of wildflowers I had put in a glass by my bed, and this time I laughed aloud. Late yesterday afternoon, when Daniel had helped me down from the tallyho and thanked me formally for a lovely afternoon, he had given me one of his teasing winks as if we shared a secret.

It had helped me enormously, my being honest with him about my uncontrollable impulse to seize certain lovely objects for myself, if only for a moment. He seemed to understand the compulsion. What was it he had said? "When the human spirit is starved, the mind ingeniously attempts to fill the void." If that were true, I wished I'd found some other way to compensate for the emptiness in my life. In any case, now that I understood what was happening, maybe I was better equipped to deal with it.

Humming to myself, I went downstairs and found

Elizabeth alone at the breakfast table. She had a pile of envelopes at her elbow and was hurriedly dipping a pen into an inkwell as she addressed them. I didn't want to disturb her, so I quietly assembled my breakfast from the sideboard and took a chair some ways down the table from her. I was surprised when she sighed and gave me an appealing look. "Deanna, would you be so kind as to stamp these invitations for me? I want to get them posted this afternoon. They're for our annual church breakfast."

"Of course, Elizabeth. I'd be happy to." My spirits were elevated even higher. This was the first time my sister-in-law had shared anything with me. We worked in harmonious silence until the job was done. "I'll mail them if you'd like," I offered.

"Oh, would you? I have a dozen things I need to do today." She looked at her lapel watch. "Oh, goodness, I'm late for the dressmaker's. And Nina is meeting me at the hotel at ten o'clock for a committee meeting on the proposed opera house." An exasperated expression crossed her face briefly as if the role of community leader was wearing a little thin. With her usual erect carriage, she swept out of the room and in a few minutes I heard the sound of the buggy rolling away from the house.

When I was certain she had gone, I slipped upstairs to the nursery like a thief bent on a nefarious mission.

"I'm going to take a little walk to the post office," I told Sarah. "I think I'll take Patty along for company."

Her eyes widened for a moment. "Oh, I'm not sure you should, Miss Deanna."

Up until then, the most I had dared was to squirrel the children away to my room for a stolen hour when their mother was out of the house. In spite of her busy

110

schedule, Elizabeth was very maternal and protective of her children. I sometimes wondered if she didn't resent all the community and church work that took her away from them.

"It's all right. I'm running an errand for Mrs. Banning," I told Sarah. That much, at least, was true. "Will you get Patty's bonnet?"

The little girl clapped her hands. "Goodie. Goodie." Then she hugged me around the legs, her little face radiant, her blue eyes sparkling. "Will you buy me some ice cream?"

I laughed. "We'll have a treat."

She wiggled so much that Sarah had difficulty tying the streamers of her bonnet under her chin.

"Now you be good," admonished Sarah, giving me an exasperated lift of her eyebrows as the little girl tugged on my hand, pulling me toward the door.

"Bye, Nicky." She gave her baby brother a wave of her plump hand as if she was a woman of the world off on important business.

"We won't be long, Sarah," I assured her. "Elizabeth has appointments all morning. I'm sure she won't be back until after lunch."

Sarah gave me a conspirator's smile. "Have a nice time, Miss."

My steps were almost as light as Patty's as she skipped along at my side. I fought the urge to lift my skirts and race her down the driveway. It was a day for foolish laughter and childish play.

Shoshone Avenue was Brimstone's main street, running east and west, and Hunters Hall was on the western edge of town. Patty and I had a nice walk to the post office, which was located in a small building that might have been someone's log cabin. The United States flag whipped over a steeply slanted roof and two worn steps led to a heavy planked door

111

that some people said had held off attacking Indians when only a few pioneer residents lived in the area. Before the white man pushed them out, Ute, Cheyenne, and Arapaho Indians frequented the mineral springs to heal wounds of battle and cure their sick with the health-giving waters.

The postmistress, Gertrude Dorf, was a widow whose husband, a railroad worker, had been killed during a winter storm when a steam engine had rolled off the track near one of the mining camps. She had been appointed postmistress out of community charity so that she would have the means to provide herself with an adequate living. Any gratitude that Gertrude may have felt was kept well hidden under a taciturn exterior. Her sharp tongue was legendary in Brimstone. I'd never seen her wear anything but black bombazine dresses without a spot of lace to soften the somber cloth. Her rather long neck and thin arms stuck out of her clothes like broomsticks and I thought her sharp nose resembled a pecking chicken's beak.

Gertrude's company didn't hold too much promise—except for one thing. She was better than the *Brimstone Herald* when it came to spreading news. In her position as postmistress she was as effective as a military general when it came to knowing most of the town's business. I knew that every letter I had sent to Steven had been scrutinized by her eagle eyes and if he had opened any of them in the post office, her pointed questions would have pecked out every bit of news.

Brass letter boxes lined one wall and a wrought iron cage with a wide counter allowed customers to conduct business with Gertrude on the other side. She peered at me through the opening. "Oh, it's you," she said in a tone that classified me as a bad penny. "Come back, have you? Had yourself a little bit of traipsing around, I'd say, from the postmarks on the letters you sent."

"I'm sorry I didn't send more postcards to keep you better informed," I said sweetly.

She didn't even flinch. Sarcasm was lost on Gertrude. "What happened to send you scooting home? After all that bad business with your brother, I'd think you'd want to stay shut of this place. People haven't forgotten, you know. Tongues are still wagging. They're waiting for the whole story to come out." A hint of a smile touched her narrow lips. "And I'm betting it will be a good one."

My euphoria was quickly dissipating. I pushed the bundle of letters at her. "Elizabeth would like these sent out today."

"Church stuff, huh? She's sure trying to become Lady Bountiful. Wouldn't be surprised if she's the one donating all that stuff to the Methodist church. That organ must have cost a thousand dollars."

My ears perked up in spite of my reluctance to engage in any kind of discourse with Gertrude. "Someone donated that lovely organ to the church?" I remembered noticing it the day I had disposed of Della Danvers' brooch.

Gertrude's eyes lit up like someone who has tossed out a fishing line and snagged a bite. "Some people try to buy their way up the social ladder, pretending they don't want anyone to know their good works." She gave a snort through her narrow nostrils and handled the invitations as if they were some kind of foul offering. "But the benefactor's name always comes out when there's a pie to be cut. Your sister-in-law could be the one."

I knew Elizabeth didn't have that kind of money, but I wasn't going to offer any grist for this vulture's gossip mill. "Doesn't the Bible advise doing good works anonymously?" I said.

"Hump!" she snorted.

"Good day," I replied briskly as I herded Patty out of the building as fast as I could. Just a few minutes in that woman's company and my bright mood had dimmed like a sunny valley invaded by gray mist. Firming my shoulders, I determined I wouldn't let the malicious old woman affect my mood, and I said brightly to Patty, "A chocolate ice cream cone, is it?"

Patty shook her head. "No, strawberry."

I laughed at her decisiveness. My niece wasn't going to meet life in a wishy-washy way. Confident, secure, and outgoing, she was already marshaling her strengths for challenges life might throw at her.

Her warm soft hand snuggled in mine. With childish honesty she said, "I'm glad you're my aunt and I'm your . . . ?" She looked at me questioningly.

"Niece."

"Niece," she echoed as if delighting in a new word. "But I'm a sister, too," she said solemnly. "To Nicky."

"And you're a daughter to your mother and father, and a granddaughter to your mommie's parents."

"Gosh, I'm lots of things," she said, wide-eyed.

"Indeed you are," I laughed and squeezed her chubby little hand. At least one member of the Banning family was going to be surrounded with ties of belonging.

The Shoshone Ice Cream Parlor had not changed much since the days when Steven and I spent our pennies there. The same round tables bore a few more scratches on their marble tops, black wrought iron chairs sported new pink cushions, and the familiar soda fountain flanked by high stools promised every delectable combination of ice cream and toppings.

The place was crowded with summertime visitors and I decided that it would be better for Patty and me to eat our cones across the street at the park.

I gave our order while standing at one end of the fountain, since there were no empty stools. Patty impatiently wiggled beside me while we waited. A young woman sitting on the next stool turned in my direction. She wore a lovely lapel watch. My eyes fastened on it. The shiny gold filigree mesmerized me.

"Aunt Deedee . . . Aunt Deedee!"

A tug on my hand and the child's voice broke the hypnotic moment. I stared blankly at Patty, then smiled—with relief. I paid for our cones, and hurried Patty outside. "Let's go across the street to the park."

Chattering like a chirping bird, Patty bounced along at my side. We found a bench under the shade of a generous oak tree. Summer visitors were like a bevy of colored birds moving among the trees and along the paths. Patty licked her cone, enthusiastically making a clown's pink smile around her mouth and dribbling spots on her pretty muslin dress. Elizabeth would scold us both, but the outing was worth it.

"We'd better head home," I said when we had finished our ice cream. Walking hand in hand we strolled down the street, enjoying the bustle around us. Patty screamed with delight when two boys rolling hoops went racing by. I could tell from her luminous expression that she longed to be big enough to keep an iron band rolling at such a speed. A cacophony of noices filled our ears. Shoshone Avenue was alive with horses shaking their harnesses and tossing their heads as they vied for passage in the narrow street.

When we passed the windows of a bottling company, I saw a glass blower busy at work and I asked Patty if she'd like to watch him for a minute. She nodded eagerly.

The Colorado Bottling Company furnished green bottles for a drink of cinnamon and mineral water that was being marketed as Spring Delight, but they also offered fancier bottles for retail business. As we went into the building, the woman clerk was busy with another customer. We watched the skillful artisan at work for a few minutes and then wandered around the tiny shop.

Patty became entranced with some small glass figures and I wondered if I had enough money to buy her one if she put up a fuss. Bright sunlight came through the window and hit a tiny amber vial, mesmerizing me with its intense sparkle. I picked it up and it felt warm in my hand. My fingers closed over it. I waited for the warm, contented feeling to invade my body. Nothing. The glass was cold in my hand. Joy surged through me.

"What's the matter Aunt Deedee?" Patty asked as I stood staring at the pretty perfume vial.

I looked down at her and then carefully set the bottle back. "Nothing's the matter," I breathed in relief. "Everything's wonderful. Come on, let's go."

I hadn't taken it! I didn't need it. I had given myself a test and had passed it. There had been no warmth sluicing through me when I held the lovely vial in my hand. There had been no desire, no impulse to take it. I knew why. When Daniel had handed me the bouquet of golden wildflowers, I had experienced true joy.

"Why are you laughing?" Patty asked, puzzled.

"Because it's absolutely a perfect day for laughing. Come on. I'll race you home."

A couple of playful puppies joined us on the way,

barking excitedly and tumbling at our heels. I ignored the scowls of more than one passerby who, obviously, couldn't believe a grown woman was skipping along in such a ridiculous fashion.

That night after supper, I sat cross-legged on my bed looking through an old scrapbook of mine that I had found tucked away in a cupboard. I grew nostalgic as I fingered colorful cigar bands that I had pasted down, along with scraps of wallpaper, ribbons, and lithographic pictures of cherubs and smiling babies. I fingered pressed wild violets that I had collected in the woods one spring. I was halfway through the book when men's voices raised in anger floated up the stairs. My mouth went dry. What on earth—?

I slammed the book shut and hurried down the center staircase. The raised voices were coming from Papa's trophy room. I recognized one of them as belonging to Brian Milburne and the other as Steven's. My mild-mannered brother seldom raised his voice. I couldn't imagine what had caused him to shout loudly enough for me to hear him upstairs.

I had just reached the bottom step when Brian Milburne burst into the hall, slamming the door to the trophy room behind him.

"What on earth is the matter?" I asked him as we faced each other in the front hall.

For a moment I thought he was going to lash out at me or shove me out of the way at the very least, but he visibly brought his emotions under control. His expression softened and he summoned up an apologetic smile. "Business matters. I was trying to hammer some sense into that brother of yours. I apologize for the disturbance." He glanced back at the room and then at me. "Is there somewhere we can talk . . . privately?"

Under any other circumstances, I would have refused an invitation that left me alone with Brian Milburne, but I couldn't miss the chance to find out what had happened between the two men.

I led the way out a side door to a small terrace where Elizabeth sometimes served afternoon tea. Steven had planted a screening of trimmed junipers around the small enclosure and filled large Grecian urns with summer flowers.

I remained standing.

"Tell me what is going on," I demanded, resting my hands on the back of a chair as if it were a safe barrier. I was well aware of the impropriety of being alone with him on a moonlit terrace.

"I told you . . . business. That fool brother of yours is going to lose the store. Things have been going from bad to worse and I've been as patient as I can."

"What does this have to do with you?"

"The bank is involved. My father did a lot of business with Bannings when your father was alive, and he continued to support Walter when he had the store. I've tried to keep that relationship going. Steven has been borrowing to keep the store in stock and his books are a complete disaster. He doesn't tend to business."

"His heart isn't in it," I said defensively.

"I hate to foreclose but—"

"Foreclose? You can't do that."

He sighed. "Yes, I can. I told him so tonight."

"Give Steven a little more time to . . . to resolve the situation." I didn't want to reveal my brother's plan to sell the store if he wasn't ready to make it public.

118

"I've been as patient as I can. I have stockholders to answer to and time is running out. I think that Bannings would be a very good financial investment for someone. I don't see any reason why it can't regain its prestige and turn a tidy profit."

I detected an eagerness in his voice. "You want the store for yourself!"

"No, of course not. I was just speculating . . ."

"Then give Steven a little more time."

"I can't. I have someone who is willing to buy the note we hold on Bannings."

"And of course that's all that matters to you. Taking care of business."

"Not all," he countered. "There are other things that have been on my mind."

I should have turned and walked back into the house at that moment, but I couldn't let him sell the store out from under Steven. Foolishly, I thought I could change his mind, but I had missed the shift in his mood. He wasn't interested in discussing business with me.

Stepping closer to me, he said, "I've been wanting a chance to talk with you, sweetheart, ever since you stepped off that train." His hand touched my arm caressingly.

I pulled back in alarm. I recognized the tone of his voice.

"Why did you run out on me the way you did, my love? We had so much going for us—then overnight you were gone. Just like that," he snapped his fingers. "It was all over. You take off for parts unknown and leave me to nurse a broken heart."

He smiled lightheartedly but I knew where the conversation was headed. "I'm glad you were able to recover so nicely, anyway," I said.

"Maybe I didn't." He took my hand and put it over

119

his heart. "Feel those dangerous palpitations. Almost critical."

I laughed, making light of his declarations. "I think Carolyn is just what the doctor ordered."

"She has nothing to do with this." His voice was suddenly serious. "Why the disappearing act? Were you worried because I never actually did the proposal bit, you know—with bended knee and diamond ring? Were you afraid that I might have decided *not* to marry you after all? Did you suspect that my intentions might not be all that honorable?"

I looked into his eyes, trying to gauge his expression. I must have hurt him more than I thought, or worse, wounded his vanity.

"Why did you leave?" he demanded. "Was it that brother of yours, getting himself cut open by some jealous husband? You might have known this old town would lick its chops over a juicy scandal like that, given that the almighty Bannings were involved. But damn it, Deanna, there wasn't any need for you to leave because of idle talk."

"I didn't leave because of Walter's murder."

"Then why?"

"It really doesn't matter. I went away—and now I'm back. You're going to marry a lovely girl. Let's leave it that way, Brian."

"Maybe it's not too late . . ."

"Believe me, Brian. It was too late a long time ago."

"You're as lovely and tempting as you ever were."

"Don't—"

"My blood still runs hot whenever I see you. Those green eyes make me crazy. I still want you."

"Please, Brian . . ." I tried to move away from him but he had approached the chair between us, kneeled with one knee on the seat, and captured me in his arms. Before I could move, he bent his head and kissed me. The past rushed back to me as his lips covered mine. But only for a moment. As he deepened the kiss, the pleasure was lost . . . like the burst of a star that leaves the sky empty.

"No . . . Brian . . . please." I turned my head to one side.

"You feel the same way as I do," he whispered huskily. "You can't deny it. It's the same as it always was."

"No. It's not."

"Is it Carolyn? I told you she has nothing to do with the way I feel about you. She's a child. Pretty and pampered and utterly predictable. Not like you. You're like smooth whiskey that burns a man's insides." He cupped my chin and pulled my face around. As he bent his head to kiss me again, I slapped his face.

For a moment he froze, stunned. Then he smiled. "That's what I like about you. No delicate protests. You always had fire in you."

"Let me go," I ordered icily. He laughed softly but dropped his arms. "You've always been a challenge, my lovely Deanna. Running away didn't change anything at all."

"Please leave."

"And if I don't?"

"I'll call my brother."

He laughed. "No, you won't."

He was right, I wouldn't. Steven had no part in the relationship I had with Brian Milburne, and I wasn't about to bring him into it. Brian had called my bluff. "Good night, Mr. Milburne," I said with cold formality.

Grinning, he gave a mocking bow, "Good night, Miss Banning."

I heard his soft laughter as he walked away from the terrace and disappeared into the shadows. I felt as if a tight band was around my chest. My legs were as soft as clabbered cream. I sat down in a chair. Putting my elbows on the table, I cradled my head, and tried to sort out the wild surf of emotions that rolled over me.

Chapter Nine

I stayed close to the house the next few days, but on Sunday morning I decided I would attend church services. I tried to explain the motivation for my sudden piety and finally admitted that the reason was simple—I wanted to see Daniel Norris again. He had been in my thoughts a good deal since the picnic at Hunters Glen. When I was reading or walking through Steven's greenhouse, I would remember something that he had said and several times I caught myself carrying on an imaginary conversation with him. In retrospect, I feared I had behaved foolishly and misunderstood his attentions, taking his interest as something personal instead of an expression of his ministry. He was, after all, dedicated to helping his flock—even though my claim to that group was tenuous.

I put on my best bonnet, a Parisian creation that Mrs. Lowenstein had given me for my birthday. I knew that she had purchased it for herself but had decided that the wide brim and matching pink roses high on the crown didn't flatter her round face. I suspected it had not garnered enough compliments the first time she wore it so it had not been difficult for her to part with it. I wasn't offended. The high fashion hat certainly cost more than I would have ever been able to pay for one. I thought the soft pink was quite lovely and it certainly added a fashionable touch to my Sunday-best gown, a sky-blue watersilk. Elizabeth nodded in approval when she saw me, and I thought there was a hint of envy in her glance as it traveled over my slender build down to my small white kid shoes.

My robust sister-in-law wore a russet hat fashioned with curling feathers dancing beside her full face and a veil piled high upon the crown. Her elbow-length gloves in brown matched a summer gown of beige crinkled pique. A lovely topaz necklace rested on her motherly bosom and she touched it lovingly when I complimented her on it. "A Christmas gift," she said.

"From Steven?"

"No, from Papa Banning."

I felt a slither of envy. My father had never given me anything so beautiful. His gifts under the tree had always been pragmatic: socks, aprons, and school supplies. There must have been a gentle side to him that he never showed me—I wondered why.

The children were quite miserable in their best bib-and-tucker. Nicky screamed in protest, trying to pull off a wide bow circling his neck and wiggling out of a layered outfit. His little suit was already rumpled and his white socks were twisted from all his kicking when Sarah brought him downstairs.

"I'm sorry, mum. He's having a bit of a fit, he is."

"My shoes hurt!" whined Patty, her little face scrunched up and her lips sticking out in a pout. "I want my black ones."

"You can't wear your play shoes to church," Elizabeth said firmly. "Now straighten up, and stop fussing. Where's my Bible? Sarah, would you run

and get it off the table? Patty! Leave those shoes on."
She shifted Nicky to her other hip. "Good gracious, I
think he's dirtied his pants."

"Why don't I take Patty and walk ahead?" I
suggested.

"Yes . . . that would be a help. I don't know why
Maude had to choose Sunday morning to be away
from the house. You'd think she could have visited
her old friend some other day." She stomped away,
calling Sarah's name. "Take this child upstairs and
make him presentable. And hurry. You know I don't
like being late."

I took Patty's hand and we made our escape from
the Sunday-go-to-church bedlam. We had only taken
a few steps away from the house when Patty began to
skip happily. So much for pinching shoes. I smiled
as she bobbed along at my side, chatting and
giggling.

We reached the church and still no sign of
Elizabeth and the black phaeton. I hesitated near the
front steps. Should we wait or go on in? I felt terribly
on display as church members gave me frankly
curious glances, nodding politely to me and then
exchanging raised eyebrows with each other. At that
moment, I regretted my impulse to attend services.

"Good morning," greeted Millie as she and
Harold arrived in his buggy. "How nice to see you,
Deanna." She gave me a knowing smile. "I can't say
that I'm surprised. Reverend Morris can be quite
persuasive, can't he? Attendance has really improved
in the few months he's been here. Especially the
feminine sector of the congregation."

Harold chuckled, massaging his goatee. "I've
never seen the Ladies Aid Society so industrious . . .
pancake breakfasts . . . everything from projects to
improve the kitchen's coal stove to a red carpet for the

vestibule. A good-looking minister certainly brings out Christian love, doesn't it?"

I wanted to turn on my heel and show my back to the lot of them, but Elizabeth arrived at that moment and shooed us inside. If any of the congregation had missed my presence outside the church, they had a good view as Elizabeth and I with Patty and Nicky in tow proceeded to the front of the packed assembly. Even as I ridiculed myself for entertaining an emotion close to stage fright, I couldn't ignore a dryness in my throat and a thumping in my chest. How I detested feeling as if I was on display!

As we took our seats, I glimpsed Nina Milburne's granite profile, Della Danvers' autocratic posture, and Carolyn's dark head bent over a hymnal. I shuddered under the older women's censorious glares, and was relieved when the organist began to play, signaling the processional. "Holy, holy, holy! Lord God, Almighty. Early in the morning our song shall rise to Thee."

Everyone in the congregation stood up, singing loudly as the choir marched in and Daniel Norris took his place before the lectern. He wore his shiny black suit, starched white shirt, clerical collar, and proper high-top black shoes. Light coming through the stained-glass windows touched his coppery hair and his vigorous features were at once solemn and joyful as he lifted his head and sang.

I suppose I was expecting him to register my presence in some fashion. A lift of an eyebrow, a smile or gesture in my direction. He did none of these things. If he were aware of my presence in his congregation, he gave no sign that would acknowledge that.

I was both relieved and miffed that he had not singled me out in some way. Blast him anyway! Not very good at lying to myself, I had to admit that I was disappointed. I had wanted to be special in his sight—not just one of the flock.

The topic of his sermon was bondage. Daniel opened a large Bible and read a scripture from the Book of John, ending with the verses, Take Away the Stone . . . Unbind him. He closed the Bible and leaned casually on the lectern as he began to talk about all the things that took away our God-given right to live life joyously. He didn't spend time on generalities, but seemed to be speaking directly to the good people of Brimstone.

"Why do we continually chastise ourselves for some past indiscretion or failure? Why are we afraid to turn away from the past? We put ourselves in bondage when we are such cowards that we refuse to live life fully." With a theatrical rise in his voice, he urged all to have the courage to enjoy the bounty of God's gifts and break free from the bondage of fear, guilt, and failure.

His remarks hit very close to home for me. Had he expected me to be in church to hear them or was I being vain to think he had had me in mind at all?

I felt Elizabeth stiffen beside me when he warned against being a slave to style and fads. He surely knew how to stick it to the fashion plates preening in the audience, I thought with an amused smile. Out of the corner of my eye I saw Della Danvers touching her string of pearls in a defiant gesture.

"Empty social strictures have no place in our lives," he cautioned. He folded his hands on the lectern and leaned forward. "Remember who we are—an expression of God! Everything that is good and beautiful lies within us. It is no sin to enjoy the abundant life promised us. Make a joyful noise unto the Lord," he quoted.

The sermon was inspiring, and I judged from the congregation's hushed reception that he had their attention. I wondered if anyone else felt that his words were being spoken directly to them.

Daniel stood at the door shaking hands with the congregation as we filed out. "Good Morning, Miss Dorf. . . . How are you today, Millie . . . Harold?" Daniel's gaze passed from them to me. "Miss Banning," he said formally, but the twinkle in his eye undermined his solemnity. "How nice to see you here this morning."

"Thank you. I appreciated your sermon."

"I thought from your expression that your mind might be wandering a bit," he chided.

A warm flush mounted in my cheeks. "That's not fair. I didn't think you knew I was here."

"I knew," he said simply.

I stepped to one side and waited for Elizabeth and Sarah to collect the children, who had run off to join some other little ones playing in the churchyard.

Nina swept forward with her sister, Della, and Carolyn in tow. "Don't forget that dinner is at two o'clock, Reverend."

He nodded and I thought his smile was forced. "I'll be there."

When the last person had emerged from the church, he closed the door and walked over to me. "Lovely day for a walk, Deanna."

"Yes."

"Are you going to be free later on this afternoon?" I nodded.

"Aunt Deedee!" Patty bounded over to me. "Can we walk home . . . please, please."

"Stop that begging," Elizabeth said firmly. "Go get in the phaeton with Sarah." Her order included me. "I'll be there in a moment, Deanna." She turned to Daniel and began talking about a problem which would affect the purchasing of a stove for the church kitchen.

A few minutes later we drove off, leaving Daniel standing in front of the church. I waved to him and he gave me a mock salute.

"What are you laughing about, Deanna?" demanded Elizabeth as she flicked the reins over the rump of the dappled horse.

"Nothing. I just feel like laughing."

She gave me an exasperated look.

My high spirits lasted until late afternoon when Daniel sent word that an elderly member of the church had died and he would be ministering to the family.

How could I have known that disaster was at that moment already lumbering toward us.

The following afternoon I was out on the front porch reading when a stranger walked up the driveway. Slight of build, the man had a brown derby hat set squarely on his neatly trimmed sandy hair and he wore a serge business suit. A gold cane swung jauntily at his side. "Lovely day, isn't it?" he greeted me as he doffed his hat. His thin, middle-aged face was pleasant to behold. "Couldn't resist taking a walk in this wonderful fresh air after my train trip from Denver. I'd like to speak with Steven Banning. The lady at the store, Miss Mildred Dillworthy, informed me that he was probably at home."

That was news to me. Steven had disappeared after lunch. If he hadn't gone to the store, I suspected that he'd sneaked off to work in his greenhouse. "May I tell him who's calling?"

"Certainly." He gave me a slight bow. "George

Babcock, Junior. He's expecting me."

"Won't you sit down, Mr. Babcock?" I indicated the porch rocking chair. "And I'll tell him you're here."

"Thank you. You're most kind. Are you Mrs. Banning?"

"No, I'm Steven's sister. Mrs. Banning isn't here this afternoon. May I offer you some lemonade?"

"That would be delightful." He sat down and sighed contentedly as he set the chair moving leisurely back and forth on its rockers.

I hurried into the house and down the long hall to the kitchen. Maude was nowhere in sight and her door off the back hall was closed. Probably taking a nap, I thought. She probably didn't know where Steven was, anyway. I'd have to search for him myself. I wondered if Mr. Babcock was the prospective buyer that Steven had written to regarding the sale of the store. Maybe my brother was finally going through with the sale.

I let the back screen door bang as I went out of the house and started down the path leading around the stables to the greenhouse. Before I had gone very far, I heard the sound of a shovel and flying dirt just beyond a dense planting of Canterbury bells.

Jericho rose up and saw me about the same instant I saw him. His bulldog glare and attack stance stopped me in my tracks. He held his shovel as if it was a weapon and he was facing the advance of a fierce attacker.

"Do you know where Steven is?" I asked, my voice a little less firm than I would have liked.

His nod was barely perceptible.

"Please go and tell him that he has a visitor. A Mr. Babcock is waiting on the front porch to see him. And hurry!" I said with as much authority in my voice as I could manage. Relief sped through me when he turned away and headed around the stable. I realized then how nervous his hostile presence made me.

In the kitchen, I searched for fresh lemons and the hand squeezer. Maude had her own idea of how kitchen utensils should be arranged and I spent nearly ten minutes assembling the things I needed to make a pitcher of lemonade. It would have taken me longer than that if Sarah hadn't come down to the kitchen and showed me a new kind of fruit squeezer that looked like a small fruit cup with a matching lid.

"I'll help you," she said, bringing out a tray and glasses. "The children are down for their naps. It will give me a bit of a breathing spell. Have you talked to the Missus about taking them more of the time?" she asked hopefully.

"Not yet. I'm waiting for the right moment," I answered—which in translation meant that I was waiting for Elizabeth's attitude toward me to change. Obviously, my sister-in-law viewed me as an unhealthy influence—she had not been happy the few times I had braved her displeasure to spend time with Patty and Nicky.

"Do you want me to take this out?" Sarah offered when the tray was ready—two glasses, a small pitcher, white linen napkins, and a plate of molasses cookies.

"No, I'll do it. Thanks, Sarah." I carried the offering out to the front porch and found the rocking chair empty. Steven and Mr. Babcock must have taken a walk, I thought. Just like Steven to want to show off his greenhouse to the visitor. I set the tray down on a small wicker table with a smile. Well, I'd leave the refreshment and they could enjoy it when they came back to the house.

I picked up my book and wandered over to a small bench at the edge of the lawn, but I decided not to read in order that I might take care of a task I had almost forgotten. Several pinecones scattered on the ground reminded me that I had promised Elizabeth to collect a sack of them for a lady who was making crafts to sell at the opera house benefit on the Fourth of July. The day was a perfect one for a stroll down to the creek, and for some reason a restlessness was building inside me. My disappointment that Daniel had not called on me the previous afternoon was mingled with a growing impression that I was putting much too much importance on his friendship.

I walked back to the kitchen door and picked up a gunnysack from a pile of them that lay there. Men's voices coming from the stable reached my ears. Steven's voice sounded slightly agitated and I wondered if the heat of bargaining had begun.

I hiked through the thick band of trees, picking up cones that had fallen to the ground and depositing them in my gunnysack. I was grateful for my summer gloves as I handled the prickly objects and retrieved them from the dry deadfall collected under the trees. In some places the scrub oak and junipers were too thick to penetrate and I circled about in a wandering pattern until I reached the creek.

I rested for a few minutes on a log, watching the gurgling water moving around glistening rocks and driftwood. Once again my thoughts centered on Daniel Norris. Like the items in my scrapbook, I mentally fingered every word, glance, and smile he'd given me. Even in memory, they brought a peculiar contentment. I sighed, knowing that he would choose a strong, dedicated woman to share his life and work. But he would be my friend. I wouldn't be so foolish as to expect more.

Dragging the sack of cones, I headed back toward the house. I had almost reached the last drift of trees when a glitter of something just off the path caught my eye. Almost concealed by a low spreading cedar, a metal object drew me closer.

I bent down. A man's ring. "I wonder whose this is?" I murmured idly as I reached out my hand to pick it up.

"No!" I recoiled. My stomach lunged.

The gold band was attached to a human hand.

Chapter Ten

My stomach lurched and bile rose up in my throat. I dropped the sack of pinecones and put my hands over my mouth. Backing up, I stumbled over a decaying log, tearing my dress and scratching up my arms before I could right myself. The hand, its curled fingers pressing into the ground, sent me fleeing, screaming in horror. I frantically pushed aside overhanging branches and stumbled across patches of deadfall, scattering needles, leaves, and dirt. With Death like a chilling breath upon my neck, I bounded through the woods. When I broke free of the band of trees and saw the house ahead, my screams rose to a frantic pitch. Several people came running toward me in alarm, having heard my cries of distress.

Steven, Elizabeth, Maude, and Jericho were talking all at once, crowding close around me, attempting to make sense of my hysterical sobbing.

"What is it?" Steven demanded.

I flung myself into his arms. "I found . . . I saw . . ."

My brother put his hands firmly on my shoulders. "Get a hold of yourself, Dee. Now tell me slowly . . .

135

what did you see?"

I bit my lip to stop its trembling. Then I said weakly, "A hand . . . a human hand . . . wearing a ring . . . sticking out from under a juniper bush."

Elizabeth gasped.

"Heaven help us!" breathed Maude.

Jericho spat an oath which seemed to express his disbelief.

"A body?" demanded Steven, looking a little pale himself.

"I don't know." My mouth was so dry I could hardly move it. "I only saw a hand . . . in the dirt."

Steven exchanged looks with Jericho. "We'd better have a look. Tell us where it is, sis."

I pointed. "Back in the trees that way . . . not far."

"All right. All of you go back in the house." The two men hurried away in the direction I had indicated.

For once Elizabeth was speechless. She didn't give orders or try to control the situation in any way. Her usually ruddy complexion was as white as bleached bone.

Maude put her plump arm around my shoulder. "Come on, Deedee. Sure and you've had a shock . . . finding a thing like that." She muttered under her breath as she led me back to the house.

I declined her offer of tea and went upstairs to my room. I shut the door and turned a key in the lock as if by shutting myself in I was safe from the horror outside. Trembling, I sat down on the edge of my bed and stared at the floor. A chilling numbness overtook me. Crossing my arms, I hugged myself as if that were the only thing that would keep me from shattering. The sight of the hand pressed into the dirt rose up in my mind's eye, clear and horrible. A half-hour later a knock at the door brought me out of my stupor.

"You're wanted in the trophy room," Sarah told me with her eyes rounded. "It's the police."

I nodded wearily.

The maid's eyes fell upon the huge tear in my dress, and then traveled to my torn sleeve and scratched arm. I realized then that I had lost my bonnet somewhere in my flight and my hair was flowing wildly around my face.

"Are you all right, miss?"

I forced a reassuring smile to my lips. "Just shaken up, Sarah. I'll be down as soon as I freshen up."

The trophy room was really Papa's room. His gun cabinets still lined the walls and the floor was covered with bearskin rugs. His hunting trophies were displayed on the dark walls. Stuffed heads of all kinds looked down upon us, bears, elk with five-point antlers, glassy eyed antelope; there were also a snarling bobcat and two mountain cougars. I had always hated the room; oppressive memories of Papa and his hunter friends rose like a black surf and washed over me as I entered. The smell of tobacco lingered in the dark wood panels.

The last time I had seen Wade Whitney, chief of police, was during his fruitless investigation of Walter's death. I had little respect for him at that time and my opinion of him had not improved when he turned to meet me now. He had a thick, square body. A few more lines were etched on his weathered face, and thinning brown hair had left a freckled bald spot on the crown of his melon-shaped head. He resembled, in his movements, a huge animal on the prowl. He was at his best breaking up barroom fights and throwing drunks into jail on Saturday nights. He'd taken a lot of criticism over the way he handled the tragedy that had occurred five years earlier, and he had lost a lot of prestige when he failed to find my brother's murderer. I had felt at the time that Chief Whitney blamed my family for his humiliation. I had the same impression now as the officer swung his bulk around to face me when I entered the room.

His antagonism was apparent immediately. A tight smile failed to soften the cold stab of hazel eyes that were shaded by thick eyebrows. His gaze narrowed to take in my appearance from head to foot.

"Miss Banning." His slight bow was perfunctory. "Please sit down. I'm sorry to bother you, but since you were the one to make the unfortunate discovery . . ." His tone held me responsible for any unpleasantness that was to follow.

Steven moved to my side and eased me into one of the chairs placed near the sofa, where both men had been sitting. My brother gave me a smile that attempted to be reassuring, but I felt the tremble of his hands on my shoulders and sensed his anxiety. He remained standing behind my chair.

"We have identified the victim," said Chief Whitney.

I moistened my dry lips. "Then there was a body."

"Of course," retorted the officer, his thick lips curved in obvious disdain.

"I . . . I thought maybe it was a dismembered hand," I explained. "I only saw the hand . . . nothing else."

"The rest of the body was stuffed under that juniper with a pile of dead needles and leaves thrown on it."

"Who was it?" I asked in a leaden tone. But I knew what his answer would be.

"George Babcock Junior. A gentleman from Denver. He might have lain there a good long time without being discovered if you hadn't come along. Only an animal would have sniffed him out. Don't you think it's quite a coincidence that you would

138

find the body while it was still warm, Miss Banning?" His tone leapt at me like the sharp report of a hunting rifle.

Steven stiffened behind me. "I don't think your tone is appropriate, sir. My sister's discovery of the body is no cause for badgering."

"Badgering?" He scoffed. "I'm conducting a murder investigation, and I'm aiming to find out exactly what's going on here. I'm sorry if I offend any feminine sensibilities," he apologized with no sincerity in his tone. "Now, Miss Banning, suppose you tell me how you came to find Mr. Babcock hidden in the woods with his head bashed in."

His head bashed in! I felt sick remembering how the man had walked jauntily up to the house, his cane swinging at his side, his face raised to bask in the summer sun. I raised my hands up and pressed my fingers against my temples. It couldn't have happened. I had left him rocking contentedly on the porch. Less than an hour later, he lay dead.

"What were you doing in that thick stand of trees, Miss Banning?"

Steven tightened a hand on my shoulder and squeezed it gently. "You'd better answer, Dee."

I nodded, took a deep breath, and put my hands in my lap. My voice trembled as I began, but as I related my search for pinecones, it grew stronger and I kept my eyes fixed on the policeman's craggy face. "I walked all the way to the creek and when I was coming back . . . that's when I saw the ring."

"Ring?"

"The ring on the man's finger. I wouldn't even have noticed the hand if it hadn't been for the ring. The metal glittered and caught my eye when I was reaching for a large pinecone close by."

"What did you do then?"

"I was curious and came closer—that's when I saw the hand."

"And—?"

"And I dropped my bag of cones and ran to the house." I locked eyes with him. "You found the bag, didn't you?"

He brushed this detail aside as if unimportant. "You knew the victim?"

"I'd seen him earlier . . . but I didn't know him. He came to the house . . ." I thought Steven's hand tightened on my shoulder in warning, but I finished, "looking for Steven."

"Your brother claims he never saw the man today."

My mouth was suddenly as dry as a hot summer desert. Why was Steven lying? My thoughts scattered like leaves caught in a devil's wind. Before I could respond, Steven said quickly, "My sister sent word to me that a Mr. Babcock was waiting on the porch to see me but by the time I had reached the front of the house, he wasn't there."

The officer's neck flushed in anger and color rose into his thick jowls. "I already have your statement, Mr. Banning. I suggest you let your sister give me hers without interruption or I will insist upon seeing her alone."

"My sister doesn't need to be harassed in this fashion."

I thought Steven was protesting too vigorously—was it possible he had something to hide? I was positive I had heard his raised voice in the stable just before I left on my walk.

"Now, Miss Banning. Please start at the beginning. At what time did you first see Mr. Babcock?" He glared at Steven. "And I want no interruptions."

I focused on a point just below the policeman's

face. "It must have been about two o'clock. I was reading on the porch and he came walking up to the house. He said he'd been at the store and that Millie had told him he would probably find Steven here."

"Did you know what he wanted to talk to your brother about?"

"No, and he didn't say." I kept my voice even. I wasn't about to tell the policeman that I had suspected the murdered man had come to see Steven about buying the store. "I asked him to wait on the porch while I called Steven and made some lemonade."

"And did you? Speak to your brother and make some lemonade?"

"I sent a message to Steven through Jericho—he's our garden man—and I made a pitcher of lemonade."

"And did your brother and his visitor enjoy this refreshment?" he asked evenly.

"I don't know . . . I mean, no one was on the porch when I brought the tray out. Mr. Babcock was gone." I wished Steven had been in front of me so I could gauge the expression on his face. I felt as if I were treading on dangerous ground with every word. Steven and I had always stood together against any trouble, united against Papa's despotism and Walter's indifference. Whatever the danger was to my brother, I must face it with him.

"And how long did it take you to make the lemonade and bring it out? Five minutes?"

"Oh, much longer than that," I said, remembering how I had been delayed in the kitchen. "I couldn't find the lemon squeezer and our maid, Sarah, had to help me. It must have been more like fifteen."

"I see. Plenty of time for your brother to greet Mr. Babcock and take him off—"

I heard a protest rise in Steven's throat but he

141

bit back a retort.

"I never saw either of them," I said honestly. "Elizabeth had asked me to gather some pinecones for a lady making oddities for the Opera House benefit. So I collected a gunnysack and left the house."

"And how long were you away on this little stroll to the creek and back?" His tone branded the whole story as a lie from beginning to end.

"Over an hour, I would guess."

"But you didn't see the body . . . or anything suspicious on your way to the creek?"

"I didn't go that way when I started out. I took a more direct route and returned in a different direction."

"And you saw no one on your little walk?"

"No."

"And heard nothing . . . a cry, perhaps? Mr. Babcock could have cried out when he was struck with the head of his cane."

"His cane? That was—?" I gulped.

"The murder weapon," he finished. "The head of the cane was a golden eagle fashioned with a sharp beak. It efficiently broke his skull. He was struck several times."

The horror of the deed came at me full force. I had only spoken with the man a few minutes but our pleasant exchange made me feel that somehow I was responsible for his demise. If only I had taken him into the house to wait for Steven, I agonized. Would anything have been different? Would he be alive now instead of lying in the woods with his head bashed in?

Officer Whitney was watching me closely. "Who else was at home . . . you, your brother, and the help, is that correct? What about Mrs. Banning?"

"Elizabeth left right after lunch . . . but she had returned by the time I came back to the house."

"She says she never saw the man," Steven said in a firm voice.

"I'll be asking her about that myself," he countered gruffly. "This whole thing seems a repeat, doesn't it? The same people having to answer questions about a murder . . . only this time, the guilty one isn't going to get by me." His eyebrows knitted ferociously in warning. He reached into his pocket and pulled out a piece of paper. "We found this letter in the gent's pocket." He looked at us as if he were sighting down the barrel of a gun. "This here letter asks Mr. Babcock to come down from Denver and evaluate the assets of Bannings Department Store. Do either of you know anything about this?"

I shook my head. I expected Steven to tell the officer that the dead man was a prospective buyer for the store, but he remained quiet. Warning bells went off in my head like the clamoring of a fire wagon racing toward a disaster.

"Brian Milburne sent the letter," Whitney said, measuring our reaction. "Apparently the bank is interested in verifying the investment potential of the store. Did either of you know anything about this?"

"Brian told me about it the other night," Steven said, his tone sharp with anger.

"So both of you knew the man was coming today?"

"No," I said quickly before Steven could answer. My heart started knocking in my chest and I knew that my voice betrayed an emotional confusion.

Chief Whitney smiled. A malicious, satisfied smile. "I intend to get to the bottom of this in short order."

"We'll cooperate in every way we can," said Steven evenly. "And now, I think my sister has endured enough for one day. I'm sure she will inform you if she remembers anything more." He offered me his arm and I rose from the chair. I expected Chief Whitney to tell me to sit back down, but he didn't. His silence was ominous and I felt his eyes boring into us as Steven guided me out of the room.

"Let's get out of here," my brother whispered in a furtive tone, and we slipped out of a side entrance of the house without taking a chance of being seen from one of the other rooms.

With his arm around my waist, Steven hurried me past the house, along a garden path, and around the stable to his sanctuary in the greenhouse. The sun had already set behind the high peaks and a gray twilight was spreading into the valleys.

Inside the greenhouse, panes of glass resembled blank, opaque eyes. Rows and rows of benches hemmed us in on every side. Pots and trays of plant life massed together in jungle-like density, filling the air with a cloying and oppressive sweetness.

Steven increased the pressure on my arm as I tried to draw away. "Here's my private workroom. We can talk here." He led me into a small enclosure that resembled a storage room and smelled strongly of dirt and fertilizer. A battered desk and a couple of chairs sat in one corner. A stack of journals topped a filing cabinet and papers spread over the desktop. Steven lit a kerosene lamp before he closed the door and motioned for me to take one of the wooden chairs. Only one side of his face was illuminated as he sat in front of the desk and faced me.

"You lied," I said in a choked voice. I couldn't believe I was challenging him—this was my dear brother, the only one who had ever offered me unconditional love. But I couldn't feign ignorance.

"What are you saying?"

144

"You *did* see Babcock . . . I heard you talking to him."

"You're mistaken."

Lantern light flickered in his eyes; at that moment he seemed a stranger. I moistened my lips. "When I was getting a gunnysack, I heard you talking."

He looked puzzled.

"Please tell me everything," I begged.

Steven ran his fingers through his hair. "When Jericho came to tell me that a man named Babcock was here, I was working on a compost heap behind the stable. Of course, the name rang a bell. I knew he was the man Brian had sent for to look over the store's books and evaluate the assets." His eyes flashed with anger. "He's going to foreclose . . . and we'll be left without a dime, Dee. The bastard!"

"I didn't know things were so bad you'd taken out notes on the store," I said, trying not to sound as if I were accusing him.

"We've had some pretty bleak months, but I thought things would turn around. Anyway, when Jericho told me Babcock was here, I knew I couldn't greet a visitor like that without washing my hands and getting out of my coveralls. So I came here and took a few minutes to freshen up and put on my jacket. When I was presentable, I walked around to the front of the house—it wasn't more than ten minutes since I'd been summoned, but no one was on the front porch. There wasn't any tray of lemonade either, so you still must have been in the kitchen. I peeked in the drawing room to see if he was waiting inside but he was nowhere in sight, so I went back outside and around the house to ask Jericho again where Babcock was waiting. You must have heard me bawling him out because I found him drinking from a jug he had hidden in the stable."

It could have happened that way. The timing was right. We could have just missed each other on the porch. And I had identified Steven's voice, but the other low rumble could have been Jericho's.

"You don't believe me?" Steven searched my face. "Good Lord, Dee, you don't think I killed that man, do you?"

Perhaps it was the day's horror, or my growing mood of dark apprehension, but suddenly Steven's presence was no longer comforting. I didn't want to be here with him . . . or anyone. Someone was wearing a mask hiding a vicious, heartless killer and I no longer trusted my instincts. I put a hand up to my forehead. "No, of course not. But what happened to him between the time I sent Jericho after you and you found the porch empty?"

"He must have gone off with someone."

We looked at each other for some moments.

"I tell you I never saw the man!" he flared as if my eyes had accused him. "I never heard his name until the other night. I suppose you heard the ruckus. Brian told me of his plan to sell our indebtedness to George Babcock and that the man could foreclose if he wanted to."

But now he was dead.

Neither of us spoke for some time. Then Steven said, "Looks bad, doesn't it?"

Steven . . . Steven. I felt my heart breaking.

"I swear to you I didn't kill him, sis." His voice cracked and I put my arms around him. Who was going to believe his innocence? Or mine? The murdered man had been going to take away our livelihood. The motive and opportunity were ours.

"There's only one thing to do," I said evenly. "We'll just have to find out who did it."

Steven sobbed in my arms.

Chapter Eleven

Neither Steven nor Elizabeth was in attendance at breakfast the next morning. I saw Sarah taking a tray upstairs and deduced that my sister-in-law was having breakfast in her room. Maude scolded me when she saw me nibbling on a piece of toast and ignoring the offerings of the covered dishes on the buffet.

"No sense in starving yourself . . . won't help nobody, you going around looking near death." Then she blanched as if regretting her choice of words. "You know what I mean. I just can't stand seeing you and Steven go through all this again. Why in God's name did such a thing have to happen on our doorstep? I bet Gertrude Dorf's mouth is rattling as fast as a corn-shucking machine. Don't think I can face going to the Ladies Aid meeting tomorrow."

"I'm sorry, Maude. You've had your share of hardship with this family."

"You don't know the half of it, child." Then she clamped her mouth shut as if she'd said too much. "But it ain't any fault of yours. An innocent babe, that's what you are."

I put my arm around her plump shoulder. "I'm

not a babe anymore, Maude. And neither is Steven. You don't have to feel responsible for us."

"And why not?" she flared. "Sure as God made green frogs, nobody else has ever made life easy for ya. And now this." Her voice quavered and her eyes filled with tears. I realized that she was no longer the staunch defender of my youth who could weather the gales of any storm, but an old woman who deserved peace.

We clung together and I murmured reassurances that I didn't feel. She swiped at her eyes and then drew herself up. "I've got some baking to see to." She patted my arm and disappeared into the kitchen. I heard the clatter of pots and pans and knew that Maude was drowning her troubles in industry.

I wished I had some demanding responsibilities that required my attention. Maybe Elizabeth's indisposition would give me the chance to spend time in the nursery. I left the morning room and made my way upstairs.

I was surprised to find my sister-in-law's door open as I passed her room, and was even more surprised when she called out to me. "Deanna, do you have a minute?"

Elizabeth was standing at a window, looking down at the grounds. I'd never seen her so unkept. Her hair was mussed under her ruffled nightcap and her morning wrapper was carelessly tied. A hint of night cream glistened on her face, which was devoid of color.

As I stood beside her, I saw what had caught her attention below. Several men were carefully examining the ground as they fanned out from the house to the drift of trees where the body had been found.

"What do you think they're looking for?" she asked.

"I don't know."

"I wonder if they've found any clues. I don't know why they're wasting time searching the grounds. We obviously don't know what happened to him. I never saw the man."

Her strident tone surprised me. I had never seen Elizabeth in such a nervous state. "I had just returned home when I heard you screaming," she continued. "Jericho wasn't in the stable to tend to the horse, so I just left it there, then saw the others gathered around you on the lawn."

It could have happened that way. *Or she could have arrived earlier than she said.* Elizabeth must have read the doubt seeping into my expression. "You surely don't think I had anything to do with this horrible incident."

"No, of course not," I assured her, perhaps too readily.

"You've never had any great love for me, Deanna. You were aligned against me from the very beginning. You didn't want Steven to marry me. I know that. And I don't appreciate offering you the hospitality of my home and having you stir things up with Steven the way you have."

"Stir things up?" My defenses went up immediately. "What do you mean?"

"You know perfectly well. Talking him into selling the store."

"That was Steven's idea—I only approved of his plan after he shared it with me. If he would be happier doing something else—"

"Like working with dirt and manure in the greenhouse!" she flared. "You know as well as I do there's no money in that kind of thing. And even if there was, Steven would never be able to make a go of it. He's an incompetent businessman. Better leave things as they are. Millie is able to manage the store and I'm sure our financial problems are only temporary. We just need a little time and we'll be able to pay off the bank's note."

"Millie is going to get married. I'm sure Harold Haines is financially capable of taking care of his wife. One of these days Millie will hand Steven the keys to Bannings and that will be that. In any case, our family has depended upon Millie long enough. Things cannot go on as they have been."

Elizabeth walked over to a chaise longue and lay down wearily as if her body and her thoughts were too heavy to carry around. "I thought everything was under control. The letter Steven wrote to his prospective buyer was never posted—I saw to that. I offered to mail it, but I tore it up. Steven does too many things on impulse. Then Brian tells us he is going to sell our note to some greedy investor."

"Then you knew Mr. Babcock was coming."

"Of course, Steven told me that night after his argument with Brian." She closed her eyes for a moment. "This is just like Walter's death all over again."

"Not quite the same. Mr. Babcock was an innocent stranger who came here on business, while Walter—"

"Why do you speak his name in that derogatory tone? Isn't it enough that he's dead? Have you no respect for his memory? Surely, he deserves that much."

Elizabeth struggled to resume her former poise, but the need for release must have been too much for her. She looked beyond me and continued, her voice strangely soft. "Walter was closer to my age, you know. He used to come out to the ranch often, helping with roundup, breaking in colts. We'd ride

150

and work together. I always thought—I always thought we made a good match. Walter liked me." Her eyes suddenly sought mine. "He really did."

"Then why—?" I barely mouthed the words.

"Why didn't Walter marry me?" A glint of tears showed in the corners of her eyes. "Papa Banning. Your father had it in his head that Steven was the one I was going to marry. He liked to play God, you know, always talking about balancing family strains to improve heredity—like we were a bunch of cattle." Her laugh became a sob pressed through tight lips. "Had everything figured out, he did. And Walter wouldn't go against him. Maybe he didn't care enough to fight for me." Her lips trembled. "But I cared for him."

"I'm sorry, Elizabeth," I said softly. It had never occurred to me that she had been in love with Walter. Anger against my half-brother and my father churned anew. "Walter wasn't worth it!"

"Maybe not." She sighed. "I knew he had other women . . . single and married . . . but I kept hoping, praying. Then he told me that he agreed with his father. Steven would make me the best husband— and Walter offered us his blessing. So I married Steven . . . and I've made him a good wife. Haven't I?"

She seemed to be pleading with me to tell her she had *not* failed in the role she played as wife, mother, and upstanding matron. I searched for words. What could I offer in honesty to alleviate some of the ugliness? Both Elizabeth and Steven had been cheated. But nothing could be changed. In an impulsive gesture I leaned over and kissed her cheek.

She looked at me, relieved and grateful. "So now you know, Deanna, why I was so distraught when Walter was killed. I knew one of his women must

151

have done it. If any one of them loved him as I did . . . they could have been desperate enough in their jealousy to want to see him dead."

"Whoever killed Walter had to have been a man. A betrayed husband or lover seeking vengeance," I said, feeling certain that the crime had to have been committed by someone strong. The next thought entered my mind unbidden. *Elizabeth was a large woman and as strong as any man.* And she might have been just desperate enough . . .

A timid knock on the open door interrupted my unsettling thoughts.

"Sorry, ma'am," Sarah said, addressing Elizabeth. "Reverend Norris has come to pay his respects. He said he would be pleased if you would receive him."

"Oh, heavens," gasped Elizabeth. "Why on earth would he come at this ungodly hour—and without any warning?" She looked absolutely devastated. Elizabeth's only security was in appearances; she was terribly vulnerable stripped of her lady-of-the-manor facade. I saw her almost fall to pieces in front of my eyes.

"What'll I do? I can't possibly make myself presentable at a moment's notice. Deanna, you'll have to receive him. Tell him I'm indisposed. Try to be polite and—for pity's sake—don't air any of our family affairs."

A little late for that, I thought, but nodded. My heartbeat quickened as I went down the stairs, pausing outside the parlor door. I took a couple of deep breaths before I went in. My feeble attempts to still the quivering in my stomach were for naught when Daniel Norris rose from a chair and quickly approached me, clasping my hands in his.

"I didn't know if I would be able to see you. Are you all right?" He stood so close to me that the warmth of his body radiated into mine. His eyes searched my face.

"Yes, I'm . . . fine."

"I couldn't believe what Gertrude Dorf told me this morning when I went for my mail. Is it true?"

I wanted to lean my head against his chest and pour out all the fears that were churning within. My emotions threatened to get the better of me, but I had learned years ago to keep my torment hidden.

I gave him a weak smile. "I imagine *some* of it is true. Considering that it was Gertrude who was doing the telling. Please sit down. Would you like some refreshment, Reverend?"

"No, I would *not* like any refreshment," he said firmly. "I would like to know what is going on." He was wearing a black suit and a clerical collar. His thick reddish hair had been neatly brushed and subdued in soft waves. Only cowboy boots under-mined his proper attire. His expression was somber and frank. "Let's dispense with formalities, shall we?"

"Elizabeth warned me to mind my manners."

"Manners be hanged!" He pulled me down on the settee beside him, keeping my hands captured in his. "You don't have to play games with me, Deanna. Whatever has happened, you aren't going to face it alone. Understand? Now tell me everything." This last was a firm command.

"Everything?" My tone held a hint of mockery as I drew my hands away. Instinctively my inner barriers went up. I had kept my secrets too deeply hidden to send them out on parade now. How simplistic he was! He was dead wrong if he thought a little Christian charity was going to change anything. "What do you think this is, a confessional?"

For a moment he just stared at me. Then the flush

of anger swept up into his cheeks and a flicker in his eyes told me I had wounded him. "Is that how you see me?"

"I'm sorry," I said quickly, feeling ashamed.

He stood up. "No, I'm the one who's sorry. Please forgive my intrusion. I had mistakenly thought that you were relating to me as a friend, but now I realize my mistake. You regard me as the *Reverend,* a person who is the sum of his religious beliefs, and nothing more."

"No, that's not true." How could I make him understand something I didn't understand myself? "I pressed the flowers you gave me."

At this feeble confession, the tenseness around his mouth eased. "Did you now?"

"Yes."

"Why would you do a thing like that?"

"Because I want to remember . . . how it was that day with us. How very happy I was." My eyes suddenly welled up with tears.

He sighed and sat back down. This time there was space between us as he turned sideways to face me. "Why do you fight like a cornered animal when someone tries to help you?"

I swiped at my eyes and shrugged. "I've spent my life fighting. I can't remember a time when I wasn't guarded and wary. You don't know how complicated and twisted everything is."

"No, I don't. And if you don't tell me, I never will."

"I can't tell you everything."

"All right. Just tell me about yesterday—please, Miss Banning," he said softly.

I related to him the events of the day in the same order I had told Officer Whitney. This time my voice was almost devoid of emotion, and I felt detached from the account as if someone else had seen the ring on the dead man's hand and ran screaming from the horror. Daniel watched me closely but he made no sympathetic gestures, and for that I was grateful. He seemed to respect my inner strength and that generated more control within me as I answered his questions.

"Then you didn't know this Mr. Babcock at all? He was a stranger to everyone in the family?"

"Steven knew his name because Brian Milburne had told him the other night that he was coming . . . to evaluate the assets of the store." I sighed deeply. "The bank was considering selling a note to Babcock, which would have allowed him to foreclose if he decided Bannings was a good investment."

Daniel let out a slow whistle. He didn't say anything for a moment, and neither did I. Then he surprised me by confessing, "When I first heard about the crime, I thought it might be connected with your brother's murder."

"Walter's? Why would you think a thing like that?"

"The chances of two murders involving the same family are so unlikely that a connection between them isn't entirely absurd. Since Walter's killer was never identified, he might have struck again."

"For what reason?"

"If we knew that, we'd be able to see the whole picture. Maybe we should make a list of people involved with Walter and with this new victim—and see if we can find a motive that would span two murders."

"I think we ought to leave the investigation to the authorities," I snapped. "Or do you fancy yourself a detective too?"

"Why are your hackles up again?" he asked evenly. "Don't you want to find the guilty party?"

"Don't be ridiculous. Of course I do."

"Maybe you're afraid it might turn out to be someone you care about?"

"No, of course not."

He watched me silently for a moment. "Better that the truth come out before someone else gets hurt. You don't seem to realize how much danger you may be in."

"Me?" I scoffed. "Why would anyone want to harm me? I don't know anything."

"Maybe the killer doesn't know that. Paranoia could drive a twisted mind to strike out at anyone who represents danger. Don't you see, Deanna, you may have the answer and you don't even know it! If you should say the wrong thing, act in a threatening way, or stumble into the truth, the murderer could turn his sights on you."

I must have paled for he reached out and traced my cheek with a fingertip and then tipped my chin up. His eyes bore into mine and his voice was suddenly intimate. "There must be something I can do. I'm a man of many talents. Remember I told you I'd had lots of jobs before wearing this collar? And I've had experience with a lot of different people."

I wanted to ask if his experience extended to women, but I curbed my curiosity. Besides, the way he lightly stroked my cheek was answer enough. I knew if he bent his head and kissed me, I would only part my lips in willing acceptance. But he didn't move closer. He slowly removed his hand, leaving me awash in tempestuous feelings. "I can take care of myself," I said rather too abruptly, disturbed that his nearness had unnerved me so.

"I don't want to frighten you, my sweet Deanna, but you mustn't trust others so blindly . . . not even those you love dearly."

"My brother didn't do it," I said quickly, even as I remembered the uneasiness I had felt with him the previous night. "I know Steven had a motive, but he's not a killer."

"Somebody is," he said flatly.

In the tense silence that followed, we heard a swish of skirts in the hall. Daniel rose to his feet as Elizabeth entered the room, perfectly coiffured, her mauve morning dress crisp and pleated. She didn't resemble the agitated woman who had confessed a short time earlier that she had not married the man she loved, but his brother.

"Reverend, how thoughtful of you to come." She held out her hand to him and then dabbed her eyes. "Such a dreadful business."

"Yes, I came to offer my support in any way possible."

"You're most kind." With a sigh, Elizabeth settled herself in a nearby chair. "Deanna, haven't you offered Reverend Norris some refreshment? I specifically told you—" then she caught herself and gave the minister an apologetic smile. "You must forgive us, I'm afraid we aren't our usual selves. Deanna, please ask Maude to bring us in a tray."

Daniel quickly declined refreshment, but Elizabeth insisted. "It has been an exasperating morning, but I'm glad you dropped by, Reverend. I wanted to talk with you about the church breakfast. I really must insist that—"

Her voice trailed after me as I headed down the hall toward the kitchen. Elizabeth's society mask was back in place. The crack in the exterior that I had glimpsed that morning had successfully been mended. I wondered if she regretted sharing her feelings about Walter with me.

Maude had company in the kitchen. Jon Duval sat

at the table eating a generous breakfast, and he raised his dark eyebrows slightly as I came in. "Well, look who's here." He made no motion to rise to his feet but gestured with his fork toward a nearby chair. "Sit a spell and have a morning mug with me."

"Thank you, I've already had breakfast," I said curtly.

Maude looked uncomfortable. "Jon's been out shooting. Brought us some quail and two rabbits."

"Just like the good old days, eh, Maude? Remember how Walter and me would come back ravenous from our early morning shoot? He was the best damn shot around. Always bagged twice my kill. And nobody can cook 'em like you, Maudie."

She colored at the compliment and then dismissed it with a wave of her hand. "Go on with ya. Eat your breakfast."

I told her that Elizabeth would like a tray in the parlor for her and Reverend Norris, and I volunteered to take it in when it was ready. She waddled into the scullery to get some fixings for sandwiches.

"So the preacher's come to call," said Duval smugly. "I saw the way the wind was blowing at the picnic."

"Don't be ridiculous."

"Sabrina says half the women in town are panting over him. Don't tell me a gal like you cottons to a weak-kneed, Bible-toting parson?" he said scornfully. "You need a red-blooded man to take you in hand."

Before I could move, he reached out and pulled me sideways onto his lap. His arms were like iron vices pressing my breasts against his chest and capturing my arms helplessly at my side. I protested loudly, but he only laughed at my cry and tightened his embrace. "I'll take a kiss now . . . kind of a down payment."

I jerked my head to one side, repelled by his moist lips. He only grunted gleefully and buried his mouth in the nape of my neck, pulling the warm flesh between his teeth. I butted him away with my head and bit his ear.

"You blasted wildcat," he swore, and I thought he was going to shake me senseless.

"Take your hands off her!" Daniel loomed large in the kitchen doorway. In two steps he was at the table. Duval's eyes registered surprise and then delight. "Well, well. Look who's come charging to the rescue. Aren't you out of your league, preacher?"

"Let her go, now!"

Duval hesitated for a moment and then released me with a scornful laugh. "Get out of the way, honey. I think the parson's getting a little riled up. He's acting mighty brave hiding behind that collar of his."

With one quick motion, Daniel jerked off the clerical collar and tossed it aside. With the other hand, he pushed me to safety.

Maude gasped from the scullery doorway as the Frenchman slowly rose to his feet. Every muscle in Duval's large body pulsed with brute strength. His thick arms and iron fists were flexed, his head jutted forward at a pugnacious angle, and he assumed a predatory stance.

Daniel never moved. He stood fast, waiting, and his steady gaze held a challenge that seemed to disconcert Duval.

"I suppose if I knock your head off, you'll just turn the other cheek," the Frenchman taunted.

"Want to try it and find out?"

Duval reached out and turned over a chair as if that was the signal for the fight to begin. It clattered on the floor but neither man moved. The silence was deafening.

"I think you'd better leave, Mr. Duval," said Daniel in an even tone.

"And who's going to make me?"

"I am—if you insist."

Duval gave an ugly snort. "No white-livered preacher is going to make me do anything."

"I wasn't always a preacher."

The statement hung threateningly in the air. Duval's expression seemed to weigh Daniel's ready stance. The ugly twist on Duval's lips wavered.

My breath caught in my throat.

After what seemed an eternity, Duval spat an ugly oath, turned, and stalked out of the kitchen.

Maude began to sob and sat down heavily in a nearby chair. I couldn't move. Daniel turned to me. "Did he hurt you?" he said angrily.

I moistened my dry lips. "No. He just scared me. Thank you."

His hands were clenched and I knew that he would have fought furiously if Duval had landed the first blow. The scandal of the fight would have rocked the foundations of the First Methodist Church, but he would have risked the ire of his congregation to protect me. I wanted to rise up on my toes and kiss his freckled cheek, but at that moment Elizabeth swept into the kitchen.

"Would someone please tell me what is going on here?" she demanded with a puzzled look. "I went upstairs to get my record books and heard an awful commotion."

"Just a little misunderstanding with Jon Duval . . . but it's all settled now," Daniel said smoothly.

I nodded in agreement, desperately wanting to believe that he spoke the truth.

Chapter Twelve

Steven was furious when he heard what had happened with Jon Duval. I tried to make light of the incident but my brother went into Papa's trophy room and loaded one of the hunting rifles. "I'll shoot the bastard if he steps foot on this property again."

"Steven, put that gun back. This is no time for heroics. Officer Whitney is just waiting for an excuse to take you in for Babcock's murder."

"I didn't have anything to do with that and he can't prove that I did. He's been snooping around here like this house is full of criminals and I've about had enough of it. Oh, I know the town's yapping that I murdered Babcock to keep from losing the store. But you know something, sis? It would be a relief to be free of the damn thing. If it weren't for you—"

"Me?"

"If we lose everything, what will you do?"

I bristled. "I have earned my own living for five years, Steven Banning. It's you and Elizabeth and the children I worry about. If the bank repossesses the store, you won't have the money you need to invest in your new business."

"I wonder why I haven't heard from that interested

buyer in Denver I wrote to."

Because Elizabeth intercepted your letter. "Write to him again—today," I urged. "I'll mail it for you." I gave his arm an affectionate squeeze. "Please put back the gun."

"No." His muscles were rigid under my touch. "I may not be the best shot in the county but if Duval shows his face around here again, I'll make him sorry for taking liberties with my sister."

My brother's mood had grown darker and more belligerent with each passing day. I was frightened by the change in him. He was no longer the mild-mannered brother I adored, but a stranger. I was afraid that the stress of the investigation and the threat of business failure had become too much for him. I was afraid he would crack under the pressure.

The house was permeated with a foreboding that threatened to envelope me. I had always hated its dark interior: black walnut woodwork, narrow windows, and thick stone walls—here was a pervasive melancholy. A frightening menace lingered in the shadows, formless and yet clearly recognized. I jumped at the slightest unexpected sound. Even spending hours in my own room could not ease the growing apprehension building inside me. I tried to find some enjoyment in the garden, but the hostile presence of Jericho spoiled my pleasure. I dared not take a walk in the woods. Just looking at the dark drifts of trees sent a chill through me. The days passed slowly and the nights brought only fitful sleep.

As far as Elizabeth was concerned, after a day or two everything seemed to be back to normal. Busy with her various projects, she spent the afternoons attending meetings, and chatted about plans for the upcoming Fourth of July celebration. I was surprised one morning when she waved two parchment envelopes in front of me. "Here's one for you."

"What is it?"

"Can't you guess? It's from Nina Milburne." She ripped hers open and then nodded knowingly at me. "A bridal tea for Carolyn Lareau. At the Miramonte Hotel. Oh dear, what kind of gift should I get? I do wish we had some way of knowing what other guests will be bringing. I'm certain that Carolyn's family will see that the couple starts off with everything. I want to get exactly the right gift. Something spectacular. What's the matter?" She frowned at the unopened envelope in my hand. "You're going to attend, of course."

"I'll send a gift," I replied. "Along with my regrets."

Elizabeth's face instantly flamed. "Regrets! Why, such a thing would amount to a deliberate slap in the face to all concerned. Surely you're not so eaten up with jealousy, Deanna, that you can't put on a polite face and wish the couple well? Everything was over between you and Brian a long time ago, you said so yourself."

A mirthless laugh rose in my throat. I wondered what my dear sister-in-law would do if she knew the bridegroom had kissed me on our terrace within the last week.

"You have to go!" she ordered. "If you don't, people will talk. You know that Nina would never accept anything less than a terminal illness as a legitimate excuse for not attending one of her affairs. I know the two of you don't like each other, but that has nothing to do with honoring one's social obligations."

"I don't care one whit about honoring social obligations."

163

"I do!" she flared. "And you'll not embarrass me by thumbing your nose at the Milburnes. I've worked too hard to gain my position in the community and I won't let you ruin it for me, so stop being so selfish and do something for someone else for a change."

I couldn't face the relentless barrage of upbraiding remarks. "All right, Elizabeth," I said wearily. "I'll go."

"Good. Now you just leave everything to me. I'll find an impressive gift, and put both our names on it." Elizabeth's mind sped ahead to the next important matter. "I hope my new summer gown will be finished by then. All my afternoon dresses have been worn much too often and it's only the end of June." She eyed me in scrutiny. "What about you, Deanna? Surely you have something more presentable than those plain governess dresses you've been wearing. Vivian, the seamstress, could sew up a gown that would be more suitable."

My wardrobe had been adequate for my uneventful life in the Lowenstein household, but I could see that Elizabeth would be embarrassed to have her sister-in-law attend a society fete in unfashionable attire.

"I'll see if I can find some material at the store," I promised. "I suppose they stock some of the new patterns."

Elizabeth's nose quivered. "With Millie in charge, I wouldn't count on it. You know what a drab bird she is. Bannings isn't anything like it was when Papa Banning and Walter ran the store. I've been sending away to the Delineator and Butterick magazines for my patterns. I'd let you use one of them but, of course, we wouldn't want to be seen in the same dress."

"Of course not," I said dryly.

Unfortunately, Elizabeth was right about the selection of material and patterns at the store. I spent an hour looking through uninspiring bolts of material and the best I could find was a pale yellow organza with tiny sprays of violets in an all-over pattern.

Millie had come down from the office to personally wait on me. Her solid, sturdy frame was a commanding presence behind the counter. While Walter was alive, she had been his best saleslady. "I think that will be very nice," she said, nodding over my selection and suggesting a heavy lace inset for the bodice. I thought the inset would have been more suitable for winter velvet than a summer gown. I murmured something vague and set the trimming aside.

"Here is a style that would work up very well, I think." She handed me a dusty envelope that must have been in the pattern drawer since Walter was running the store.

As politely as I could, I declined Millie's suggestions and did the best I could with my limited choices.

"Of course, we don't have the selection you're used to, Deanna," she said testily. "But I'm certain that any one of these patterns would do. I think they would provide some needed padding. You're much too thin, you know. Men like women to have a full figure these days. I would suggest a tournure. They lift a peplum nicely."

She put a horrid-looking contraption on the counter. The bustle was made by placing steel springs in a shirring across the back of a petticoat and tying the ends together with tape across the front. I had watched women trying to sit down gracefully in this encumbrance and would have none of it. A modest bustle of gathering cloth was style enough for me.

I knew from Millie's slightly pursed lips that she was offended that I didn't take her suggestions. She didn't approve of my idea of combining a bodice pattern with the skirt of another gown, but I didn't see any other way to achieve a fashionable look. With lavender glass buttons and a trimming of grosgrain ribbon, I thought Elizabeth would not be ashamed of my appearance. I was glad she had a seamstress who could make up the dress for me.

Millie handed me my purchases. "I've been invited to the bridal tea, too."

I would have never expected Millie to be on the invitation list and I guess my expression betrayed my surprise. "Oh, I know everyone will be wondering why I was included." She set her square chin. "Carolyn is not stuck up like some people. The day of the picnic, I offered to order some special things for the wedding and she's been in almost every day adding to the list. She told me she was going to include my name on the guest list. I didn't expect her to really do it, but I got an invitation from Mrs. Milburne in the mail." Millie's plain face broke into a broad smile. "Except for church, I never have been included in anything that had to do with the Milburnes. People like that have never taken the least notice of me."

"I envy you that," I said wryly. It seemed to me that my life had always been tangled up with the Milburnes. I'd even fled Brimstone in order to escape them.

"I heard that the murdered man they found on your property was a friend of Brian Milburne," Millie said in a conspirator's tone.

"Not a friend . . . a business associate. Mr. Babcock had come down to look over Bannings at Brian's request. I guess you know there's been talk of the bank foreclosing."

She nodded. "Harold and I have been waiting to see what's going to happen. I hate leaving Steven in the lurch by getting married."

"You've been very loyal to the family, Millie, and we appreciate it. We could have never kept the store this long without your help. I think Steven is ready to sell . . . if we can find a buyer. He has other business plans which will suit him much better."

She eyed me with interest. "What about you? Are you sweet on the preacher?" Then she clamped her mouth shut as if she was appalled that she had voiced such a question.

I hoped the dimly lit store put my face in enough shadow to hide the warm color that I felt rising in my cheeks. "Reverend Norris and I are friends."

"I saw the way you two were looking at each other at the picnic. But I can't see you in the role of a minister's wife," she said with her usual bluntness. "You don't even go to church regularly."

She had put her finger on the mark, that much was certain. What could I say? Daniel detested people relating to his collar and not to him as a person, but I knew it was utter foolishness to separate the two. And yet, in my daydreaming, that's what I had been doing. But Daniel Norris was a minister and required a woman fit to be a minister's wife.

"People have been known to change," I said defensively.

"The Bannings never change," she said in a bitter tone that surprised me. She handed me my package without saying anything more. I wished everything was as black and white for me as it was for her.

167

Carolyn's bridal shower was held in a private hall off the hotel's public dining room. As Elizabeth and I made our way through the lobby of the Miramonte Hotel, I observed that the tourist season was in full swing. People surged in and out, engaging carriages for sightseeing excursions in the area, or standing in lines to sign up for any number of activities. Posters proclaimed the wonders of the numerous bath-houses, and maps were offered for a walking tour to all the natural springs in the area. The excitement of a donkey trip up to Sunshine Falls was offset by the more leisurely wildflower-and-butterfly search. An afternoon concert presented by a string quartet drew guests to a lovely music room fashioned with mirrors and free-standing ferns. The chamber music offered a respite from the bustle and chatter of the crowds.

"Good afternoon, ladies," Joe Sawyer, Sabrina's husband, said, greeting us with a polite half-bow. He wasn't the kind of man whom you would expect to host a hotel full of fashionable pleasure-seeking guests. His dull hair receded from a high forehead, small eyes peered through round gold-rimmed glasses, and a black coat and gray trousers hung on his bony frame with only slightly more aplomb than they would have on a wire hanger. He looked like a man who was weak and self-effacing, but he wasn't. Too often a freeloading guest would mistake Joe's laissez-faire appearance for an easy touch, only to discover to his chagrin that nobody cheated Joe Sawyer out of a dime. The hotel owner employed several burly men who took care of such unpleasant details as collecting unpaid bills.

"Nice to see you again, Miss Banning," he said to

me. "Sabrina was delighted that you were able to attend the picnic at Sunshine Falls."

I doubted that very much, but I nodded and smiled.

"I understand everyone had a good time?" He waited for my reply.

The remark was obviously a question. Was he trying to find out how his wife had behaved? He must have known that Jon Duval had been a member of the party—or maybe not. Maybe Sabrina had left the hotel with David Kirkland and Jon was picked up later.

"It was very pleasant," I said noncommittally. "Hunters Glen is one of my favorite places."

"You're having a busy season," Elizabeth commented as a flow of guests mounted the wide steps to suites on the second floor.

"Yes. Business is good. And I'm making plans to expand." For several minutes, Joe chatted on about a new casino he planned to open soon. I was ill at ease in the man's company because I knew that Walter had enjoyed the pleasures of his wife. I was even more uncomfortable when Sabrina joined us.

She gave me a perfunctory nod, smiled at Elizabeth, and then addressed her husband. "Joe, darling, you don't mind if I join the ladies this afternoon, do you? If I hear one more complaint about lukewarm baths or noisy children running in the halls, I will go mad." She smiled at him playfully. "Besides, my watercolor class begins today at four o'clock so I'd appreciate a little time to enjoy myself." She feigned a petulant tone as if she was the most put-upon creature imaginable.

"Of course, my dear. I'll have one of the other girls take the desk. You enjoy yourself." Sawyer's expression was so adoring that it made me sick to my stomach.

I didn't look at Sabrina as we made our way down the hall to a private parlor that looked out upon a small terrace. The doors were open and tables had been set out under the trees. Women gathered in groups in the parlor or were sitting in the midst of greenery on the terrace, looking like a bevy of colorful birds, as ostrich plumes and other elaborate decorations danced on their hats.

"Hello, Elizabeth . . . lovely dress . . . very becoming . . . beautiful day, isn't it?"

The greetings were for my sister-in-law. I felt the same kind of scrutiny that had come my way in church. Elizabeth was immediately appropriated into a chattering circle, leaving me standing alone. Millie sat with some church ladies and I perceived a smug smile on her lips as she nodded in my direction. *See, I belong—and you don't.*

Sabrina floated over to an elaborate tea table where Carolyn stood with her soon-to-be mother-in-law, greeting guests. For a moment I fought the urge to turn around and flee while I had the chance, but Nina Milburne's eyes had already found me. From her startled expression, I knew then that she hadn't expected me to come. Her eyes narrowed dangerously and for a moment I thought she might raise an imperious finger and order me out. Carolyn must have insisted on sending the invitation, and not wanting to show her malicious intent, Nina had addressed one to me, certain I wouldn't dare intrude. Her obvious anger only fueled my stubbornness, and I felt some dubious sense of satisfaction that I was there, in a new gown, with my head held high. I doubted she would try to shame me in this company, so I kept my smile fixed on the pretty bride-to-be as I approached them.

"How nice of you to come, Deanna," Carolyn

greeted me with undisguised sincerity. "And you look lovely. Doesn't she, Nina?"

I smothered a laugh. Nina would have rather died on the spot than give me any kind of compliment. I ignored the woman's seething glare and told Carolyn how lovely she looked in her pink tulle dress and wide-brimmed hat.

"Thank you. Mother Milburne had it made in Denver for me, and my wedding gown too."

I wondered if Nina had picked out the honeymoon nightgown as well.

"Carolyn will make a beautiful bride, don't you agree, Deanna?" Nina addressed me haughtily.

"Yes, she will. Brian is very lucky." I hoped my smile was as firm as my voice. Carolyn was more than welcome to Brian Milburne.

Sabrina watched the exchange between us closely. Her dark eyes shifted from me to Carolyn to Nina and back again, as if testing any vibrations between us. I was satisfied that she didn't pick up any hint of jealousy from either Carolyn or me.

I accepted a cup of tea from Della Danvers, who was pouring. She was her usual aristocratic self and barely nodded when I complimented her on her blue gown made of a twilled silk fabric which must have come from India. She wore heavy loops of pearls on her rather flat chest and one finger flashed a diamond-and-pearl tea ring. The ring caught my eye but there was no avaricious urge or longing to possess it even for a moment. Apparently the empty spaces in my life were no longer demanding fulfillment by my former compulsion. I was confident I had overcome my addiction.

I took my cup of tea and found a chair from which I could view the festivities without being a part of them. After all the guests had arrived, Carolyn took

171

her place beside Nina in the center of a circle of gifts and her pretty face was luminous with happiness as she opened them. I wondered what Millie was thinking as she sat solidly in her chair, a rather homely woman in her gray silk dress, and watched Carolyn's every movement. The "ohs" and "ahs" as each gift was held up for display were like an orchestrated chorus. Elizabeth beamed when our gift of a gold ormolu clock received an impressive response from the assembly.

As soon as the gathering began to break up, I whispered to Elizabeth that I was going to walk home and gratefully made my exit from the room.

I was halfway down the hall when a familiar voice greeted me. "Deanna. What a nice surprise. Are you coming to the painting class?"

I turned to see David Kirkland descending the stairs with a paint box and easel under his arms. He seemed genuinely glad to see me, and I thought again what a nice man he was. I had forgotten his invitation to join the class. Now that I knew Sabrina was involved, I was glad I hadn't given in to the impulse to try my hand.

I explained that I had been attending a prenuptial tea for Carolyn to celebrate her upcoming marriage to Brian.

"Oh, yes. Lovely couple. They were quite the stars of a dance held in the hotel the other night. My goodness, they made these old bones weary just watching. Never seen so many different kinds of dances—waltzes, fox-trots, two steps . . . and did you ever hear of a schottische? They did something I'd never seen before to 'Wrap Me in a Bundle.'" He laughed. "Most risqué, I must admit. But quite enjoyable. You really should join the young crowd,

172

my dear. You seem much too somber for one so young."

Long ago, in another world, I had danced until midnight in the same hotel ballroom. I could have told him that Brian and I had mastered all those steps, and that once people had told us that we were a lovely couple.

"Forgive me," he apologized quickly. "I can tell from your expression that I'm being an old fool again. It's just that I would like to see you happy. It would mean a great deal to me. You see, you remind me of someone I once knew. She was a very giving person and deserved happiness . . . just like you."

He looked at me so tenderly, I impulsively reached up and touched his cheek. "Thank you."

For a moment I thought his eyes were going to fill with tears, but he gained control of his emotions and said, "I wonder if I could ask a favor of you? The other day when we picked you up for the picnic, I saw a beautiful flower garden at the back of your house. Would it be too presumptuous to ask if I could come and try my hand at painting some of those lovely roses?"

"Oh, please do. I'm sure it would be fine with my brother. He's the one responsible for the garden. I bet Steven would even give you a guided tour of his greenhouse."

"I would like that very much." He hesitated and a shadow crossed his face. "Please forgive me for asking, but I read in the *Brimstone Herald* about the unfortunate tragedy near your house and I wondered if they had made any progress finding the guilty one?"

"I don't know. Officer Whitney hasn't been at the house for a few days but I know he's still working on the case." The question brought back renewed uneasiness. I had never thought my brother could be capable of any misdeed, but his brooding behavior of late and the fact that he had cleaned and loaded one of Papa's rifles continued to disturb me.

"If there's anything I can do . . ." The lines in the older man's face deepened. "Please call on me." Then he looked distractedly over my shoulder with a frown.

I turned and saw Nina Milburne standing in the hall watching us, and I wondered how much of our conversation she had overheard. She looked as if she was sitting in judgment of us, and when I met her eyes there was naught but condemnation.

Defiantly, I turned back to Mr. Kirkland. "Please come and see us anytime," I told him, and quickly took my leave. As I exited the hotel, I shivered. I knew that it was only my state of mind, but Nina Milburne had conjured up in me the image of a vulture circling hungrily overhead.

Chapter Thirteen

Fourth of July promised to be a perfect Colorado summer day. The sun rose brassy and bold, peering over the high mountain peaks and heralding a new day in colors like the blast of a trumpet. In the Colorado Rockies, the warm valleys were cooled by breezes descending from the high snowy mountain peaks. As I sat beside my open bedroom window, summer smells of freshly cut grass and rose petals mingled with the heady scent of pine needles and wild berries.

Downstairs in Maude's kitchen, an array of baked pies and heavenly cakes were lined up like a confectioner's army ready to be taken in baskets to Wateredge Park, a stretch of land on both sides of the creek about a mile west of town. The park offered large cottonwood trees, picnic tables, and a covered band shell for entertainment and dancing. Decorated booths, colorful signs, paper streamers, Chinese lanterns, and long tables of food had been brought in special for Elizabeth's fundraising celebration.

The last few days of preparation, Elizabeth had been impossible to live with. She sent everyone within range scurrying, delivering orders in the strident tone of a general. I sympathized with her, given the enormous responsibility she had assumed, but whenever possible I contrived to stay out of her way. The feverish tempo in the house put us all on edge. I was glad when the holiday finally arrived.

Breakfast was a brief affair. The children were positively delirious with excitement. Elizabeth's patience was short. Steven had made two trips in the wagon to deliver items to the park grounds before the rest of us were ready to leave.

After helping Maude unload her bakery offerings in the cake booth, I took charge of Patty, and Sarah held onto Nicky. The toddler insisted upon navigating over the rough ground on his own bowed legs, landing on his padded derriere with every other step.

"Why don't you take Nicky up to the bandstand, Sarah, and let him play there until the music starts?" I suggested. "He'll be happier there and Patty and I can look around."

The maid nodded gratefully, hoisted Nicky up on one hip and set off on her own.

"Let's visit the lemonade stand and the penny pitch," I suggested to my niece.

"Will we win a prize?" she asked eagerly.

"We can try."

With a squeal, Patty grabbed my hand and pulled me along at an enthusiastic pace. "Look, Aunt Deedee. Look! A balloon. I want a balloon. A red one!"

The pathways were crowded, picnic tables were already heavily laden, and firecrackers and other Fourth of July explosives were popping loud enough to send dogs scurrying away with tails between their legs. The park resembled a county fair. Lines of people waited to partake of various offerings. From all indications the amount of money raised for the opera house would be impressive, I thought. Elizabeth would surely get the community recognition she yearned for after this affair.

Patty decided she would rather have ice cream than lemonade. Two ladies in a pink and white booth were dipping cones as fast as they could. Patty spent a lot of time deciding which of the small freezers offered the flavor she liked best. She finally decided on chocolate, and after a few licks of the treat, she had a brown mustache.

Sarah had dressed the children in play clothes; Elizabeth had been too busy to notice that they didn't look like they had just stepped out of a Maude Humphrey painting. I was comfortable in a sheer lawn white bodice and walking skirt. My straw bonnet shaded my face and allowed the cool air to circulate around the thick coils of hair on my neck.

"Win me a doll," ordered Patty when we stopped at the penny pitch and she saw a row of stocking dolls offered as prizes. Numbers and tiny cups were set out on a large board and I did my best to fling a coin into the winning-number cups, but without any success. "Let's try something else," I said quickly, knowing my chances of winning a prize in that game were slim.

At the next booth, I bought three balls to throw at some cardboard ducks floating on cardboard water, but I was only able to nick one duck and it didn't fall over.

"Well, it's a relief to know I won't have to duck if you throw something at me," said an amused voice behind me.

Feeling a spurt of joy, I turned around. "Don't be too sure, Reverend. I'm just warming up."

"Aunt Deedee pitched a dollar's worth of pennies and didn't get anything," Patty told him with childlike honesty. She cocked her yellow curly head. "Will you win me a prize?"

"I'd be honored to try, Miss Patricia," said Daniel with mock dignity.

Patty pointed to a large stuffed rabbit with floppy pink ears. "I want that one."

"Patty, that's not polite," I chastised.

"I like a woman who knows her own mind," he said with a wink at me. "The rabbit it shall be."

He missed the first four throws.

I covered a smile with my gloved hand.

"Just practicing," he said solemnly to Patty.

She nodded as if she understood completely. I was skeptical. He needed six out of ten throws. When he hit the next six in a row, I swallowed my smile.

"There you go," he said, handing Patty the soft furry animal and accepting a kiss on the cheek from her chocolate-covered mouth.

"Where did you learn to throw like that?" I asked as we walked through the crowd.

"I once pitched for a baseball team made up of a bunch of West Virginia miners. On our one day above ground, we played baseball."

"You dug coal?"

"Not by choice, believe me. It was the only job around that would bring in enough money to feed us after my pa died." He shuddered. "I hated it. You can't imagine the complete absence of light underground. The darkness is absolute. No shadows . . . just black. I thank the Good Lord every day for the miracle of light." He lifted his face to the sun as if trying to make up for all the sunlight he had missed. Then he smiled at me in an apologetic way. "Sorry. I didn't mean to talk about such morose things. This is not a day for dark thoughts." He took Patty's hand and put a guiding touch on my arm. "Ladies, I believe the races are about to begin. Let's find a nice spot under one of the trees and cheer the courageous contenders."

Potato-sack races, egg-and-spoon relays, and three-legged contests drew the crowd like spectators to a national sport. Amid cheers, jeers, and boisterous laughter the combatants tried valiantly to reach the finish line without tripping, dropping eggs, or falling on the ground in jumbled heaps. I laughed and yelled as loudly as anyone. Daniel's eyes met mine in shared pleasure.

After the races were over, we wandered back to the center of the park and found families beginning to sit down to their picnic feasts. Everything looked and smelled wonderful. Several families and community groups shared potluck offerings and others sat in small groups on the ground around a blanket or tablecloth.

Elizabeth was directing the placement of food on one of the single picnic tables. I could tell from the way she was fretting that she was not enjoying herself. She acknowledged Daniel's presence with a fleeting nod and gave Patty a hurried "How nice" when her daughter held up the toy rabbit. "Deanna, please unpack these hampers. Reverend, you must join our gathering. We have more than enough food." She took a deep breath. "I think it's going smoothly, don't you? The booths seem to be doing well—"

"Very well," Daniel assured her. "You're to be commended, Elizabeth. I can appreciate the amount of work you've given to this project."

"I'm afraid the booths won't bring in as much as we'd hoped. We really need the dance tonight to be a success. If people go home before the evening activities begin—"

"Elizabeth," I interrupted sharply. "Try to relax. You're going to make yourself ill. Stop worrying about every little thing. You've done a marvelous job—now enjoy it."

"I agree," said Daniel. "Let other people take over now."

"But what if . . . if something goes wrong?" She bit her full lip nervously.

"What can possibly go wrong now? The whole town has turned out."

"I don't know, I just have this feeling that I'm overlooking something. And Steven . . . he's not himself. He disappeared after bringing things over in the wagon this morning. Doesn't he understand I need him today?" For a moment I thought her eyes were going to tear, but she caught herself. "After this is over—" she began, but her voice trailed off as she took herself in hand and began giving Sarah instructions about feeding the children.

"Where *is* your brother?" Daniel asked me as he helped me set out the table service.

"I don't know. He must be here somewhere. I'm worried about him, too. He's been acting peculiar ever since . . ." I faltered. "Since Babcock was killed."

Daniel nodded in understanding. "Murder is always a shock, even when the victim is not a loved one. In this instance, I'm sure Steven must feel responsible for not having been able to prevent the tragedy." He eyed me candidly. "Or do you think he had something to do with it?"

"Of course not!" I snapped, but I kept my face turned away from his. He was too blasted perceptive.

"I didn't mean to distress you," Daniel said quickly. "I know how much you love Steven. All of this must be a great worry to you."

180

Later I thought it might ease my mind if I shared my concerns with him, but Millie and Harold arrived at that moment and engaged him in conversation.

Millie's face was flushed and smile lines radiated around her eyes as she greeted him. I remembered how she had warned me that whoever married Daniel Norris would have to be suitable to church life. The thought was sobering enough to dissipate the morning's enjoyment in his company. I was letting myself get too involved with a man I was not suited for. Millie had been right to warn me.

I filled my plate and sat with Sarah, Maude, and the children on one side of the long table. Millie and Harold joined Elizabeth and Daniel on the other, and they kept the conversation going, mostly about church affairs.

I missed Steven. Where was he? Was he avoiding the celebration because he couldn't face the public after what had happened? A growing uneasiness made me decide to accompany Sarah back to the house with the children to look for him. I sensed danger in the air, the way I had in childhood when my brother was hurt or frightened.

"Take the buggy, Deanna," ordered Elizabeth. "And then come back after the children are down for their naps. If Steven doesn't appear, I'll need some help later this afternoon. Reverend Norris, if you would be so kind, I need someone to sell tickets for the baseball game."

Sarah and I herded the children across the park to the place where our horse was tethered under an oak tree, contentedly chomping on a clump of buffalo grass.

Nicky set up a howling protest, striking out at Sarah with flailing arms when she put him in the buggy, a true sign that his afternoon nap was overdue. Patty fussed about leaving and let it be known that she considered herself too old for baby naps.

I flicked the reins upon the rump of the horse and set it trotting briskly back to the house. Since Hunters Hall was not far from the park, we reached it in a few minutes. Circling the house, I reined the horse in the clearing in front of the stable.

"Can you manage, Sarah?" I asked as she and the children piled out of the buggy.

"Yes, mum." She had Nicky on one hip and she firmly pulled Patty toward the house with the other hand. They disappeared through the back door.

Lifting my skirts, I hurried through the garden to the greenhouse. If Steven had not returned to the park after making his deliveries early that morning, I guessed he would be in his hideaway. Calling his name, I walked through the greenhouse to his office but found it empty.

Some sixth sense fueled my uneasiness. Since childhood a psychic sensitivity had existed between my brother and me. More than once we had come to each other's aid during childhood. The perception that my brother was in trouble was as strong as it had ever been.

"Steven!" I ran out of the greenhouse. A side door of the house was closest. With my heart pounding and my mouth dry, I burst into the house as if being pursued by some unseen beast. I bounded down the hall. The smell of whiskey assaulted my nostrils at the doorway into Papa's trophy room.

"Steven!" I screamed, and lunged into the room.

My brother held a gun to his head.

My hand pushed the gun frantically aside. The gun discharged. A bullet tore into the wall behind his head.

For a moment he looked at me as if befuddled by what had happened. His eyes were blurry with drink.

"Oh my God, Steven," I gasped and eased the gun out of his hand. Then I drew him into my arms and stroked his head. He trembled and shivered as though suffering from palsy. "Why? Why would you do such a thing?" I sobbed.

His voice was choked and husky with drink. "Had to. No way out." I saw a half-empty bottle of whiskey beside the chair.

My fright mingled with a surge of anger. "There's always a way out—and killing yourself isn't it!" Tears streamed down my cheeks. "I don't care what you've done. We'll figure out some way to handle it."

He raised his face and a feeble smile touched his lips. "You always did pull my bacon out of the fire, sis, but this time, you're only going to get burned."

"I don't care. We'll face this together—the way we always have. Just don't lie to me." I found enough breath to continue. "Tell me. Did you kill Babcock?" I asked.

Steven's eyes looked beyond me. His mouth drooped sadly as his head lolled to one side. I braced him against me as he succumbed to the effects of the alcohol and passed out.

Chapter Fourteen

I sat on the arm of the leather chair and cushioned Steven's head against my breast. I felt as if I had been engulfed in a wave of dark, dense water. The hated room was oppressive, filled with Papa's condemnation and ridicule. Glassy-eyed animals looked down upon us, their open mouths showing sharp jagged teeth. The room reeked of whiskey and an insidious smell of tobacco smoke that had remained in the walls even after Papa was long gone. I leaned my fair head against my brother's, our hair so much alike in color and texture, and I remembered how our father had rejected Steven and me with such vehemence. His lashing tirades echoed in my ears. He had brought us to this moment. I had learned to deal with my feelings of displacement and loneliness, but the gun lying on the floor beside Steven was evidence that he had not.

I don't know how long I sat there. The room grew dark as afternoon shadows lengthened. The echo of noise from the nursery upstairs told me that the children had awakened from their naps. I heard their scampering footsteps as Sarah took them out for a walk. I knew I had to get back to the park. Elizabeth had requested my help in collecting tickets for the evening dance in the band shell.

"Steven!" I gave him a sharp slap on his cheek and shook his shoulders. He groaned and slowly lifted his heavy eyelids. His head wobbled and he slid further down in the chair. "Wake up!" I slapped him again.

He worked his mouth and I knew he was regaining consciousness. As the events of the day flooded into his mind, he sobered up before my eyes. He sat up and leaned forward, resting his head in his hands.

"Come on. I'll help you upstairs. We can't let anyone see you like this." I wanted to rant and rave at him but I held my tongue. "Go to bed and sleep it off—then we'll talk!"

Somehow I got him upstairs and shut the door of his room as he sprawled on the bed. I went back to the trophy room, returned the pistol to its place in the gun cabinet, locked it, and pocketed the key. Then I returned the half-empty whiskey bottle to the cupboard. No one would have known what had taken place there—unless I had been two minutes detained and my brother's brains had been splattered all over the walls.

I changed my dress, which was wrinkled and smelled of whiskey, and put on a pale blue gown with a matching jacket. When I reached the park again, I saw that the lanterns had been lit. They twinkled through the trees like multicolored fireflies in a Japanese garden. Faint orchestra music floated above the soft gurgling of the creek and I wondered if I was too late to help Elizabeth with the dance tickets.

The park was still crowded, and I had difficulty finding a place to leave the buggy. I finally reined the horse some distance from the center of the celebration. I was collecting my beaded bag and shawl from the seat, preparing to alight from the buggy and tether the horse when I heard a gruff laugh.

I froze in the seat as Jon Duval grabbed the bridle strap of my horse. "Well, look who's here. Miss Uppity herself."

I jerked on the reins, trying to set the horse in motion, but the Frenchman held the bridle firmly. "Whoa, boy!" The animal stomped his hooves but didn't bolt. Duval jerked the reins away from me and tethered them securely on a nearby branch. "Now then," he sauntered around the buggy and reached for me. "Let me help you down."

"I don't need your help. Please leave," I ordered with as much composure as my pounding heart would allow.

He laughed. "Never let it be said that Jon Duval turned his back on a lady . . . especially one in need of my protection."

"Isn't that like a weasel offering to guard the chicken house?"

His smile turned ugly. "You always were a smart one with that tongue of yours. I used to tell Walter you needed a lot of taming."

He moved toward me and I lifted my crop. "Don't touch me."

With a foul oath, he jerked the whip out of my hand before I could raise it. The next moment he had his hands on me and jerked me harshly out of the buggy.

I cried out but this time there was no one to hear me. His iron embrace held me helplessly against him. With his face poised close to mine, he held my arms tightly. My efforts to push against his chest only increased his mirth. His lustful animal ardor turned my stomach. I knew that if he dragged me into the bushes, there would be nothing I could do to stop him.

He laughed again, seeing the terror in my eyes. "One kiss and I'll let you go," he bargained with cruel amusement. Before I could jerk my head back, he had put his mouth harshly upon mine. Lust was like a fire in his eyes. His fingers bit into my flesh in a mauling caress. When he broke off the cruel kiss, he gave a growl like an animal in heat. He kissed me again and then pulled me into the darkness of the nearby drift of evergreens.

I screamed, but my cries were lost in the roar of the creek. All sounds were muffled by the tunnel of interwoven branches he pulled me through. Duval threw me to the ground and pinned my arms above my head. He pressed his body upon mine and I felt the hardening surge of his desire as he reached for my skirts.

At that moment of utter terror, I looked beyond him and saw some movement in the trees, a flash of color perhaps. I tried to scream but he muffled my cry with his open mouth and plunging tongue. When he lifted his head for a moment I spotted two forms over his shoulder. "Brian!" I gasped.

Brian Milburne stood with his arm around Carolyn, both of them taking in the scene before them with rounded eyes.

Duval swung his head around, not moving his body from mine. "What the hell do you want?"

Brian stammered. "Sorry . . . didn't mean to intrude . . . just taking a walk . . . excuse us." He grabbed Carolyn's arm and led her quickly away.

Duval gave a bawdy laugh as he rolled off me, his lust dissipated as his entire form shook with mirth. "That should take care of your reputation,

Miss Holier-Than-Thou. You'll be glad to have me for a friend after this story gets out."

I knew how it must have looked to Brian and Carolyn in that one brief moment as they came through the trees. The couple's quick retreat had assured me of the assessment they had made of the situation—that I was a willing participant in a lover's rendezvous.

Duval remained sitting on the ground with his arms cradling his pulled-up knees, laughing uproariously as I fled in the same direction that Brian and Carolyn had retreated.

"There you are, Deanna!" Elizabeth's voice lashed out at me like the snap of a whip when I reached the center of the park. She was oblivious to my disheveled condition. "Where in God's name have you been? The dance is ready to begin and I had to impose upon Millie to collect the tickets. I don't see why you can't assume some responsibility when someone requests your help. Did you find Steven?" Her voice cracked and I knew she was physically and emotionally exhausted.

"He's home. Elizabeth—" I began, but she cut me off.

"Here." She handed me a roll of tickets. "Ten cents a dance. Go relieve Millie and for heaven's sake, try to make yourself useful for a change, Deanna."

My impulse was to throw the tickets on the ground and lash out at her. *Your husband almost killed himself. And I was almost raped.* I struggled to control my hysteria.

"Well, don't just stand there gawking." She gave me a little shove. "Good Lord, why on earth are you and Steven so undependable? Papa Banning must be turning over in his grave to see what a mess you've

189

made of yourselves. God knows, I've tried to carry on." She seemed ready to burst into tears.

I had no choice but to fight the hurricane of emotions swirling within me. The orchestra was already playing and the band shell was full of dancers when I arrived. Paper streamers and lanterns, American flags, and colorful banners moved in the evening breeze as patriotic music blared from the bandstand.

Millie didn't bother to hide her displeasure when I entered the ticket booth to relieve her. A few curt remarks implied that while I had been enjoying myself, she had sacrificed her time with Harold to take over my duties.

"I'm sorry, Millie. I was . . . detained."

She gave me a scathing look and I wondered if the distress of the afternoon showed in my face. I couldn't believe that I could successfully keep it hidden, but Millie flounced away with Harold, leaving me alone in the booth. I smiled mechanically as I dispensed tickets and collected money.

"Ten tickets please," a familiar voice ordered coldly. I looked up and my heart plummeted to my toes.

"Brian—I need to talk with you," I said in a rush.

He smiled tightly. "Are you sure you aren't too busy?"

"You have to believe me. Duval attacked—"

My words were broken off when a burly man pushed against Brian in the line. "What's holding things up?" he demanded over Brian's shoulder. "The dance is going to be over before I get my ticket. Let's get a move on."

Brian took his tickets and with a cold stare in my direction walked away. I looked beyond him to where

Carolyn stood waiting. She caught my eyes for an instant before her gaze fell. A quiver of nausea churned in my stomach. *No one was going to believe me.*

"Mind if I keep you company?" Daniel asked toward the end of the evening. I had watched him moving around the edge of the crowd, listening to the music but not dancing.

"I'm too busy to be sociable," I said flatly.

"In other words, my company isn't welcome?" he asked with a frankness that irritated me.

"People might get the wrong idea."

"Heaven forbid," he said in mock solemnity, but I didn't laugh. He gave me a steady, measuring look before taking his leave of the ticket booth. I felt both relief and despair.

David Kirkland bought several tickets and danced with some of the matrons, who acted as giddy as young girls as he led them around the small dance floor. He chatted with me, asking me to save him a dance when my duties were done. At any other time I would have enjoyed the festivities, but the evening was one long nightmare. When the final waltz was played, my nerves felt like they were stretched as tight as the strings on the orchestra's instruments. I collected the money and was just leaving the booth when a shadow fell over me.

"Steven!" I said in surprise. My brother was neatly dressed and freshly shaven, though his color was poor and deep shadows ringed his eyes. "I—I'm glad you came."

He stared at me with some uncertainty. I don't know what he expected me to do or say. Words were inadequate to describe the hell I had felt when I found him on the verge of committing suicide. The

191

horror of it swept back upon me and I reached for his hand.

"Don't ever scare me like that again!" I ordered. "Promise?" I searched his pained expression and he nodded.

After the last dance, Elizabeth bustled up to the booth and handed Steven a leather bag. "Please, take this and put it in the store's safe," she ordered. "I've bundled the currency but haven't counted it. Deanna, do the same with the proceeds you've collected. We'll take the money to the bank in the morning."

"How did it go?" Steven asked sheepishly.

She glared at him. "I'm going home in the buggy, you take the wagon."

Her husband nodded.

I told Elizabeth where I had left the horse and buggy, thankful that I could accompany Steven in the wagon. I hadn't seen Duval at the dance but I sickened every time I remembered how close I had come to being raped. I didn't dare tell Steven about the attack. In his present state of mind, I feared he would hunt the Frenchman down and shoot him. My stomach twisted with new apprehension. I prayed he never found out about the incident, but it was unlikely that Carolyn and Brian would keep their silence.

Steven gave his wife a weak kiss on the cheek before she sailed away amid a chorus of congratulations from the departing merrymakers.

I looped my arm through Steven's, glad for his company as we walked through the park. When we reached our wagon, we heard several men swearing and women's voices raised in dismay and protest. "What's happened?" asked Steven of a woman who was standing nearby.

"Some pranksters have taken the lugs off the wheels of the tallyho. Can you imagine such vandalism . . . right here under our noses. The culprits are in for a good tanning if the men ever find out who did it."

Steven quickly checked our wagon and found all the wheels intact. Daniel came by as Steven was helping me up into the seat. "How about a lift?"

"Sure, climb on."

In the next few minutes we picked up a wagon load. Several people who had been depending on the hotel conveyance flagged us down. I was disconcerted to find that Brian and Carolyn were among them, as well as Millie and Harold. We were just about to leave the park when Sabrina waved us down. "Do you have room for two more?" Apparently she didn't want to wait for her husband to come back with the wheel bolts to fix the hotel's tallyho. David Kirkland was with her and guided her into the top-heavy wagon.

"All aboard?" Steven called out, making certain everyone was seated before he gave the strong dray horse full rein and we lurched forward.

A chorus of laughter and chatter floated from the wagon as we made our way back into town. Someone started singing, and we rolled merrily into town amid the rollicking strains of an old folk song.

I remained removed from the gaiety around me. I had no energy, no interest in social banalities. Daniel tried to include me in the gaiety but I ignored his efforts. I heard Brian and Carolyn laughing together and a deep chill coarsed through my body. Would they ever give me a chance to explain? Duval would brag about his conquest, and if Nina heard the story, she would spread the poisonous scandal with relish.

193

Steven stopped in front of the store. "I'll just be a minute," he told everyone. "Have to put some money in the bank."

"I'll come with you, Steven," I said quickly, not wanting to be left in the wagon of merrymakers.

"Look," said Sabrina, pointing across the street. "The Conifer Café still has its lights on. Let's have a midnight snack."

A positive roar greeted her suggestion. Steven helped me down from the front seat and I stood beside him at the front door to the store. There was a flurry of confusion as women collected their belongings.

"I've lost my fan," wailed Sabrina.

"Here it is," said David Kirkland, holding up a peacock-blue object.

"Thank you." She gave the fan a flirtatious flutter as she smiled at him.

All the men hopped out first, some over the sides, others over the back and front. Then they reached up and swung the ladies to the ground.

"I think I'd best get on back to the hotel," said the artist. "And leave the night to you young people."

"You'll join us, won't you?" asked Daniel to Steven and me as he lingered beside the wagon.

"Sure we will," answered Steven before I could. "We'll be with you in a minute." He fumbled for his keys. "I guess I left them home." He called to Millie and asked to borrow hers.

"Do you want me to unlock the safe too?" she asked without hiding an edge of irritation as she untied her reticule and searched out a ring of keys. She opened the door and pulled a cord on a front light.

"No, I can manage the combination. Thanks, Millie."

She made a side remark under her breath to Harold. He nodded and I knew that her comment had been disparaging from the way her fiancé looked at Steven.

I followed my brother along the shadowy aisle and up the center staircase. The store always brought out uneasy feelings in me but in the middle of the night, the oppression was even more disquieting. Too many feelings came to the surface and triggered memories that still had the power to tear me apart. I followed Steven into Papa's office. Even in the silence, I heard my father's voice resonating to the rafters. *Just like your mother! I'll not have it. Do you hear?*

My heart made the familiar sickening plunge. After all these years I couldn't escape. He had hated me, and I had been unable to protect myself against his ire. It was pure irony that for most of my life I had thought him the most wonderful man in the world, the smartest, the strongest, and I had reached out for his love and approval as a plant turned its face to the sun—only to be withered by its heat. "Please hurry, Steven."

"The safe's open. Give me the money bag."

"I don't have it." I held out my empty hands.

"I saw you pick it up in the wagon," he countered. "I thought you were going to bring it in."

"I just wanted to see how heavy it was. Then I set it back down in the seat between us."

Steven started out of the office. "Stay here. I'll run out and get it." He disappeared into the shadows.

Wearily I sat down on the black horsehair sofa and leaned my head back against the wall. Tomorrow I would face the horrors of the day. Whatever Steven had done, I would find the strength to stand beside him.

A clatter of footsteps halted my thoughts. I raised my head just as Steven came back into the office followed by the group we had driven back to town.

"The café was closed," explained Sabrina.

I barely heard her or the excited chatter of the others. Steven's bewildered expression tightened a band around my chest. He held out empty hands. "It wasn't there. The bag's not on the seat."

"What do you mean?" I asked, uncomprehending.

"I mean—the money's gone!"

Chapter Fifteen

I couldn't sort it all out afterward. The police were called and Chief Whitney took charge of things. He questioned everyone again and again about what had happened from the time Steven placed the leather bag between us on the seat. No one had seen it after that—except for Sabrina, who told Whitney she had watched me pick it up just before we arrived at the store.

"I thought my sister had it," said Steven. "But after I opened the safe, we realized that it had been left in the wagon."

The wagon had been searched from one end to the other. All the hampers, ice cream freezers, and carnival prizes were searched, even the women's summer bags were subjected to investigation. If it had been left in the seat when everyone left the wagon, any passerby could have taken it.

If it had been left in the wagon. That was the unspoken doubt that was reflected in everyone's eyes as they looked at Steven and me. Millie pursed her lips in an accusing way. Brian and Carolyn wouldn't meet my eyes. Sabrina had a knowing smile as if her distrust of me had finally been vindicated. I knew what all of them were thinking. Steven and I could have stashed the money bag somewhere in the store and pretended that we had left it in the wagon. Everyone knew about Bannings' financial problems, and the murder of a man who might have taken the store from us had occurred almost on our doorstep. I couldn't blame them for thinking the worst.

Even Daniel kept his distance from me—his eyes showed resignation as they caught mine. He had not volunteered any comments to Wade Whitney, but I read his thoughts as clearly as if he had aired them. At the front of his mind was my guilt over the stolen brooch. I wondered if he were waiting for me to make a confession, either about the brooch or the money. Did his pensive manner imply that he had already made up his mind that this theft was just another one of my compulsive acts? Finally I couldn't stand it any longer. I moved to where he stood near the doorway. With my back to the others, I said in a hushed tone, "I didn't take it."

His expression remained stern.

"You have to believe me," I pleaded in a husky whisper. At that moment, I knew I couldn't bear it if he turned away from me.

"I want to, Dee. But—" Doubt suffused his features.

"I would know if I did—I always know!" But even before I voiced the words, a new fear rose up to possess me. *Maybe I didn't.* Could I have blocked out the whole thing?

He must have seen the doubt in my eyes for he prodded gently. "Are you sure?"

"Yes," I lied. At the moment, I wasn't certain about anything. I turned away so Daniel couldn't see my confused expression. Maybe I didn't know any more when I took something. Had I picked up the bag and dropped it somewhere in the store as I followed Steven to the office? I pressed my fingers against my temple. The pressure inside was excruciating. *Remember! Remember!* My thoughts whirled. Steven had placed the money bag on the seat. I remembered picking it up and thinking how heavy it was. There had been no sense of warmth, or contentment as I touched the leather pouch. No aching need to possess the bag or the money it held. *Had I kept it in my hands?* I couldn't remember either putting it back down in the seat or keeping it in my grasp.

"All right. Let's go over it again," commanded Chief Whitney. "Tell me exactly what happened after Steven stopped in front of the store." Everyone started talking at once and Officer Whitney held up his hand. "One at a time. I'll get to each one of you, never fear."

Without hesitation, Brian told the officer in crisp tones that he had simply helped Carolyn down from the wagon and that they had walked across the street to the café.

The others had the same story. When the wagon stopped in front of the store, they had all climbed out together. Except Sabrina.

"I lost my fan and David Kirkland helped me find it."

"What happened after everyone was out of the wagon?"

Brian told the officer that all of them had collected in front of the door of the Conifer Café trying to persuade the owner to open up.

"All of you?" questioned Whitney.

"Well, not Steven or Deanna . . . they went inside the store," said Millie.

"And not David Kirkland," said Sabrina.

199

"Where is Mr. Kirkland?" asked the officer.

"He walked on to the hotel."

There was a silence. The man wasn't there to protect himself against the instant suspicion that landed on him. "I see," said the officer meaningfully. "I'll have a talk with Mr. Kirkland."

Everyone seemed to entertain for the moment the same thought. *Had David Kirkland taken the money bag while everyone was across the street or in the store?* He was the only outsider. The rest of us were hometown.

"I'm sure he had nothing to do with it," flared Sabrina. "He's a very nice man."

"What do you know about him, Mrs. Sawyer?"

"Well, really nothing . . . except he's been staying at the hotel, and he's interested in painting."

I was sure the older gentleman would establish his innocence, and for the moment I was grateful the finger of suspicion was pointing in another direction —away from Steven and me.

When Officer Whitney finally let us go home, it was nearly dawn. I lay stiffly in my bed and watched the grayness of night escape before the wash of watery pink across the sky. Barn swallows landed on my windowsill, chirping merrily. Their optimism mocked my heavy spirits. Even when I closed my eyes, I kept seeing Daniel's face, stony and judgmental. *"Are you sure?"*

It was obvious that the minister had made up his own mind about what had happened to the money. How long would it be before his conscience demanded that something be done to put the matter right? I didn't think he would betray my confidence, but I knew he wouldn't rest until he found out the truth. I searched my mind for any hint that I might have taken the money bag, and a surge of confidence rose within me. No. I was innocent.

Wearily, I dressed and went downstairs to face the day. I would have remained in my room if it hadn't been for Steven. I didn't want him to take the wrath of Elizabeth and the community all by himself.

Elizabeth was already sitting at the table, staring at some point on the tablecloth while her breakfast grew cold in front of her. The previous night she had taken the news as I would have expected—furious, lashing out bitterly at the carelessness involved, and then collapsing in a state of shock.

"Good morning, Elizabeth."

She didn't answer. From the deep lines in her forehead and the sagging muscles in her cheeks, I knew she hadn't been able to sleep either. Her beautiful hair was dull and without its usual elaborate coiffure, and she slouched in her chair, strangely silent as I took my seat beside her.

The morning paper was open beside her. OPERA FUND MONEY STOLEN. My fingers trembled as I picked it up and read the brief account. Thank God for the position Papa had earned in the town. The article gave Steven the benefit of the doubt, stating that informed sources believed that the money bag had been taken out of the wagon while Mr. Steven Banning and his party were absent from the scene. A list of the people who had been involved followed. I was certain that mention of Brian's name would help to keep hounds like Nina Milburne from baying at our heels. And then, of course, the most respectable Reverend Norris was listed as one of the party. A thief couldn't be in better company, I thought.

"Where is Steven?" I asked. I had made certain that he retired with Elizabeth when we all finally

201

went to bed. "Still asleep?"

She nodded. Her pained eyes turned to me. "He doesn't care about the humiliation."

"That's not true," I said firmly, remembering the events of yesterday. "I'm sure he's devastated by everything that has happened." I wanted to lash out at her. Steven had already reached the end of his endurance. *He tried to kill himself!* I thought angrily. I tried to voice the words and couldn't. A protective instinct kept me silent. Steven had trusted me with his secret. I couldn't betray his confidence even though I knew that his wife's attitude was in part responsible for the heavy burden that had almost crushed him. If he lost the store, she would be disgraced, and her social standing would be as threatened as the family assets. The only thing Elizabeth seemed to cherish in her marriage was Steven's surname! Surely, she wasn't blind to her husband's state of mind. Maybe she suspected that he was responsible for the horrible things that had been happening, and in her own mind believed that Steven had stolen the community money.

Elizabeth took a tremulous breath of air. "It was bad enough having that man murdered on our doorstep," she lamented. "And now this." She clearly rated the loss of the money above the earlier tragedy. "I'll never get the nomination for Community League president now."

I couldn't believe it. Elizabeth's whole life was organized around community status. The effect that the recent tragedies had had on her husband didn't seem to matter. "How am I going to face everyone?" she wailed.

I didn't know . . . and I didn't care. I had to fight battles of my own. I left Elizabeth at the table, slumped and defeated, unable to face herself or anyone else. I couldn't bring myself to pity her.

After slipping on my gloves and tying the streamers of my bonnet, I left the house. I had made a decision. Facing Daniel was the first battle. Putting it off would only make things worse. Whatever else happened, I wanted him to know that I was innocent of this latest thievery.

The parsonage was a small house located behind the church. Ivy vines softened the stone exterior with a tracery of shiny green leaves, and newly painted white shutters and a cedar roof added a homey look to the cottage, transforming it from the rather somber dwelling I remembered from my childhood.

I opened and shut a picket gate, glancing about at the neatly trimmed lawn and a border of purple verbena. Lifting my skirts, I mounted wooden steps to the front door. A polished brass knocker fell loudly upon the wooden panel as I dropped it twice and then waited, trying to command a foolish quickening of my heartbeat.

The door swung open and Daniel stood facing me in his shirt sleeves, open collar, and brown nankeen trousers with grass stains on the knees. He wasn't wearing shoes. A gasp of surprise accompanied his welcoming smile. "Good morning. I thought it would be Mrs. Elbert, my housekeeper. She's always forgetting her key."

"I need to talk with you."

"Come in, come in."

I hesitated. "Maybe we should walk over to the church."

He gave me a teasing smile. "Don't worry, we won't be alone for long. Mrs. Elbert will be here momentarily." He stepped back, grabbed a black coat off a hall rack, and hastily smoothed back his hair. He slipped his stocking feet into a pair of black boots. "I wasn't expecting any visitors this early." He eyed me frankly. "I doubt that any of us got much sleep."

"I dozed off for a couple of hours but I saw the sun come up."

To the right of the door was a formal parlor, filled with somber furniture and done up in muted wallpaper the color of putty. A huge Bible and a stack of hymnals had been placed on a large library table and an assortment of chairs were arranged for church meetings.

"No, not there," he said as I took a step forward toward the room. "In here."

He opened a door on the opposite side of the hall, and I saw a room that was twin to the other parlor, only this room was anything but neat and formal.

"Here, have a chair." He swept a pile of books off the seat of a fireside chair and threw aside a sweater that had been draped over the back. A ginger colored cat was curled up in the largest chair. The furry creature opened one eye at our intrusion, stretched leisurely, and then went back to sleep.

"Ebenezer. He's been out all night courting the ladies," said Daniel with an affectionate chuckle.

A child's room wouldn't have been any messier, I thought in amazement and wanted to laugh as I looked around. The Reverend Daniel Norris was a pack rat. Piles of rocks and ores sparkled in mass confusion in an overflowing collection upon a scarred table. Small pieces of driftwood naturally twisted in various shapres were lined up along the mantel and on each side of an old clock. One piece of wood resembled a long-necked goose, another a coiled snake. One piece looked like a figure with a humped back, and another was remarkably like a turtle with its head stuck out of its shell.

"You like my sculptures?" he asked as my eyes traveled over the wood pieces. "I never take a walk without bringing back a treasure of one kind or another."

"I believe it," I said dryly, eyeing the clutter in the room. It was as if he had taken in the whole outdoors, wood, rocks, and flowers.

"Look at this." He showed me a wide-bottom glass bottle that had been planted with miniature blossoms smaller than a fingernail. "Found every one of them along the creek. I sat down to rest and there were these flowers as lovely and delicate as anything I'd ever seen. I'd have walked right over them, crushed them underfoot without even knowing it." As he turned the bottle in his hands, sunlight was refracted from the glass into his face and his expression was one of pure joy.

Love surged within me. I was moved in some mysterious way that startled me.

Daniel put the terrarium back on a shelf in the midst of wild violets and forest fern growing in an assortment of chipped pots. Laughing, he gave a wave of his hand. "Free for the taking."

I stiffened. Just a moment ago, I had related to him on some pure level, but now reality swept back with the force of a lashing wind. The same dark secrets that had made me flee from my home five years ago could also destroy this man if I allowed my emotions to encourage any intimate feelings between us.

He pulled up the chair where the cat was sleeping and lifted the animal onto his lap as he sat down. Ebenezer gave a protesting meow at being disturbed. He kneaded Daniel's legs with his flexing paws as he circled a couple of times before flopping down on Daniel's lap to resume his morning nap. Daniel automatically scratched behind the cat's ears as he waited for me to speak.

"I want some advice."

He nodded and went on stroking the cat's neck.

"I want to talk to you about the theft of the money," I said evenly, my gaze steady. "I think my brother might be responsible."

A slight flickering of Daniel's eyelids told me he had been expecting a confidence of a different sort. Obviously, he thought I had come to confess and seek his help, perhaps to return the money in the same way I had the brooch. "I told you last night I wasn't guilty," I lashed out, as if he had accused me again.

"And what makes you think Steven is? Did you see him with the leather bag after we all left the wagon?"

"No, but I wasn't paying that much attention to him. The store was poorly lit and shadowy and . . . and I was fighting some unpleasant memories as I do every time I'm in that place. Steven could have stashed the bag anywhere on our way up to the office and I wouldn't have noticed."

Daniel frowned. "I was one of the first ones off the wagon. In the confusion, I didn't notice whether or not the money bag was lying on the seat. I suppose anyone could have climbed out of the wagon with the bag hidden under a wrap."

"I can't remember if it was there when Steven lifted me down. I never gave it a thought until we reached the office and he had the safe open. Then he asked me for the money. He could have been pretending that he left it in the wagon, when really he had taken it off the seat without anyone seeing him."

Daniel nodded. "I didn't notice whether or not he had the money bag when he asked Millie to unlock the door. I guess nobody else did either, or they would have said something to Chief Whitney. Have you talked with Steven about this?"

I shook my head. "I'm afraid."

"Afraid of your own brother?"

"Not afraid for my safety, but for his." I bit my lower lip. "Yesterday Steven tried to shoot himself."

Daniel's eyes widened in alarm. "Steven attempted suicide? Are you sure?"

As steadily as my voice would allow, I told him about returning home with Sarah and the children and finding Steven in the trophy room with a loaded gun to his head. "He was drunk. From what I could tell, he'd been drinking since early morning. My brother never could hold his liquor. When I went back to the carnival, I left him to sleep it off."

"Why didn't you tell someone?"

"I was going to and then—" My voice faltered. I couldn't bring myself to tell Daniel about Duval's attack on me. I didn't want to put him in a position of having to defend my honor a second time. I didn't want to be responsible for any fight between them. "I was going to tell Elizabeth but she was in such a state, she didn't give me a chance. And then Steven showed up at the end of the evening and I couldn't betray his confidence by telling anyone what had happened. Elizabeth asked him to put the money in the store's safe. I wish to God he'd stayed home."

"I can't believe that things are so bad that Steven thinks suicide is the only way out."

I didn't answer.

"There's more to it isn't there? It isn't only the money?"

I nodded.

He reached over and took my icy cold hands in his. "What is it, Deanna?"

Pulling my hands away, I shook my head. "You can't help. I was wrong to come here." The tick of the clock on the mantel was as loud as cymbals in my ears.

207

"No, you were right to come," he said softly. "You think Steven might have killed Mr. Babcock."

I wanted to shout a denial. The idea was preposterous, too horrible to be true! Steven said he'd never seen the man. I wanted to believe him. But my brother had changed. He wasn't the Steven I knew. He could have lied.

"Why don't you tell me about it, Deanna? You said you came for advice. I can't give any if I don't know the whole story," Daniel said in a reasonable tone.

Fighting the feeling that I was betraying my brother, I poured forth my suspicions. "Steven could have found Babcock on the front porch, taken him around to the stable where I heard them talking, and then led him into the trees on some pretext and killed him." I sent a look at Daniel which pleaded with him to tell me I was wrong.

"As I understand it, the bank was ready to sell the loan note to Mr. Babcock if he was interested in the store?"

I nodded.

"Killing Babcock would only delay matters . . . not solve the financial problems for good," he reasoned.

"I know, but Steven thinks he has a prospective buyer who will make a good offer. He needs time. He might have taken the money to keep the store in operation for a little longer."

"Do they know how much money was in the bag?"

"Several thousand. All bills. Elizabeth kept the coins." I passed a hand over my eyes. "I don't know what to do."

A clatter of dishes in the kitchen announced the arrival of Daniel's housekeeper. He handed me the cat. "I'll be back in a minute."

Ebenezer accepted my lap with a disgruntled

meow. His soft fur and warm body was soothing under my hands as I stroked him. I'd never had a pet. Papa only allowed hunting hounds when I was growing up, and they were kept in kennels. I don't know how long Daniel was gone but by the time he came back my raw-edged nerves had been eased by the purring cat.

I was surprised to see he had changed his attire. He wore trousers that matched his black coat and his white clerical collar was in place. "I'll walk you home," he said.

Daniel laughed as I settled the leggy cat in the seat of my chair and patted its head. "Sweet dreams," I said.

"He's quite the family man," Daniel told me as he guided me to the front door. "Come around to the shed and I'll show you something wonderful."

The something was a litter of five kittens, so new that their eyes had just opened. The mother was a long-haired white cat with lovely blue eyes. Daniel talked to her in soothing tones and she allowed him to present each of her offspring to me. Three of them had Ebenezer's ginger stripes and the other two were white like their mother.

I laughed to see the way they wriggled about, tumbling over each other and scrambling for their turn at sweet dribbles of milk.

As Daniel knelt beside the box, his movements were gentle and loving, and in a moment of fantasy I saw him as a caring, proud father, holding a newly born baby. The vision filled me with an inexplicable pain. The mother of his children would of necessity be without reproach. Deanna Banning would never measure up.

"Take your pick," he ordered, smiling up at me as he settled the balls of fur back in the box. "In a few weeks, they'll be tumbling all over the place."

"Thank you, but I couldn't—"

"Of course you could. When they're big enough, you can have two, one for you and one for Patty. Nothing like playful kittens to lighten the spirits." He stood up. "You have my permission to come over every day and watch them grow." His face was in shadow under his narrow brim hat but the shine in his eyes was as warm as the sun.

"We'll see," I said, turning away. I knew I had to refuse his gift. After my fantasy, a kitten would be a constant reminder of something that could never be.

I knew he saw the shadow on my face. He thought it had to do with the purpose of my visit. "I think I should talk with Steven. Maybe he'll open up to me."

"And if he does?"

"Anything he tells me will be in confidence, you know that. He's the one who must decide what must be done. I can only offer my support. With God's help, I'll try to keep him from trying to take his own life again. You'll have to trust me to do the best I can."

I felt his strength as he walked beside me and I knew I could depend on him to stand by Steven. "I trust you," I said, grateful for the courage his presence filled me with.

He gave me a smile that for a moment sent all dark specters fleeing, but when we reached the front steps of my house, the illusion was shattered.

There was no mistaking the sound of gunfire that came from behind the house.

Chapter Sixteen

Daniel bounded into a run. "Stay here!" he ordered over his shoulder, but I ignored his plea.

Steven. Steven. My brother's name was like a lash at my back. I don't know what I expected to see as I rounded the back corner of the house, but for a moment my eyes wouldn't focus. It was as if I had already seen Steven stretched out on the ground with a bullet hole in his head.

"What is going on here?" demanded Daniel as he confronted Jericho, who was standing with his bandy legs stiff and a rifle smelling of gun powder in his hands. I followed Jericho's black eyes to a figure cowering behind a tree trunk at one end of the garden.

David Kirkland!

A splintering of the tree bark showed where the bullet had hit. I screamed and ran over to the visibly shaken man. He must have scurried for the protection of the tree, leaving his drawing pad and pencils scattered on the ground and the tiny stool he usually sat upon turned over on the flagged stone path. "Mr. Kirkland, are you all right?"

His reassuring nod was weak.

Fury exploded in my head. I swung around to Jericho, unleashing my pent-up rage. "Have you taken leave of your senses? Stupid lout! You should be locked up. How dare you—!"

"Easy, Deanna," Daniel cautioned me as I waved my arms at the beady-eyed man, who met my gaze with contempt. Jericho glared at me, tightening his grip on the gun as if he were tempted to jab the barrel into my stomach if I came a step closer. "Let the man explain."

"Yes," I hissed, my breath hot. "Please do, Jericho. Explain this outrageous behavior."

"He was trespassing! Wandering around Mr. Steven's greenhouse. I warned him. Told him to leave, but he ignored me. Some people need a little persuasion."

"He was *not* trespassing! I gave Mr. Kirkland permission to draw in Steven's garden any time he liked. You should have had the sense to inquire before treating my guest like a common criminal. You could have killed him!"

"I wasn't aiming to hit him . . . just scare him a little, make him think twice before coming around again." He lowered his voice to a husky whisper. "This ain't the first time he's been snooping around here. I've seen him, huddled down in the trees watching this house. If you want to know, I think he's the one who bashed that fellow's head in."

"What!" I gasped, appalled. I glanced at Mr. Kirkland, who was some distance away, picking up his materials. I hoped he hadn't heard the ridiculous accusation.

"When did you first see him near the house?" asked Daniel, as if he put some credence in Jericho's words.

"A couple of months ago. Before Miss Banning came home. I warned him then that this was private property, but that didn't seem to impress him none. Kept my eye out for him and today I found him as red-handed as a fox in the chicken house."

"Did you see him here the day of the murder?" prodded Daniel.

"Shhhh!" I said, as David Kirkland cautiously approached us. I was angry with both Jericho and Daniel for even suggesting that the amiable gentleman was connected with any wrongdoing.

I could tell that the man was quite disturbed by what had happened. His voice shook as he apologized. "Please forgive me for causing this unpleasantness."

"It is not you who needs to apologize," I assured him quickly. From the first word we had spoken to each other, I had instinctively liked the gray-haired gentleman. He had always been kindly, friendly, and eager to share his love of art with me. There was nothing devious in his manner, nor any inconsistency in his behavior. Every time I had seen him, he had been the same. Even now, when he had been unnecessarily assaulted, I felt his deep concern for any trouble he might have caused. "Jericho was under the misapprehension that you were trespassing. I assure you that you are most welcome at Hunters Hall at any time."

"That is very kind of you."

He smiled at me in such a way that my anger with Jericho flared again. I challenged the yardman's black, hostile gaze. "Do you understand, Jericho? Mr. Kirkland is to be a welcome visitor here anytime. And you will treat him accordingly."

"I take my orders from Mr. Steven, not you!" the man spat. "He says who can come around and who can't." The gardener then turned his back on me and stomped back into the stable, the gun still held firmly in his hand.

"I am sorry," said Mr. Kirkland again. "I never wanted to cause any trouble."

"Please, don't apologize. I am mortified that such a thing should happen. Jericho is like a pugnacious bull when it comes to Steven and his flowers. I can't even pick a bouquet without his permission." I tried to lighten the moment with a wry laugh. "Please, let's try to forget this unpleasantness. Will you join me for lunch . . . both of you."

"Do you think Steven's at home?" he asked, and I knew that Daniel was hoping for a chance to talk with my brother.

"I don't know. He was still sleeping when I left this morning."

We entered the house through the kitchen and found a note in Elizabeth's handwriting on the kitchen table. *Maude and I have gone to market and won't be back until after lunch. Sarah and the children are picnicking at the park. There's cold mutton and fresh greens in the cooler for lunch.* I didn't know whether the message was meant for me or Steven.

"Excuse me, and I'll see if Steven's here."

"Wouldn't he have heard the shot?" asked Daniel in his practical manner.

Of course he would have—if he hadn't been drinking again. I ran up to his room and was relieved to see that his bed had been made up and his watch and cuff links were gone, indicating that he had dressed and gone to the store. I didn't know whether he would come home at noon or not, and I wondered if I should rescind my invitation to the two men for lunch.

I might be overstepping my bounds, offering such hospitality without asking permission. I knew that

214

both Maude and Elizabeth kept tight reins on the larder. Would the cold mutton stretch to unexpected guests? And if it didn't, should I presume to fix something else that was planned for another meal? This was Elizabeth's house, after all, and Maude's kitchen. I didn't think either of them would take kindly to my invasion of their territory.

With a decisive lift to my chin, I went downstairs and set about playing hostess. The two men sat comfortably around the oak table, chatting about places they had both traveled to. Daniel was guiding the questions as if endeavoring to learn something about David Kirkland's background. I only half listened as I attended to preparing a tray of cold mutton and sliced cheese, which I hoped wasn't being saved for some special occasion. I added some mushrooms, tomato slices, and chopped hard-boiled eggs to a bowl of spinach greens. Maude always kept a bottle of vinegar dressing made up, which gave a tangy zest to the salad. I sliced a new loaf of bread and took a mound of golden butter from the scullery cooler.

"I've spent most of my life in Connecticut. Although I love the sea, I'm partial to the mountains, especially the Colorado Rockies," I heard Mr. Kirkland say.

"God's country, without a doubt," agreed Daniel.

"After I sold my company a couple of years ago, I decided to do some traveling."

"And how did you happen to land in Brimstone?"

"Someone recommended it to me."

"Lunch is ready," I announced. Rather pleased with myself, I asked my guests if they would like to adjourn to the dining room, but both men said the kitchen table was just fine. I knew that Elizabeth would be horrified, but I was pleased with the informality that the spacious, red-bricked room offered. I sat down at the round table between them and joined in the conversation with an ease that surprised me. Until the discussion turned to the disappearance of the carnival money.

"I suppose Officer Whitney questioned you about it," said Daniel with an encouraging smile.

"Indeed, he did." His gray eyebrows furrowed. "Even went through my things at the hotel to make certain I hadn't stashed it away somewhere. I told the officer that I never touched the money bag, but I'm not certain he believed me. Apparently my early departure that night was suspect. I assured him that weariness was the only motivation for my decision to return to the hotel."

"Did you notice whether or not the leather pouch was on the seat when you were searching for Sabrina's fan?" asked Daniel.

"I'm afraid not. Do you think it was still there when we all left the wagon?"

Daniel shrugged. "No one seems to know."

I didn't look at him. My suspicions of Steven seemed to hover in the air. I was relieved when the unpleasant subject was put aside and the conversation moved on to general topics.

"And what business were you in, Mr. Kirkland?" asked Daniel.

"I inherited a small freight business from my father and was able to expand it into a profitable shipping line. I've done very well, as Officer Whitney discovered when he made inquiries into my financial status."

"And do you have a family? Wife? Children?"

"I never married. And you, Reverend? How did you come to the ministry?"

"Unexpectedly."

We all chuckled.

"I must be honest with you, Reverend Norris," said Kirkland. "My idea of a clergyman doesn't quite fit a vigorous, physical young man like yourself."

"Really?" Daniel cocked his reddish head thoughtfully. "That's interesting, sir. I've always pictured Peter and Paul, the disciples, as being rather vigorous men. Strong. Dedicated to a conviction that the golden rule was part of the answer to life's happiness." He leaned forward on the table. "Do you really think of Christianity as being for the weak, Mr. Kirkland?"

The older man laughed fully. "I stepped into that one, didn't I? Please forgive my prejudice. You are right, of course. A young man like yourself needs a lot of courage to follow his convictions. I expect the church could use a lot more men like you."

Daniel smiled. "Well, you may be in a majority of one in that opinion. I'm not sure my congregation would agree with you." He looked at me. "Some think I need the influence of a good woman."

Heat swam up into my cheeks and I felt Kirkland's eyes moving from my blushing face to Daniel's bold wink.

The silence was finally broken by the older gentleman clearing his throat. "Well, now, I think it's time I thanked you for this fine lunch, Miss Banning. I enjoyed it immensely. I really must be going." He stood up and shook Daniel's hand. "Perhaps we can continue this pleasant conversation some other time."

"You know where you can find me," answered Daniel pointedly.

Kirkland laughed and nodded. "You may yet be seeing me at services, Reverend."

I accompanied him to the front door. "Please visit

217

us again. I hate to think that Jericho has destroyed your interest in Steven's garden. I know he will be as furious as I am that you were treated so shamelessly."

"Having lunch with you and Reverend Norris was well worth any momentary discomfort," he responded warmly. "Hotel life gets pretty lonesome. Perhaps you and Reverend Norris could join me for lunch sometime soon."

I thanked him and assured him that it would be a pleasure. When I came back to the table, I said, "Nice gentleman, isn't he?" Daniel didn't answer and I searched his pensive expression. "What's the matter? Don't you like him?"

"He seems sociable enough."

"Then what is it?"

"I don't know. I just have a feeling that he's holding something back. On the surface he seems to be a successful businessman who's enjoying a spot of travel and leisure activity in his old age."

"I don't see anything wrong with that."

"There's nothing wrong with being what he seems to be," agreed Daniel.

"Then what's the matter?"

"He's lying."

"Lying?" I exclaimed. "He's a man in his sixties who is enjoying himself on a summer vacation, doing a little amateur painting, and being friendly. For heaven's sake, what's he lying about?"

Daniel's forehead creased thoughtfully. "I don't know." He sighed. "It sounds silly, I know, but I've always had an intuitive sense about folks. Not everyone is what they seem to be. Mr. Kirkland's behavior sent up a few red flags to my way of thinking."

"I think you're imagining things."

"Maybe I am. But I'm betting his simple, straightforward manner is a subterfuge. I think I'll talk to Sabrina. Do a little inquiring."

"Don't you mean snooping?"

He laughed. "Never let it be said that you ever hesitate to call a spade a spade, my dear. All right, snooping—but only because I believe in gossip."

"What?" I was appalled.

"If people didn't chatter about other people and what's going on in their lives, I'd never know how to help. I always listen to idle talk, it's where I get my information. If a man drinks up his wages and doesn't feed his children, I want to know about it. If the community is ostracizing someone, I offer my friendship at a time when it's needed."

"I see. Is that why you've gone out of your way to stand by me and Steven? Christian charity?" There was a coolness in my tone that didn't escape him.

"I didn't say *all* my motives were philanthropic." His lips eased into a gentle smile. "You're not the first one to question my intuitive wisdom. I hope you'll learn to trust it in time."

"I think you're bragging."

"No, just making you a promise. And I'll try to have a talk with Steven later today." Very gently he leaned over and kissed my hairline. "Thanks for the lunch, my dear Miss Banning." He sauntered out of the kitchen with infuriating casualness. I had to control my emotions where Daniel Norris was concerned!

As I put the kitchen to order, my mind gingerly explored the possibility that I would be responsible for a catastrophe of my own making if I didn't do some quick backtracking with the Reverend. He was beginning to know too much. I had gone to him in desperation because I didn't know what to do about Steven. Even now I wondered if I had done the right thing. I had just finished when I heard voices from down the hall and the front door closing.

I looked up as Maude came through the doorway with string bags filled with purchases hanging from her arms. She heaved them up on the table with a weary sigh and then plopped down in the kitchen chair that Daniel had just vacated. "I don't know why we can't have Alpert's market deliver," she complained. "No sense in spending half a day haggling over every cut of meat and tinned can. I don't know why I have to tag along anyway. *She* makes all the decisions."

I knew who *she* was. I could hear Elizabeth's voice coming from down the hall. I raised a questioning eyebrow. "Who's with her?"

"Some people wanting to talk with you."

"Me?"

My complexion must have drained to a sickly white pallor because Maude said hurriedly, "Don't know what it's all about, honey. Probably nothing. We've told Chief Whitney all we know."

"He's here?"

She nodded.

"Tell them I'm not here."

Maude shook her head. "Don't do no good to run away, Deedee. Haven't you learned that by now? Better to grab the bull by the horns than be gored to death."

I didn't like her metaphor.

When I reached the parlor doorway and saw who was among the group assembled, I shrank inside.

"Oh, there you are," said Nina Milburne in a tone which indicated I had deliberately kept them waiting. Even Elizabeth sent me a look of utter exasperation. Carolyn Lareau was sitting on the flowered settee beside her future mother-in-law, and the young

220

woman's discomfort was obvious. Carolyn twisted a lacy hankie in her gloved hands and avoided my eyes. What was this all about, I wondered.

Brian! Had he said something about our tête-à-tête on the terrace? Surely not. Why would he confess to any feelings about me with the wedding only a few weeks away? He wouldn't be that much of a fool.

Chief Whitney stood up as I entered, nodding at me. His mouth was set in a stern line and his eyes were like those of someone squinting down the barrel of a gun. "Miss Banning, won't you sit down. Some new information has come to light which involves you."

I chose the closest straight-back chair to the door. The atmosphere in the room couldn't have been any more dire. They were like a pack of coyotes eyeing their prey. I guess I knew even before he spoke, what it was he had to say.

Chapter Seventeen

An ugly smile hovered at the edges of Nina Milburne's lips. I knew that whatever had brought the officer to my doorstep pleased her immensely. That knowledge alone was enough to send my blood running cold. Her dark eyes were like those of a poisonous snake ready to strike.

Officer Whitney sat back down, took out his weathered notebook, and flipped through the pages. When he raised his eyes, his look was as sharp as a skinning knife. "You left Brimstone five years ago and were in the employment of a Mr. and Mrs. Isaac Lowenstein, is that correct?" At my stiff nod, he continued. "And you remained in that household until June of this year?" I nodded again. "Why did you leave your position as governess with that family, Miss Banning?"

"I wanted to come home."

Nina Milburne's eyes glistened triumphantly.

Officer Whitney cleared his throat. "No other reason?"

I could feel a shudder creeping up my legs and settling in the middle of my stomach. My hands curled over the edges of my chair in an effort to keep myself steady.

"No other reason?" repeated Whitney. The police officer's voice contained the subtle excitement of a sportsman about to reel in an elusive fish.

"I told you she was a liar," spat Nina. "And now we have proof." She turned to Carolyn and patted the young woman's hand in a reassuring way. "Don't we, Carolyn?"

Chief Whitney held up a silencing hand. His glowering expression showed that he didn't appreciate the lead being taken out of his hands by Nina Milburne. When his cutting glare returned to me, he said, "I warn you, Miss Banning, it's time to tell the truth. Why did you leave your position with the Lowenstein family and come back to Brimstone?"

"I was homesick."

Nina gave another triumphant snort. My gaze slipped to Carolyn's flushed face. I knew at that moment that her discomfort had nothing to do with Brian. The matter that had brought them to my house like vultures after carrion was something else entirely.

Chief Whitney unfolded a piece of paper. "I have been given a letter that was sent to Miss Carolyn Lareau in which a young woman in New York, Miss Anita Clayborne, writes that you were dismissed as governess to the Lowenstein children because of an act of theft."

I closed my eyes for a split second. When I opened them I saw that Carolyn's expression was disconcerted, apologetic and accusing at the same time. "I'm sorry, Deanna."

"I don't understand," I said, as if my words could possibly keep the truth from coming out.

"Don't you remember?" she answered quickly. "I told you when we were introduced that my friend

224

Anita Clayborne knew the Lowenstein family. I asked you if you'd met her. When I wrote to Anita about the wedding, I mentioned your name and—" Her voice broke off.

"And she wrote back that you had been dismissed for thievery," finished Nina, giving the last word the cutting lash of a whip.

"It was a misunderstanding," I countered with as much poise as I could manage.

"I'm sure," the older woman smirked.

Chief Whitney leaned forward. "Miss Banning, do you deny that you were responsible for the theft?"

"I do. The charge is false. One of the maids had stolen an emerald ring and when it was discovered in her possession, the girl told the Lowensteins that I had given it to her."

"Obviously they believed her and not you," said Nina in a tone that dismissed my defense as an obvious lie.

"Do you deny that you took the ring?" demanded Chief Whitney.

I looked him directly in the eyes and said, "Yes, I deny it. I never stole Mrs. Lowenstein's ring."

"But you were dismissed because of the incident?"

"Yes."

He stabbed an impatient blunt finger at me. "Seems a little too much of a coincidence that other things show up missing the minute you show your face around here again."

Nina lashed out. "My sister's brooch! My pencil! She could have taken them! And the carnival money, too."

Elizabeth gave a strangled gasp. "Deanna! How could you?" Horror was written on my sister-in-law's face. She looked ill enough to faint.

Like an animal backed into a corner, I struck out as

best I could. "For heaven's sake, Elizabeth, I didn't steal the money! Surely you believe me?"

"Why should Elizabeth believe you?" demanded Nina.

"Because it's the truth." I moistened my dry lips. "I know that I make a perfect scapegoat, but someone else stole that money. Not me!" I met Chief Whitney's level gaze and said as firmly as I could, "I never stole Mrs. Lowenstein's ring, and I never stole the carnival money." That much was true. I only prayed the omissions would go unnoticed.

Carolyn put her hankie up to her eyes and sobbed. "I'm so sorry. I never meant to cause trouble. Mother Milburne made me turn the letter over." Carolyn's wet eyes met mine. "I'm sure there was some mistake, Deanna, about your dismissal. I shall write back to my friend, Anita, and tell her so." The young woman straightened her back and gave me a reassuring smile.

Brian didn't deserve such a jewel, I thought.

"Where there's smoke, there's fire," said Nina tritely. She turned to the policeman. "Chief Whitney, I suggest you look very carefully at all the evidence surrounding the missing money pouch."

"Mrs. Milburne, I don't need you or anybody else telling me how to do my job," he responded curtly.

"Really?" she said in a scathing tone. "You seem ready enough to dismiss the evidence you hold in your hand. That letter verifies that Deanna Banning is a thief."

"No, Mother Milburne," protested Carolyn. "I'm sure that Anita was just repeating what she'd heard."

"I'll need more than this to level a charge of thievery against her," admitted Whitney. His eyes narrowed as he shook his finger at me in warning. "I aim to get at the bottom of this, Miss Banning. Don't take a bucket of brains to know where all this business of dead bodies and stolen money has its roots in matters which concern the Banning family."

Elizabeth gave a sob, covered her face with her hands, and then fled from the room.

"I wouldn't be so certain, Officer Whitney, that someone isn't taking a great deal of pains to make you think exactly that."

"Well, I never!" spat Nina.

"What do you mean by that remark?" demanded Whitney.

"I think you should look outside the Banning family for your culprit. Every single person riding in that wagon had as much opportunity to steal the money as Steven and me. And throwing suspicion upon us will only let the guilty one get away. You should—"

"Don't be telling me, young lady, what I should be doing," flared Chief Whitney.

I stood up. "If you have no more questions, please excuse me."

I swept out of the room, leaving Nina's indignant voice vibrating in my ears. My breath was coming in short gasps by the time I reached the top of the stairs. I bolted into my room like a harried animal searching for cover. I shut the door and paced the floor. Had I handled the situation in the best way possible? There was no way Whitney could build a case against me just because of my dismissal from the Lowenstein family. He would have to find new evidence. But at least he was concentrating on me instead of Steven.

I wondered if Daniel had gone to the store to talk with Steven. When I heard my brother's voice coming from downstairs, I smoothed my hair, straightened the lace collar and cuffs of my dress, and took several deep breaths which failed to loosen the tight band around my chest. My moist palm trailed on the banister as I went downstairs.

Steven was in the library with Elizabeth and Millie. I could tell from their expressions when I came in that Elizabeth had just completed her recital of the latest events.

"Dee, is this true?" Steven demanded with a look of open astonishment as he sat behind his desk . . . or I should say, Papa's desk.

I smiled at him and my calm, undisturbed posture surprised even me. The scent had been drawn away from my brother and I felt a surge of relief even as my own position became more perilous. I nodded a greeting at Millie, who was waiting for Steven to sign some papers she held in her hand. I thought her expression was somewhat smug. Elizabeth avoided my eyes completely and turned to the window, looking out with her back to me.

"Is what true?" I asked evenly.

"That the Lowensteins dismissed you . . . for stealing?"

"Yes, that part is true. But the charge was false. A maid in the household stole the ring and lied about it."

"Why on earth didn't you say something?" he lashed out. "Now it looks like you were trying to hide the truth from all of us."

"I didn't see any reason for anyone to know. It was my business, after all."

Elizabeth swung around angrily. "But now it's *our* business, because your disgrace has fallen on all of us!"

"Liz!" Steven swung on his wife. "Don't you talk to my sister like that."

"Well, it's true! Why don't you take the blinders off

your eyes? Ever since she came, nothing has gone right. You've even changed. Never smile or tease the way you used to. Brooding. Always going off by yourself. You don't even care what happens to me and the children.''

"That's not true. I—I've just had things on my mind.''

"I don't even know you any more,'' she wailed between deep sobs. "Heaven knows I've tried to do my best . . . be a good wife. A credit to the community. It wasn't easy to hold my head up in public even before all of this happened. Now it will be all over town that Deanna Banning is a thief! Everyone will know she's the one who stole the money. Oh, the shame of it all. How can I bear it? You have to do something, Steven. I'm your wife, and I don't want Deanna under my roof another day bringing disgrace upon us all.''

"This is *my* house, Elizabeth, and you won't drive my sister out of it. Dee's more important than those cackling women you call friends. Don't you see the writing on the wall? We're going to be broke, Elizabeth! I'm writing letters right now trying to put off our creditors. The books are so full of red ink they look like the Red Sea. Tell her, Millie. Tell Elizabeth it's time to come off her social merry-go-round and face the facts.''

Millie swallowed hard as if being brought into this domestic quarrel was the last thing on earth she wanted.

"Bannings has always done a good business,'' Elizabeth protested. "How did it happen that there's no profit being fed back into the store? When Walter was alive there was a good living for all of us. He wouldn't have let the store slump into bankruptcy. Walter—''

"I'm not Walter," growled Steven.

Elizabeth was silent for a moment. Then she lifted up her tear-streaked face and looked Steven straight in the eyes. "You're certainly not." The words cut into her husband like the flick of a smarting whip. Elizabeth walked out of the room without a backward glance.

Steven groaned and cradled his head in his hand. I realized then that he loved his wife deeply, passionately, and the marriage between them had been of his own choosing even though Papa had pushed them together. All these years Steven must have known in his heart that Walter would have been a better match for Elizabeth, but he had taken the vibrant, strong-willed Liz for his own and had tried to be what she wanted. His own nature had betrayed him. He would never be a businessman, a community leader, nor a vigorous outdoorsman. He would always be Steven, sensitive, caring, and in harmony with the softer aspects of nature. My heart ached for him.

Millie looked at me as if waiting for me to say something that would put everything right again, but Elizabeth's vindictiveness and Steven's emotional response had left me shaken. I tried to ease the moment as best I could. "You mustn't blame Elizabeth for being upset, Steven," I said in a faltering voice. "This must be very hard on her."

Steven slowly rose to his feet. "Excuse me," he said, brushing past me and following his wife upstairs.

"That bunch of community do-gooders would scalp their own mother," said Millie, as if she knew too well what it felt like to be ostracized by Brimstone's elite. She collected the papers from the top of the desk. "I'll be glad to see the last of them when Harold and I get married."

"You're leaving Brimstone?"

She nodded. "Harold's been offered a bookkeeping job with a bottling company in California." Her face took on a glow that made her eyes a pretty shade of blue. "We're going to have ourselves a life!"

"I'm glad for you, Millie." I hoped the deep envy I felt didn't show. What a lucky woman she was. Her future was filled with excitement and love—and mine? Every day seemed to narrow the boundaries around me, leaving me little room and chance to find my own happiness.

After she left I went into the kitchen, needing the comfort of Maude, who met every crisis the same way she handled cakes that collapsed in the oven—a quick flick of her failure into the trash, and a fresh mixing bowl.

The kitchen was empty, but I heard Maude's voice coming from the scullery. I started toward it—then stopped. Jon Duval! My skin crept at the sound of his deep voice. What was he doing here? Steven had threatened to shoot the Frenchman if he showed his face at Hunters Hall again. I remembered his harsh mouth on mine, the lust of his hard body pressed against me.

I heard Maude's light laughter as the back door closed. She was still smiling when she came through the kitchen door. The smile froze on her lips when she saw my expression.

"What was Duval doing here?" The sound of his voice had sent tremors through my bones.

"He just brought by a mess of trout—"

"Don't take one more thing from him," I ordered. "You know what kind of man he is."

Maude's ample bosom rose and fell in quick succession. I had never raised my voice to her. "I know he's put meat on this table when there wasn't

231

enough household money left to buy a mess of pigs' feet. After your father and Walter died, there wasn't any venison to keep us through the winter until Jon shared his kill with us. I don't hold with his carousing around, but he's been a friend to this family ever since Walter was in knee pants. I know he's always had calf eyes for you, even though you never treated him any better than dirt under your feet. I can't help thinking he might have turned out differently if he'd found the love of a good woman."

I was too aghast to even speak. Jon Duval had always been a bounder, a drinker, a rogue. How could Maude accuse me of being unfair to the wretched man? The swine had even accosted me in her kitchen—and he had nearly raped me in the park! My lips trembled. I had always depended upon Maude as my confidante and bastion of strength, but even she had turned against me.

She must have seen the anguish in my face, but it did not cause her to hold out her warm arms to engulf me. "Who among us is beyond reproach?" she quoted. From her tone, I knew that she too believed I had stolen the carnival money.

I turned and blindly fled up the stairs. At that moment, I knew I had to leave Hunters Hall. No one except Steven wanted me there, and I wasn't even certain that he wouldn't be relieved to see me go. I worried about his despondency, but maybe I was responsible for that as well. Maybe Elizabeth would be more loving if I were gone.

But where would I go? With Whitney's investigation in full swing, I couldn't leave town. The hotel? I knew that the Miramonte had some small apartments for permanent guests. Tomorrow I could go to the bank and withdraw enough money for a month's rent. If I was frugal, I could manage for a few months. My mind couldn't conceive of any plans beyond the immediate. Thank heaven I had banked most of my wages when I was with the Lowenstein family.

I would tell Steven in the morning and leave right after breakfast. With my thoughts racing, my emotions running the gamut from anger to sadness and fear, I packed my things and stripped the room as bare as it had been upon my arrival. I wanted to go to the nursery and give Patty and Nicky a goodbye hug, but I was afraid of another confrontation with Elizabeth. She had made it clear how she felt about me.

Through my bedroom window, I saw Steven with his head down walking despondently toward his greenhouse. My first impulse was to run after him—perhaps we could comfort each other. But then I saw him stop at the door of the stable. He spoke with Jericho for a moment. Jericho handed him something and Steven raised it to his mouth and took a deep swig out of a jug. He handed it back to Jericho and then went his solitary way to the greenhouse. I was terribly disheartened. If Daniel had talked with him, the counseling hadn't done any good.

That night I turned restlessly in my bed as the day's happenings flooded my mind with the arbitrariness of a kaleidoscope. All the scenes ran together, faces overlapped, a myriad of voices raised in anger assaulted me. Had it only been that morning that I had felt so much at peace at the parsonage? The thought of Daniel hearing about my disgraceful dismissal made me close my eyes tightly as warm tears trickled down the curve of my flushed cheeks. How would I be able to face him again? And what would he do now that I had been branded a thief? As a clergyman he had little choice but to keep himself removed from scandal.

I must have dozed off after midnight. In the midst of a torturing dream, I was suddenly stiff and wide awake, as if an alarm had gone off and jolted me back to full consciousness. The room was in darkness. No light came through the windows; before I went to bed I had drawn the drapes and closed the door. But the room seemed somehow alive, full of malicious intent. I listened like an animal feeling the air with his nostrils, not moving a muscle. Nothing happened. No sounds except the branches moving gently in the night wind, and the familiar crackling of boards settling in the old house.

What was it? Why was I rigid and tense? Then I knew! I sensed another presence in the room.

Someone was standing close to my bed.

An uncontrollable reflex brought a muffled sound up into my throat. In the darkness, moving air brushed against my cheek. I swung out and knocked over the hurricane lamp on my beside table. Shattering glass, the crash of a chair being knocked over, and then, before I could focus my eyes, the door into the dark hall opened and closed. I screamed, threw back the covers, and stumbled across the room, pressing my body against the door as if I expected the intruder to push his way back into my room.

I cried out hysterically, "Steven! Steven!" My voice bounced back at me. I prayed it would carry through the door and down the long hall to the master suite at the front of the house. It seemed like an eternity but finally I heard steps on the stairs and a band of light from the hall suddenly spread under my door.

"Dee? What is it? What's happened?"

I jerked open my door and grabbed Steven. "Someone was in my room."

"Now, now," he soothed as I trembled uncontrollably against him. "You must be having a nightmare. Nobody's in the house. I was in the library and I didn't hear anyone come or go."

"Someone was here!" I cried. "Right by my bed."

He lit another lamp. A pile of broken glass was scattered beside my bed and a small chair lay tipped over in the middle of the floor. One of the drawers of my dressing table had been pulled open.

"Is anything gone?"

I looked into the drawer and nearly fainted.

"What is it?" Steven was at my side in an instant, staring down into the open drawer. "Oh, my God." He took out a wad of bills that were banded together.

I stared at the small bundle. *The carnival money.*

My brother raised stricken eyes to me. "What kind of a trick is this, Dee? There was no intruder. Why have you staged a break-in? What did you do with the rest of the money?"

Chapter Eighteen

Steven sat down on the edge of my bed as if all the strength had been drained from his body. "It's true then."

I flung myself down beside him and grabbed his arm. "No! I didn't take the money! Don't you see, someone wants you to think that! I didn't put it in that drawer. Somebody else did."

He shook his head as if he couldn't find a thread of truth in what I was saying. *What had happened to us?* We used to be able to complete each other's thoughts and communicate without words. Now all the words in the world couldn't bridge the gap between us. I had thought Steven guilty of taking the money and now he was harboring the same suspicion about me. We were both innocent—unless Steven had been in my room a moment earlier, and pretended to come from downstairs. Oh, how could I even think such a thing?

I felt sick. Sobs built in my throat.

"None of this makes sense," he said wearily.

It had to make sense, but not if I was going to allow my emotions to color the truth. Steven would not deliberately throw suspicion on me by putting the money in my drawer. It had to be someone else.

"It's like a nightmare." He put his arm around me and held me close. I allowed myself the comfort of his embrace for a moment and then I drew away.

"Someone was here . . . in this room."

"But who?"

I could tell from his tone that he thought my story too fantastic to be believed. I grabbed my quilted wrapper off the bottom of my bed, thrust my arms through the sleeves and started out the door.

"Where are you going?" he exclaimed.

"To find out who was in my room." I had to convince my brother that I wasn't lying. There had to be something that proved I was telling the truth. The intruder couldn't have vanished into thin air.

I bolted down the hall in the opposite direction from the main staircase. There was more than one way to come and go from this floor. A small sconce dimly illuminated the hall, which stretched from my room to the older part of the house. The only room at that end was the bedroom that Steven and Elizabeth occupied.

"You don't think that Elizabeth?" Steven hissed as he joined me.

I shook my head. Just beyond the bedroom door was another door which opened to a servants' stairway curving downward to the kitchen hall below. Only someone who knew the house well would have known about the back hall and the servants' staircase. The intruder could have used it to avoid the main staircase, I thought, as I carefully descended the narrow passageway with Steven at my heels. The passage was dank and musty and I was surprised when I felt a draft of night air surging up the staircase. A dim light below showed that the door at the bottom of the stairs was open.

My steps slowed as we reached the bottom landing. What if someone was waiting there, weapon in hand, just outside the door?

"Let me go first." Steven brushed past me in the narrow passage. He cautiously looked in both directions before stepping out into the hall. "The outside door's opened," he said, motioning me forward. The small hall opened into the kitchen at one end, and an outside door on the other.

"I know that was shut when I left the kitchen about an hour ago," Steven said. "I would have felt the cold air coming in. Besides, Maude always locks up this end of the house."

He started to go out the door but I grabbed his arm and held him back. "Whoever it was is long gone. No use chasing around in the middle of night."

"I suppose you're right. I don't see how anyone could get in without a key." He shut the door and I knew from his expression that he thought I had cleverly left the door open to support my story about an intruder.

"There *was* someone!"

Just then, Maude padded out of her room off the kitchen and peered into the hall. She wore a nightcap on her gray head and had a voluminous wrapper pulled over her ample flannel gown. "What on earth is going on here?" She eyed my loose hair, carelessly tied wrapper, and wild expression.

I opened my mouth to tell her, but Steven put a restraining hand on my arm. "Just getting some air, Maude," lied Steven. "Neither of us could sleep. Sorry to have awakened you."

Her old eyes narrowed. "I haven't taken leave of my senses just 'cause I've put on a few years," she snapped. "You two never could lie your way out of a bowl of mashed potatoes."

"Well, we're not children and you don't have to worry about us anymore," Steven assured her in a calming tone.

She snorted. "And the world's made of green cheese! Look at the two of you. It's a sad sight that meets these poor old eyes." Her eyes raked Steven. "Swilling rot-gut night and day, walking around with eyes as glassy as marbles. Makes a body sick, it does." Her lips quivered. "I never thought I'd see the day when my babies couldn't spit in the face of anyone who called them names."

Steven smiled ruefully. "I guess she's right, Dee. We've forgotten how to stick out our tongues and throw green apples."

For a moment, we regained some of our past closeness. Tears swelled into my eyes. "I guess we can take on the world if we've a mind too."

"Now, that's more like it," beamed Maude. "Now, git yourselves in the kitchen and I'll fix some hot chocolate."

"Thanks, Maude, but I think I'll pass," said Steven. "Are you going to be all right?" he asked me.

I nodded and gave his arm a squeeze before I followed Maude into the kitchen. I was glad to delay going back up to my room. Maude eyed me as she bustled about warming milk and dissolving a bar of chocolate. "Want to tell me what this is all about?"

I knew that Steven had not wanted to tell her about my intruder, and I couldn't help but wonder if his reluctance was his lack of faith in the truth of my story. For my own peace of mind, I needed to talk to someone, and Maude had always been that somebody when I was growing up. Except for her support of Jon Duval, I had always felt she would take my side of any story.

I moistened my lips.

"Well?" she prodded.

From the curious glint in her eyes, I knew that even if Maude had the best intentions in the world, she wouldn't be able to keep the story to herself. If Chief Whitney learned that a bundle of carnival money had been found in my room, all my denials would be for naught. My mind raced for some plausible explanation for Steven's and my presence in the back hall at one o'clock in the morning. "I—I was sleepwalking," I lied. "Steven found me wandering around downstairs and stopped me from walking right out the side door."

"Heaven protect us!" she gasped. "You could have hurt yourself." Maude's protective response was comforting. "I remember once when your mother was found outside in her nightclothes. Such a frail thing, she was." Maude shook her head. "And now you're following in her footsteps."

"Tell me again about my mother," I urged, relieved to have turned the conversation down a less dangerous path. "I didn't know she was a sleepwalker."

Maude set down two steaming mugs and eased into a chair beside me. "There's not much to tell. I didn't know her for very long. You see, Mr. Banning advertised for help after you twins were born. Your mother was peaked and worn out just from the birthin'. Hired me to take care of you and Steven. Beautiful babies you were too. Blond angels—but don't think that you acted that way. Many's the time you both needed your fannies paddled for keeping me up all night. Neither of you had an ounce of patience. Both of you screaming your heads off to be fed first—"

"But my mother—?" I interrupted, trying to get her back on the subject. The stories of our up-

241

bringing were familiar ones.

"The poor dear was buried before you children reached your first birthday. So you see, I just knew her for a few months."

"What was she like . . . as a person?"

"Reckon I couldn't say," said Maude. "She kept to her rooms most of the time. I was busy in the nursery and didn't see her too often. One of the upstairs maids said she was very talented when it came to drawing and singing. There was a piano in the drawing room then, and I heard her playing sometimes."

"Did she have any friends?"

Maude frowned. "Not that I remember. Your father never said how he met her. He just married her on one of his trips back East and brought her here. Some folks said he was terribly jealous and that's why he kept her so close to the house. But I don't hold with that. Anyway, she was a lucky woman. A devoted husband, two wonderful children of her own, and a stepson to raise. And after her death, your pa changed. Forbade her name to be mentioned in the house as if his grief just wouldn't heal."

Hunters Hall had always been possessed by shadows, and even in death, my father's presence was a heavy pall over the house. I suppressed a shiver, stood up, and thanked Maude for the hot drink.

As I started back upstairs, I saw a light shining out into the front hall from the trophy room. Steven slumped in the same chair as before, only this time he didn't have a gun to his head. He was staring into a half-empty whiskey glass. Obviously Maude's chastising hadn't done any good. He looked up as I came in. "I thought you'd gone to bed."

"Why did you lie to Maude?" I asked.

He shrugged.

"You don't believe my story, do you?"

He sighed. "I don't know what to believe."

"Someone came in that door and went up those stairs and planted the money in my room."

"But that door was locked. I came in that way earlier from the greenhouse—I locked it myself."

"Either someone had a key or someone in the house wanted to make it look like an outsider . . . and it wasn't me."

A soft smile eased the tight corners of his mouth. "Are you accusing me?"

"Are you accusing *me?*" I countered without returning his smile.

"Damn it, Dee, I don't know what to think. This business of your being dismissed for thievery has knocked me sideways. Why on earth didn't you say something when you came home? We've never had secrets between us before. If you didn't take the ring—?"

"I didn't."

"Then why—"

How could I explain that two other incidents had labeled me as a thief? Even though I put the things back before the Lowensteins had missed them, the kitchen maid had seen a gold snuffbox and silver fan in my room. The wily girl took the emerald ring, and when she was caught she put the blame on me, telling everyone I had given it to her and swearing she had seen the snuffbox and fan in my room. While Steven watched my face, I searched for words to explain the compulsion, and to assure him that I had overcome it since I returned home. The explanation wouldn't come. *He wouldn't believe me.* Once a thief, always a thief.

"I'm moving out of the house tomorrow," I said.

"And as soon as Whitney completes his investigation, I'll be leaving Brimstone."

Steven leaned across the table. "What about the money, Dee? There must be a hundred dollars in that bundle in your drawer, but Elizabeth thinks there was close to a thousand in the bag."

"Maybe she took it."

Steven jerked back as if touched with a branding iron. "How can you say such a thing? She wasn't even with us on the wagon."

"She was right behind us in the buggy. She could have driven by the wagon. Seen the money pouch lying on the seat. Taken it while we were in the store and everyone else was across the street."

He looked at me sadly. "You have never liked Liz, have you? I remember how ardently you tried to talk me out of marrying her. And God knows, I haven't been much of a prize."

I wasn't in any mood for his self-pity. Of all the people in the world, I thought my twin brother would never doubt my word and I felt betrayed. Maybe it was time that we said some honest things to each other. "Drinking isn't going to put any marks in the plus column."

"I don't know why she married me," he said with lowered head.

"Why did *you* marry *her*?"

He looked up at me in surprise. "I wanted Elizabeth as my wife . . . mother of my children."

"She must have married you for the same reason. She must have wanted you as the father of her children. It seems to me that you both have been trying to be something that you aren't and letting the most important things go by the wayside."

"She hates me for everything that's happened."

"Nonsense. Stand up to her—it's about time.

Maybe losing the store will be a blessing. Give you two a new start."

"If it isn't too late," he said wearily.

I reached over and touched his hand. "It's never too late for a new beginning." I couldn't believe my own words—look who was talking! I myself had never heeded such counsel.

I went back up to my room and stared at the broken lamp and turned-over chair. The fear returned and a cold chill prickled the skin on my neck. What should I do now? Like someone playing chess with an invisible partner, I wondered what the next move against me would be. One of the bundles of money had been planted in my room to compound the suspicion that had already been raised against me. I had to get rid of the money before Chief Whitney was alerted that it was in my possession.

Grateful for an activity that would silence my thoughts, I quickly dressed. When I heard Steven's steps on the stairs, I held my breath. He passed my room with a slow tread. When I was sure he had entered his bedroom, I left mine, and scooted down the stairs to the front door. Pulling the hood of my long cape over my head, I fled down the driveway.

At two o'clock in the morning, I was only another shadow moving along the deserted streets. A few sporadic barks from unseen dogs broke the night's stillness. The scurrying rustle of a nighthawk ended in a dark-winged flight as I disturbed its nocturnal hunt. A lone wagon rumbled toward some unknown destination at the edge of town.

When I reached the church, I literally prayed that the doors would be open. "Dear God, please . . ." The heavy doorknob turned and I slipped inside.

The sanctuary was like a cavern with only muted moonlight dispelling the shadowy darkness. A nighttime chill penetrated my cloak. Rows of pews were dark and empty, and my footsteps sounded hollow in the empty building as I made my way to the center of the back wall.

The slot of the contribution box was too narrow to accommodate the bundle of bills. My hands trembled as I began stuffing in as many at once as I could. Daniel had protected me once before. Would he do it again? If the intruder alerted Chief Whitney that the money was in my possession, the burden of silence would be upon Daniel. My brother wasn't convinced of my innocence and the clergyman already knew I was a thief. Maybe he wouldn't believe the story of an intruder, either. This attempt to rid myself of the damaging evidence might be for naught.

I had my back to the front door and because I was covered from head to foot with my heavy cloak I didn't feel any movement of air. Only a sixth sense gave me some warning—but too late.

A burst of fiery pain shattered the back of my head. Darkness exploded behind my eyes. A swirling cauldron of nothingness drew me down, down, down.

Chapter Nineteen

Voices assaulted me from a distance, then became a painful clamor of insistence in my brain, calling me back to myself. I realized as I regained consciousness that it was only one deep voice calling my name— "Deanna . . . Deanna . . . wake up."

My eyelids opened slowly. Daniel's face swam into focus, his eyes, mouth, and nose rippling as if I was viewing his features under water. For a brief moment, he looked like a gargoyle. I cried out in an expression of horror.

"It's only me, Daniel," he soothed.

I couldn't think. My skull was ready to burst. I closed my eyes again and again drifted away. The next time I opened them I was lying on a comfortable sofa with Daniel's face hovering over mine. This time his features were not distorted. His eyes searched mine anxiously and his mouth was tense. "Dee? Thank the Good Lord you're coming around! I'll send for the doctor."

No! I tried to sit up but he eased me back. A wet cloth lay across my forehead, and a lingering odor of smelling salts assaulted my nostrils.

"No, don't move," he ordered. I realized that

everything was going to be ruined! No one could know that I had been in the church. Panic leant me strength. "I . . . I have to go."

"You're not going anywhere," he said firmly. "Now tell me what happened. I went into the sanctuary at dawn for morning prayers and couldn't believe my eyes . . . or ears. I heard a groan and there you were, unconscious on the floor."

I moistened my dry lips. What kind of a story would be believed?

"What on earth were you doing in the church at that hour?"

He didn't know about the money.

"Praying?" I said hopefully.

The deep lines in his face eased into a grin. "I think not."

I swallowed hard. "I . . . I couldn't sleep so I took a walk."

"Try again." Then he reached in his pocket and drew out a fistful of bills. "I found these scattered on the floor. And that knot on the back of your head is the size of a goose egg. What happened?"

"I fell."

His expression darkened. "Do I have to shake the truth out of you? I know patience is a virtue but I swear, Deanna, I've had it with you. Now you're going to tell me everything—now!"

"You won't believe me," I said sadly.

He put his hands gently around my face and looked deeply into my eyes. "I will. And when I see the truth shining in those green-blue depths, I'll know it. Now, what were you doing in the church?"

"Putting money in the contribution box."

"What money?"

"From the carnival. But I didn't steal it. You have to believe me."

"Then how did you get it?"

"Someone came into my bedroom and put a packet of the carnival money in my dressing table drawer. I had to get rid of it before . . . before Whitney found it there." My head was pounding deafeningly. "Steven said he locked the side door, but we found it open."

"How did someone get in?"

"I guess whoever it was had a key." *Unless it was someone in the house.* I wasn't going to point the finger at Steven or Elizabeth even though my brother had leveled the same suspicion at me.

"Did you get a look at the person? Any impressions?"

"No. I just sensed a presence near my bed. I cried out and whoever it was fled into the dark hall. Steven heard me yell and came up from downstairs. We found the money in my dresser drawer." I took a deep breath. "But I don't think Steven believes me."

"Why not?"

"Chief Whitney found out about my penchant for taking things." I told him about the officer's visit and the letter that Carolyn had received from her friend.

"You stole an emerald ring from your employers?" Daniel brushed back an unruly shock of reddish hair in exasperation.

"No, I never stole the ring!" I exclaimed, losing my patience. In a belligerent tone, I told him how I had been made the scapegoat. "An upstairs maid verified that a gold snuffbox and silver fan had been missing for a few days last winter, and when the kitchen maid said she'd seen them in my room, the Lowensteins believed that I had taken the ring, too."

"I see." He got up and paced around the room. "And whoever stole the carnival money decided to use that information to his advantage."

My heart was suddenly light. *Daniel believed me.* It didn't matter that my head was throbbing. Strength flowed back into my body. "What should we do now?"

"We?" He raised a sardonic eyebrow.

"You're my accomplice, remember?"

He let out a long breath. "Well, I guess it wouldn't be right for me to abandon ship at this late date. But how can I lie about the money?"

"You don't have to lie. Tell the truth. You found it in the contribution box."

"But if everyone knows you were in the church last night—"

"Who's to know—except you and the one who struck me?" I frowned. "The same person who broke into the house must have followed me to the church."

Daniel massaged his chin thoughtfully. "It could have happened that way."

Gingerly I put my legs over the side of the sofa. My walking skirt and white blouse were wrinkled and my white stockings were twisted. My shoes lay on the floor beside the sofa. "I have to get back to the house before anyone knows I'm gone."

"Are you sure you're well enough? Maybe you should rest here for a few hours—"

"And have your housekeeper spreading the story all over town? Who would believe I hadn't been here all night? And then there's the money. If anyone connects it with me—"

He sighed. "I guess you're right. I'll take you home."

"No! Don't you see that would ruin everything! If someone saw us together they might suspect something when you return the carnival money."

"But—"

"Please, just let me go." I sat up and for a moment the room spun around me. Then strength flowed back into my rubbery limbs and except for a gigantic headache, I seemed to have recovered from my period of unconsciousness. The early morning sun touched the array of plants on the windowsill. Ebenezer sat on a nearby chair preening himself with an energetic pink tongue. Books and papers were scattered about in homey confusion and a mug of coffee still steamed where Daniel had left it. Ordinary, wonderful sights. Somehow they put the terror of the night into a bearable perspective.

"Are you sure I shouldn't call Dr. Hardcastle?"

"I'm sure." I gingerly touched the tender bump on my head and realized my hair had fallen in a wanton fashion upon my shoulders. Heat flared up in my cheeks. I was embarrassed that he had seen me in such a condition. I pinned up the heavy strands as best I could.

Daniel knelt down, brazenly lifted my ankles, slipped on my shoes and buttoned them up. As he knelt before me, I gave in to the impulse to smooth the top of his head in an affectionate gesture. "I'm really sorry to put you in this position."

"What, on my knees?" he teased.

He looked at me with such tenderness that I blinked rapidly to hold back tears in my eyes. Every ounce of my being wanted to deny the circumstances that would always hold us apart. If only by some miracle I were given a different past. But such thoughts were folly. There was nothing I could do to change the way things were.

He stood up. "What kind of an explanation are you going to give for being out this time of morning?"

"I'll say I went for an early morning walk."

"Maybe someone's already missed you?"

My laugh was short. "Not likely. No one pays that much attention to me. Steven is lost in a morass of self-pity, Elizabeth hates the sight of me. Besides, I'm moving out of the house today."

"You're what?"

"I have to. My presence is causing trouble between Steven and Elizabeth. She blames me for everything that's happened—even for the change in Steven. Maybe she's right. If I hadn't come back, maybe none of this would have happened."

He picked up my cape from a chair and laid it on my shoulders. As his hands rested on my arms, I leaned back against him. He bent his head and his lips trailed across the nape of my neck. "You could come here," he said softly.

I wanted to lean back into the sweet length of his vigorous body, but instead gave a choked laugh. "Of course, I could. I'm certain your congregation wouldn't object at all, Reverend Norris."

He swung me around to face him. "Will you marry me, Deanna?"

My mouth was suddenly dry. "I can't."

"And why not? We're both of age and I know you're not afraid of challenges. Is it because you don't love me?"

Storm clouds threatened us with hurricane force. If I gave in to my heart, I could destroy this man. He would be forced to give up his church and his position in the community and scandal would follow him wherever he went. I cared for him too deeply to ever marry him.

"I don't love you," I said as firmly as I could.

He only laughed. "Do you know that when you lie you blink?"

"Everyone blinks."

"Not two times in one second. Are you afraid of

being a preacher's wife?"

"Yes." That time I didn't blink. Millie had been right about me. "I'm not cut out of the right stuff. Your wife needs to—"

"—be a caring, sensitive person who would make me a better man and be a loving mother to our children. You're perfect. Please, love, I know we could be happy."

"People would . . . would—" I stammered.

"Would what?"

"Never accept me as your wife."

As we stood inches apart, his hands on my arms and his touch inviting and warm, he pleaded softly, "Deanna, love."

"No." My voice was firm and I turned my head, denying him my lips. I pulled away. "Please let me out the back door. I'll take the long way through the cemetery."

"Please—"

"No!" I said with heated finality. His mouth tightened and his eyes narrowed. I knew the pain in my heart was greater than any physical pain I could have been asked to endure in a dozen lifetimes.

He held open the back door. I couldn't leave him this way. "I'm honored that you would take me to be your wife, but it's impossible. You don't know . . . you don't know . . ." I floundered.

"What you're hiding? That's right, I don't. Something sent you running away five years ago, and you're still running. I'm going to find out your secret." He looked at me determinedly. "And when I do, I'll ask you again."

I gave him a sad smile. "No, you won't."

With my head lowered and tears spilling down my cheeks, I hurried away through the churchyard and slipped out a back gate. I prayed no one saw me as I left the church behind and began climbing a path that led past the cemetery. The early morning air was cool on my heated cheeks. Drifts of pinyon pines and low-growing cedars flanking the twisting path hid me from view as I stumbled over the rough ground and tried to keep my gaze steady.

Perhaps out of habit, or some deep need to reach out to my mother's spirit, I went to her grave and knelt beside it. All the years of indoctrination in which Papa had taught me to despise my mother had taken their toll upon me. Desperately needing my father's approval I had fought to overcome the heredity which had been so distasteful to him, but as I knelt beside her grave, tears dropping on the dry dirt, I accepted the fact that her blood coursed through my veins. Pouring out my anguish in tears and sobs, I sought to communicate with a mother I'd never known. Once more the brevity and inadequacy of her epitaph wounded me and I vowed I would add "Loving Mother" to the bleak inscription.

Somehow strengthened by this wordless communion, I rose to my feet and continued my way down the hill that led to our property. The pain in my head had receded to a dull ache. Thank heavens I had been wearing my hood when my assailant struck me. The heavy cloth had cushioned the vicious blow. I was certain that whoever had planted the money in my room must have followed me to the church and hit me from behind. If anyone but Daniel had found me, it would have been impossible to convince the authorities of my innocence. Even Steven wasn't convinced I hadn't staged the break-in.

I paused a moment before entering the house. Then I firmed my shoulders and quickly passed through the kitchen, thankful that the household wasn't yet astir.

*   *   *

Later that morning, I moved into the Miramonte Hotel without any vigorous protest from Steven or Elizabeth. My brother even put my trunk on the back of the buggy and drove me to the hotel himself. I sensed an undercurrent of relief in his manner. He hated being pitted between his sister and his wife, and it was only right that he should stand by Elizabeth now.

"You can always come back, Dee, if things don't work out."

"Yes." But we both knew I wouldn't. The ties between my twin brother and myself had been severed beyond repair. That part of my life was over. I thought with some sadness that never again would we feel the special kinship that had seen us through a difficult childhood. Both of our eyes were misty as he helped me down from the buggy.

Sabrina's dark eyes glowed with suppressed curiosity when Steven asked about accommodations. "Of course. I'm certain your sister will find the Miramonte very comfortable. Will you be wanting a suite or single room?"

"Single," I answered evenly.

"I see." Sabrina almost licked her lips. "Let's see now."

Steven exchanged an impatient glance with me. Making us wait for several minutes, Sabrina examined the register and advance reservations with the air of someone who was enjoying a moment of power. I felt terribly on display with my baggage piled up beside me and people coming and going. My head ached and the nervous drain of moving out of the house had sapped what little energy the sleepless night had left me.

255

Finally Sabrina nodded in an officious way. "Of course, we are at the height of the tourist season, but we still have some lovely spacious rooms at the back of the building on the second floor. Most of our regular guests prefer that location because they have a little more privacy." The gleam in her eyes was almost blinding. "Are you interested in privacy, Deanna?" I knew what her question implied.

"My sister is just wanting a little peace and quiet," said Steven impatiently. "With the murder and all, things have not been very pleasant for her at Hunters Hall."

"I suppose after things settle down, you'll be moving back?" she asked with a frankness that invited more confidences. "Or do you consider the move to be permanent? If so, perhaps you would like to sign a lease?" Her dark eyebrows raised questioningly.

"It really depends on how suitable I find hotel life," I said sweetly. "At the moment, a week-by-week engagement of the room will do nicely." I paid her with funds that I had just withdrawn from the bank. Fortunately, Brian hadn't been anywhere around when I made my transaction.

"I'll have a boy take you up to 214," she said, eyeing Steven. "Unless you would like to see her settled, Mr. Banning?"

Steven took out his pocket watch and made a pretense of looking rushed for time. "I'd best get to the store. It's nearly noon and I have to check on some shipments coming in this afternoon. Millie and I will be working late tonight on the books." He gave me a quick peck on the cheek. "If there's anything you need—"

I assured him that everything was taken care of and waved him on his way. A deep sense of relief came over me. I hadn't realized how much living at Hunters Hall had weighed on me.

"Perhaps we can get together for tea this afternoon," suggested Sabrina as she rang a bell summoning a porter.

"Perhaps," I said noncommittally. Giving her a cool smile, I turned and followed the uniformed bellman into the wrought-iron cage of the elevator. My stomach dipped as we made a halting ascent to the second floor.

What Sabrina had referred to as a lovely, spacious room was half the size of my bedroom at Hunters Hall. Two high windows looked out upon a circular drive used by delivery wagons. The walls were done up in dove-gray paper, and the dark walnut furniture must have been in the hotel since the first guest arrived in Brimstone. A towering wardrobe dominated one wall. The bed's headboard was carved with serpentine vines and flowers that resembled lilies. A marble-top washstand stood in one corner, complete with pitcher, basin, and white towels. The only homey touch was a rocking chair placed in front of the two high, narrow windows which had been dressed with ecru lace curtains and pull-down shades.

The bellboy, who was in his fifties, dropped my trunk off his shoulders and wiped the sweat from his brow. "Will that be all, miss?"

"Yes, thank you."

He brightened at the tip I gave him and showed me the bell I could pull if I needed anything.

After he had gone, I sat down on the hard bed and tried to recover the strength of will I had experienced in the lobby. I had made the right decision, I told myself for the hundredth time. But in so doing I had deliberately cut myself off from the people who meant the most to me. My need for family had brought me back to Brimstone, and now I was alone again. The bleakness of the situation threatened to envelop me. *Get a hold of yourself,* I scolded, feeling my spirits plunge.

With a force of will I unpacked my things and set some of my personal belongings out. But the room remained empty and cold. Now what? I couldn't possibly fill the hours in the confines of this small room. I desperately needed to be with people . . . even strangers.

I freshened myself at the wash basin, made a quick trip down the hall to the large bathroom, and then went downstairs to the dining room. I had been prepared to sit alone, but welcomed the sight of David Kirkland rising from his chair at my entrance. I went to his table like a homing pigeon.

"What a lovely surprise," he said in his usual warm, polite manner. "Could I be fortunate enough to have you join me for lunch, Deanna?" His glance moved beyond me, as if he expected to see a companion following me into the room.

"I would be delighted," I said and gave him a grateful smile as he guided my chair into the small table.

He beamed at me. "I never expected I would be able to repay your hospitality so soon. I thoroughly enjoyed our lunch yesterday. It is always such a joy to be with you, Deanna. You don't know how you brighten an old man's day."

I wondered at his pleasure at seeing me. I thought of what Daniel had said about David Kirkland—*He's not what he seems.*

I was suddenly self-conscious about having lunch with him, but he carried the conversation in an easy and entertaining way and I soon relaxed.

258

The dining room was quite crowded, but I didn't see anyone I knew as I glanced about. An air of festivity permeated the dining room as guests chatted and laughed in relaxed enjoyment. Efficient staff in black and white uniforms threaded through the elaborately set tables and dispensed full trays of food with easy elegance.

Once again, my spirits rose and I found myself selecting with enthusiasm baked almond trout, creamed chives and peas, and fresh berry pie.

"I always have a little wine with lunch. Would you—?"

I hesitated. If there was ever a day that I could use the lift of a glass of wine, this was it, I thought. But ladies didn't drink spirits in the middle of the day. There was a sparkle in David Kirkland's eyes that challenged me. Oh well, what could it possibly hurt?

"Yes, please." I was in the mood to be reckless. This was a celebration of sorts, after all. It wasn't every day a girl received a proposal of marriage— even if she had to refuse it.

"To your happiness," he said, touching his goblet to mine. He watched me wince slightly as I sipped from the glass—I was used to pink lemonade. Daniel would not have approved of my luncheon companion, but more than ever I was grateful for the older man's friendship.

"I'm staying at the Miramonte," I informed him, wondering if the town was already buzzing with the news of my move. He seemed genuinely surprised. "I needed to get away from Hunters Hall," I said bluntly.

He nodded as if he understood completely. "I found the atmosphere rather . . . oppressive."

I laughed at the man's tact. After all, Jericho had nearly dealt him a lethal blow. Then I sobered and

259

took another sip of wine. "Yes, very oppressive."

"But it's your home. You must have some deep feelings about it."

"None pleasant. Hunters Hall really belonged to my papa and half-brother . . . not to Steven and me. Even now, I don't think my brother would hesitate to move somewhere else if he had the opportunity." I told Kirkland about Steven's dream of starting a nursery and experimenting with new strains of carnations.

We ate our lunch in leisurely fashion and I was forced to admit that Maude's offerings couldn't match the delicately seasoned dishes that the white-coated waiter set before me.

"And what about you? What about your dreams?" asked my companion. "A lovely young woman like yourself must have eligible men competing for your hand. If I could be so bold, I thought you and Reverend Norris . . . ?"

I knew my cheeks were suddenly pink. "I could never marry Daniel . . . even if he asked me."

"And why not?"

"Because a minister's wife must be beyond reproach. I could never measure up to such a high standard. There are too many skeletons in the family closet."

"Surely no scandal can stand in the way of true love," he countered.

"I wish that were the case," I said. "But I'm afraid there are past events that control my future."

"How unfortunate. Still, I don't see why a young person like yourself should have to sacrifice happiness because of some indiscretion of the past. You and the reverend seem happy together."

I shook my head. "It wouldn't be fair to Daniel to besmirch his life so."

"I see," he said thoughtfully, but didn't pursue the subject. Instead, he began talking about some drawings he had made that morning.

"How is the watercolor painting come along?" I asked.

He looked pained. "I don't think Sabrina is impressed with my accomplishments. Most of my efforts turn out to look like a wash of muddy water. I guess I'd better stick to oils."

The wine sent a warm glow through my veins. By the time we finished lunch I felt almost content.

"We will have to do this again. Since you're staying at the hotel, I hope to see a great deal of you." He squeezed the hand he had on my arm and I stiffened.

Surely he didn't have any amorous feelings for me. "Yes . . . yes," I stammered.

"Maybe you can be the daughter I never had," he said quickly as if sensing my unspoken concern.

"I would like that," I said sincerely. As David saw me to the elevator I felt quite relaxed—and sleepy. "And now I think I'll have a nap."

He smiled at me as if he was somehow responsible for easing my anxious mind. I wondered if that's why he offered me the wine.

"I'm glad you're here, Deanna," he said.

And for the moment, so was I. Once more in my room, I stretched across the hard bed and was sound asleep before I had drawn a dozen breaths.

A light but insistent knocking awakened me. For a minute I couldn't remember where I was. I sat up on the strange bed and looked around. The windows were opaque with descending twilight. Then I remembered. I had slept the afternoon away.

The demanding knock sounded again. I sat up on the edge of the bed and stammered a startled, "Just

261

a minute." Quickly I straightened my hair and smoothed down my skirts. I couldn't control the hopeful expectation that it was Daniel, but when I opened the door, my hopes plummeted.

It was Brian.

"You!"

"Yes, sweetheart."

His ugly smirk took my breath away.

Chapter Twenty

Brian leaned cavalierly against the door frame. "Hello, love. Aren't you going to invite me in?"

"No." My mouth was dry. "It's not proper."

"Don't be stuffy, Dee." He brushed past me and shut the door before I could protest. "Save the maidenly modesty. I saw you in the woods with Duval, remember?"

"And you did nothing to stop him!" I lashed out.

"Stop him? And why would I intrude on such an exhibition of wild passion? I bet Duval had scratches on his back the way you were clutching him."

"I was fighting him!"

Brian laughed derisively. "Not from where I stood, sweetheart. You were writhing under him like a bitch in heat."

"Get out."

A mocking smile twisted his lips. "Not very hospitable to an old friend, my love."

"I am *not* your love!"

"You really had me fooled. I never would have guessed you preferred Duval's style of courtship to my own. But no matter, I came to remedy past mistakes."

I backed up. "I told you, Duval was in the act of raping me when you stumbled upon us."

"You're lying. And I'm in no mood to be made the fool—you've already done that quite nicely."

"I'll call the desk," I warned him, positioning myself near the bell cord and glaring at him.

He leaned up against the door, still smiling. "No you won't, love. You see, my mother told me everything."

Silence. Shock. I couldn't move. I was engulfed by the desperation that a condemned man must endure the moment they blindfold him. Helpless against the final torture, my voice was barely a whisper, "She promised."

Brian straightened up and sauntered toward me nonchalantly. "But you didn't keep your part of the bargain, did you? You came back to Brimstone. My mother told me everything this afternoon."

I had gambled and lost.

"But there's no reason that everything has to be over between us." Brian's grin was the same one that had sent my heart pounding when we were keeping company—only now it left me cold and defenseless. "Just because your mother was a whore and cleverly cuckolded dear old Papa Banning."

I felt as if my body had been submerged in ice.

A glint of excitement narrowed Brian's eyes. "No wonder mother was horrified when she thought she might have grandchildren with tainted blood in their veins. What a scandal that would have been. She blackmailed you into leaving, didn't she?"

I stared at him feeling as if I was caught in a dream.

"But you came back. Why did you? Weren't you afraid she'd talk?"

I moistened my dry lips. "Nina had kept her silence for years. I didn't think she would disgrace

264

Steven and me unless I provoked her by taking up with you again."

"Don't you see it doesn't matter to me, sweetheart? Of course, I'm going to marry Carolyn. She offers the kind of respectability that I need in a wife. My mother need have no fear that her daughter-in-law isn't beyond reproach."

"Then why—?" I didn't understand why Nina Milburne had broken her silence. If her son was safely out of my clutches, what did Nina have to gain?

"Carolyn told Mother about you and Duval." His mouth twisted in an amused smile. "I think it's safe to say she was horrified to hear about your wanton behavior. Especially since everyone knows the preacher's getting sweet on you. My mother decided it was her Christian duty not to hold her silence any longer."

Daniel's voice rang in my ears. *I'm going to find out your secret.* He wouldn't have to wait long for enlightenment now. I was certain that Nina Milburne would carry out her self-righteous duty with missionary zeal.

"Don't bother keeping up the pretense with me, Dee. My mother told me everything . . . the whole story. How she was on that stagecoach the night your mother was fleeing with you and Steven. Your mother was on her way to Denver to meet the lover who had fathered her fair-haired twins."

"No," I protested. "It's not true." Gut-wrenching denial lurched through me as it had five years ago when Nina first told me the story.

Brian smirked. "Papa Banning had made the mistake of leaving his young wife alone for two months the year before, while he went back East to do his yearly buying for the store. When he came back, his pretty wife was pregnant. To save face in the community he had to acknowledge you and Steven as his own. Your mother told mine the whole sordid tale when a blinding snowstorm stranded the stagecoach they were on midway between Brimstone and Denver. For several hours, it seemed that they might freeze to death. That's why your mother talked. She feared for your lives, exacting a promise from my mother to see her babies to safety if she didn't make it."

"But Papa caught up with the stagecoach," I said in a leaden voice. "And brought us all back."

"But by then your mother had caught pneumonia, hadn't she?"

Pain twisted like a knife in my chest. "Papa hated Steven and me because we were a constant reminder of her unfaithfulness. In a way, it was a relief when your mother told me everything. Not knowing why I could never get his approval had almost destroyed me.

"Five years ago, when Nina threatened to reveal the truth of my parentage if I didn't leave Brimstone, I finally understood why my father had never loved me and Steven. He couldn't change our looks, our fair hair and greenish-blue eyes. He made us pay every day for our resemblance to his unfaithful wife. He rejected us as though we were creatures spawned from the devil. Even as small children we had recognized his deep hatred. Walter had been his only true child."

"My mother kept her silence until it seemed that I might marry you," agreed Brian. "She didn't know the name of your father, but she thinks from the description your mother gave her that he was shot in Colorado Springs a short while later for his adulterous behavior with someone else's wife."

266

I shivered. "My mother was a victim."

He laughed. "She was an actress at the Winter Garden Theater when your father met her. He was taken in by her feminine charms—you know what stage actresses are like, love. They ply their favors to the highest bidder. Your father must have triumphed when she accepted his proposal of marriage. No, sweetheart, your mother was no innocent—and neither are you. But I don't care what you've done . . . or what your mother was. I just want you."

I lowered my head, all the fight within me gone. What did it matter now if the story was spread all over town?

Brian put his hands on my arms. "Don't worry, Dee. I've never been able to get you out of my mind. And now that I know what fiery blood flows in that delicious body of yours, there's no reason to deny your past . . . nor deny me the pleasure of taking care of you in a discreet way. Don't you see, sweetheart? Now that I know the truth, you don't have to hide anything from me."

His arms enveloped me in an embrace so tight I could hardly breathe. His voice was husky. "God, how I've wanted you. When I saw Duval having his way with you, I could have killed you both. But now I realize it's better this way. There are some women better without a wedding ring. Your mother was one of those."

I tried to shove him away but his arms captured me greedily against him. The smell of spicy bay rum hit my nostrils with sickening force as he bent his face close to mine. Lust sprang hotly through his body as he leaned into me. His mouth plundered mine with savage kisses. The paralysis that had come over me with his admissions was suddenly replaced with fear.

I jerked my mouth from his. "No . . . *no!*"

He pinned my arms at my side. "Yes, my dear Deanna. I'ts time you shared your pleasures with me." He dragged me to the bed, forcing me down upon it.

I screamed before Brian's hand closed roughly around my throat, shutting off my air. With the other hand, he grabbed the neckline of my dress and underclothes and ripped them to my waist. My breasts spilled out of the torn bodice and cold air assaulted my nakedness. I fought him to no avail. He lifted my skirts.

Throwing himself upon me, he buried his mouth against a hardening nipple and pressed his face into my flesh.

His hand was clamped over my nose and mouth, choking off my breath. My chest burned. My head swam dizzily. He forced my legs apart. In desperation, I bit the soft flesh of the hand he held on my mouth.

He cried out.

I brought my knee up instinctively. The vicious blow to his groin caused him to twist sideways. I got myself off the bed and across the room to the door.

"No, you don't." Before I could open it, he had grabbed my skirt and pulled me back. The fabric tore as I twisted away, crashing into the wash stand. With a frantic cry, I grabbed the water pitcher from its perch and threw it at him.

Water spilled from the pitcher as it sailed over his shoulder—and crashed through the window. The shattering of glass was followed by the shout of someone on the ground below. Brian froze. He knew someone would be up to investigate.

My breath came in short gasps. "Are you going to get out before I yell rape?"

"And who would believe you?"

"You want to wait and find out?" I walked over to the broken window.

"No . . . I'll go. But you'll be sorry. You turn your back on me and this town will peel the skin off your bones when the story gets around about you and your brother. Think about it!" With that, he bolted from the room. I heard him taking the back stairs in a rush.

I just had time to put on a wrapper and kick my torn bodice under the bed before Joe Sawyer knocked on the door.

"I'm sorry," I apologized, explaining that I had accidentally dropped the water pitcher.

The hotel owner raised an eyebrow as if unable to imagine how such an act could have caused a window to break—but Joe was gentleman enough not to question me. He offered to hang a heavy curtain over the broken pane until it could be fixed.

I thanked him, and when he had gone, I lay down on my bed and wept. My tears were not only for me and the degradation which Brian's behavior had reaped upon me, but I shed tears for my mother, who had lost her life and children because she had loved unwisely. My grief was for Papa Banning, who had suffered her unfaithfulness every day of Steven's and my life. And my sorrow was also for Daniel, the man I loved, who would soon learn about my parentage—along with the rest of the town.

The only new information that Brian had given me was about my real father. I had always fantasized that he had been an upright, moral man even though he had chosen a married woman to love, but Brian's revelation that he had been shot by an outraged husband only increased my pain.

Five years ago I had submitted to Nina Milburne's

blackmail and had left Brimstone to protect Steven and his family as much as myself. Knowing how much her social standing meant to Elizabeth, I had tried to keep the sword of scandal from falling upon the family. I had gambled when I came back, but I knew that continuing to be an exile would destroy me. I reasoned that everything was over between Brian and me and that his mother would have no reason to follow through on her threats to tell the sordid story. I had gambled and lost.

Steven! I had to tell him before he heard the story from someone else. There wasn't any doubt in my mind that Brian's pride would drive him to seek revenge.

With great force of will I attempted to pull myself together. Cowering in my room was a luxury I couldn't afford. It was already near the dinner hour. If I hurried to Hunters Hall, I might be able to see Steven before he left for the evening. He had told me that he would be working on the books that night with Millie.

I changed clothes and braided my hair as best I could, given my trembling fingers. I flung a summer cape around my shoulders and pinned a small straw hat atop my head, put on my gloves, and took the elevator down to the lobby. I moved mechanically, as if I had been programmed to complete the tasks ahead.

As I stepped out of the elevator, guests were leisurely drifting toward the dining room. I heard the clatter of tableware and the faint strains of a violin.

Sabrina looked at me with a quizzical expression on her face as I crossed the lobby. Excusing herself from a group of ladies, she joined me as I walked toward the front entrance. "Wasn't that Brian Milburne I saw go upstairs a while ago?" she asked.

"It was," I said with a shrug of disinterest.

"I thought . . . I mean, I didn't see him come down. Is he still in your room?"

"I didn't know you kept such close tabs on your guests, Sabrina. I was unaware when I took a room here that I was forfeiting my privacy." I knew I sounded childish, but I was in no mood for her insinuations. She would know everything soon enough. I didn't have to be gracious about it.

Her black eyes shot daggers at me. "Walter always said you were a spiteful piece. You and Steven never treated him right. Jealous, he used to say, because your father loved him best. Walter was a man." Her lips quivered. "There's never been anyone like him."

I suddenly felt pity for her, remembering her husky laughter and happiness that day I came upon her and Walter in the woods. Maybe Sabrina was still searching for someone to take his place. "You loved Walter, didn't you?"

"Yes."

"Who do you think killed him?"

"I don't know," she said, and I believed her. "I used to think it was Elizabeth. She loved him, you know. Wanted him over Steven, but Walter wouldn't marry her. Elizabeth wanted to be a Banning enough to accept second best. I knew from the beginning Walter wasn't the marrying kind . . . but that was fine with me. Joe's a good provider and he's always let me have a long rein."

"He's a good man. You should appreciate your husband, Sabrina."

"Don't use that moralistic tone with me, Deanna Banning. You have no business acting so righteous. I think you and Steven stole that carnival money. Sidling up to the preacher the way you've been doing isn't going to help you a bit."

271

Any pity I felt for her at that moment was washed away by the anger that coursed through me. I turned my back and walked out the door.

Early evening strollers were enjoying the soft light of a rising moon. Stars flickered in the deepening sky. Gaslights mounted high on lampposts lent a glowing serenity to the park across the street.

For a moment, I was tempted to veer into those paths, lose myself in the protective shadows, drink in the tranquillity while I had the chance. But the impulse to delay was quickly dispelled by the fear that Steven would hear the story from someone else. Maybe I had been wrong not to tell him five years before. He had been emotionally stronger then, and perhaps better equipped to deal with our sordid parentage. But I hadn't had the courage then, and my protective instincts were still strong. Even now, if there was a way to protect him and his family, I would. But it was too late.

I walked quickly down the street, not paying much attention to my surroundings until I was in front of Bannings. I glanced in the windows of the closed store as I passed, and when I saw a light inside, I remembered that Millie and Steven would be working on the books after dinner. Maybe they were already there. Good, I thought. I'd prefer to talk to Steven without Elizabeth.

I knocked loudly on the front door, peering inside through the glass. In a moment Millie appeared, her frown easing when she saw me. She quickly unlocked the door. "I thought it was Steven forgetting his keys again."

"He's not here then," I said disappointed.

"Should be along shortly. I told him we had to get started early if we were going to finish tonight."

"Do you mind if I wait for him? It's important." I

didn't tell her that Steven wouldn't be in any shape to work on the books after he heard what I had to tell him.

I followed her along the dark aisles. The heavily laden counters and tables were indistinct forms stretching to the far walls of the store. As always, the familiar smells were cues to the past. I remembered how I had often waited inside the store for my father—no, not my father. None of his blood ran in my veins, and he had hated me for it.

"Would you like a cup of tea while you're waiting?" asked Millie as she led me into the business office. From the stacks piled high on the desk, I could see that she was already at work. Ledgers were open and invoices carefully arranged. An ink pen was drying where she must have put it down hastily when she heard my knock.

My stomach rumbled. I'd forgotten all about eating. "It is dinnertime, isn't it?"

"I was just about to go across the street and get something. As soon as the store closed, I started in on these ledgers, and I thought I could eat while Steven and I worked. Would you like me to bring you back something?"

"Yes, thank you. A sandwich would be fine."

She nodded and left.

I felt weak . . . from lack of food or nervous exhaustion, I didn't know which. Maybe Steven would come while she was gone and we could put the ordeal behind us. I couldn't even think what we would do next. How can preparations be made for a hurricane one knows will level everything in one's life?

I sat down at the desk and put my head in my hands. The pain of rejection was unbearable. I had lived with it so long it had become a part of me.

Attempting to shake off a new wave of self-pity I rose from the desk and brushed at my eyes. In my haste to leave the hotel room, I had forgotten my handkerchief. I pulled open a desk drawer, hoping that Millie might have kept a clean one in the desk.

A lovely silver box caught the lamp's light. It was familiar to me somehow. Yes, I remembered, it had once been filled with chocolates. Two layers. I had seen Walter showing it to Maude in our kitchen years ago, telling her that it was a gift. At first, I had thought it might be for me. He had laughed and said it was for his lady love.

"Put that back!"

I was so startled by the sound of Millie's voice behind me that I dropped the box.

"Oh, I'm so sorry," I said, stooping to reach the scattered contents. Letters and—my hand froze. "No," I whispered as I recognized the leather money bag. I slowly raised my gaze to Millie's marble face.

"You had to meddle, didn't you?" she said in a vicious tone.

"Millie!" My thoughts were like the sudden flight of birds. She must have read the comprehension flooding my eyes.

"Everything was going along fine until you came back," she snapped. "I've kept the store going all these years while Steven played with his flowers. If you hadn't stirred him up about selling the store, I wouldn't have had to try and cover the missing amounts."

I rose to my feet and pressed back against the desk, trying to process the new information that in my wildest dreams I would never have guessed at. "*You* killed Babcock," I said.

"I had to. I couldn't show the books to anyone until I figured out how to get some of the money back

274

into the accounts. Babcock came here looking for Steven, told me he was interested in the store as an investment. I sent him to the house and followed him there. While you were inside, I told him that I remembered Steven had said he was going fishing that afternoon. I offered to walk him to the creek and then tripped him so he fell in the woods. I grabbed his cane and—" She gave a dismissing wave of her hand.

"—bashed in his head," I finished as the horror hit me like a blow.

She shrugged her square shoulders. "All I needed was a little more time," she said innocently. "I took the money bag off the wagon seat and put it in my large hamper before I joined the others across the street at the café. When we came back to the store I secretly hid the hamper on one of the merchandise tables before we joined you and Steven in the office." She gave a satisfied snort. "Chief Whitney didn't think to make a search of Bannings."

"And then you left some of the money in my room, and followed me to the church."

"When the story got out about you being dismissed for stealing, I decided to make use of the information. The plan would have worked if you hadn't caught me in the act. Smart of you to scurry to the church with the money. I knew all along you were sweet on the preacher, but I didn't know he was fool enough to cover for you."

"How were you able to break in to Hunters Hall?" I asked.

"Walter gave me a key years ago," she said. "I know the servants' stairs by heart. It's how I used to get to his room."

It was at that moment that the truth dawned on me. "Did Walter give you this?"

For a moment her expression softened. "On Valentine's Day."

"You were lovers?"

Her eyes slid to the black horsehair sofa. The involuntary movement spoke volumes. *Walter had had his way with her in this very room.*

"Yes."

I felt sick to my stomach. My half-brother had taken his pleasure wherever he could get it, and poor homely Millie had taken his lust for love. "You killed him, didn't you, Millie?"

The softness in her eyes turned flat and hard. "Yes. The night he told me he preferred a redheaded tart across town to me. So I followed him. When he came out of the saloon and headed for the prostitute's crib, I stabbed him in the back with a knife from the store. He turned and looked into my eyes just before he died," she said with smug satisfaction. "Afterward I washed the knife and put it back in the display, just like before. Somebody bought it the next day."

Then her smile faded. "You really should have minded your own business, Deanna. Steven would never have caught on to the fact that the store profits were disappearing. It was all so easy. I'm wealthy now, you see. I even bought the organ for the church." She gave a satisfied chuckle. "Everyone thought it was Nina Milburne's gift. Wouldn't Brimstone society be surprised."

"But if you hadn't taken the money, Steven wouldn't have had to take out a note at the bank."

"I was going to put some money back but I didn't have time. Not with that Babcock fellow coming to look over the books and Steven wanting to sell the store. Anyway, all the profits of the store *should* be mine! I'm the one who's kept the doors open. Walter should have married me! Papa Banning told me a hundred times, 'Millie, you've got a good head on your shoulders. No foolishness like I have to put up with at home. A good, solid girl—that's the kind I like.' Papa Banning always said that Walter and I made a good team. But he had to go and ruin everything for some two-bit whore."

"But murder, Millie? Murder?"

"Righteous indignation shall find favor with the Lord," she quoted. "My faith makes me strong enough to do what I have to do." Her eyes narrowed. "And now I have to kill you."

Chapter Twenty-one

"You can't get away with three murders," I said as firmly as my racing pulse would permit. "And the embezzlement won't remain hidden forever, Millie. Either Steven will sell the store or the bank will take over."

She smiled in a cold, confident way. "I've fixed the books. Tonight I was going to show them to Steven. All I needed was time."

"And you were willing to do anything . . . even murder?"

"Of course. I'm not stupid, nor a coward when it comes to looking after myself. Nobody has ever cared a plug nickel about me."

"What about Harold? He loves you."

She snorted. "He wants a wife who has enough money to get him out of Brimstone. I bought him just the way I've had to buy everything. And he'll give me the alibi I need when they find you slumped over the desk with a knife in your back."

She reached into her brocade bag and drew out a long silvery blade. "I came prepared just in case Steven had found something wrong with the books and accused me of siphoning off profits into my own account. So you see, Deanna—"

I didn't wait for her to finish. With a lightning-speed thrust I threw the silver box at her and darted toward the door.

She was after me in seconds.

Pain flared in my side as her knife cut into my flesh. A crimson stain instantly dyed the folds of my summer dress.

In desperation, I grabbed the closest thing—Papa's antler coat rack—and flung it in her path. Millie cried out as she fell into it.

I clutched my bleeding side and fled like a wounded animal from the office toward the center staircase. If I could only make it to the front door—!

But she was out of the office and in pursuit.

Taking two steps at a time, I fled down the stairs. Before I reached the bottom my long skirts twisted around my legs and I fell. My breath was knocked out of me as I lay in a heap at the bottom.

I looked up.

Millie stood at the top of the dark stairs looking down at me, a satisfied expression on her face. She must have thought I was unconscious, or dead. The knife glistened in her hand. I didn't have a moment to lose.

I bolted to my feet.

She gave a cry of surprise.

Stumbling, I fled in a half-crouch behind the nearest counter. Dark as a rabbit warren, the small passage provided momentary concealment. I moved swiftly along the counter until it terminated at the far wall.

"It's no use, Deanna!" Millie called. Her voice was strangely gleeful, as if she was enjoying the hunt.

The door was still far out of my reach. I'd never make it. I was cornered in the women's section of the store. Half-crawling and running I dove under a nearby table and scrambled out the other side. It felt as if a hot poker burned in my side where the knife had slashed my flesh.

A stack of displayed merchandise fell over with a crash as I pushed my way through loaded tables. Any hope of concealing my whereabouts was dashed by the commotion I left in my wake.

I heard Millie's laughter. The store had been her home. She could have found her way around blindfolded. My clumsy flight was no more than a game for her. Only time was on my side. I had to evade her clutches long enough for Steven to arrive to work on the books. But time was a luxury I didn't have. The loss of blood was rapidly draining strength from my body.

I had to find a place to hide until help came. But where? Racks of clothes, like a maze, offered temporary concealment, but Millie's systematic search would soon prove successful.

I knocked over a display of women's shoes. My breath was coming in loud gasps. My own blood bathed my side. I pressed my hand over the wound, fighting a weakness that was seeping into my limbs.

I heard Millie methodically tracking me, shoving aside the merchandise I had frantically sent tumbling in my flight. I screamed when a fully dressed store dummy rose up in front of me, and struck out wildly, sending it tumbling. All the time blood was oozing through the fingers of the hand I held pressed against my side.

My cream colored summer dress denied me the obscurity I needed in the dusky, dimly lit store, but Millie's dark working dress blended into the enveloping shadows. *I had to find a hiding place!* I rolled under a round table and stuffed a fist into my mouth.

If only Millie passed the table by I might have a chance to remain undetected. I prayed she wouldn't see the movement of the fringed tablecloth that gave me some concealment.

I felt her skirts brush by the table and I thought my prayers were answered. Then she stopped. A waiting silence told me she was listening.

Please go on . . . please go on. This time my prayer wasn't answered.

She came back. I heard her touch the tablecloth. Then suddenly she jerked it up.

I scrambled out the other side. She gave a wild cry and lunged at me. The knife blade sliced across my arm.

I bolted behind the closest thing available, one of the tall free-standing mirrors. She would be after me in a split second. No place to run now. Trapped between the mirror and the wall, with strength born of desperation, I pushed on the huge mirror with all my weight.

It resisted all pressure. With one frantic gasp, I shoved all my weight against it. The mammoth piece of furniture budged, tilted—and then toppled over with a crash.

I heard Millie cry out above the shattering of glass and the splitting of the wooden stand.

Then silence.

I pressed back against the wall, waiting. If Millie had come at me that moment slashing a knife I doubted that I could have moved. My head was as light as a floating balloon and my arm and side were bathed in sticky blood, draining life from me. The moment extended into an eternity of breathless waiting.

Was it a trick? Was Millie waiting for me to step forward? I remembered that the mirrors stood in one corner of the store. I had boxed myself in. Was she smiling gleefully, knowing that the kill was imminent?

"Millie?" I whispered. Maybe I could reason with her. Keep her talking until Steven came. "Let's talk, Millie."

No answer.

My strength was running out. I had to do something before I fainted. Gingerly I moved around the fallen mirror, crunching pieces of slivered glass under my shoes. Then I hit something soft with my toe. My stomach turned over.

Millie wouldn't be coming after me. She was pinned under the mirror. No sound of breathing came from her crumpled body.

I don't remember how I made it to the front door. I only know that I had only a few more yards to go when the door swung open. Three men stared at me as if I were a bloody apparition stumbling forward with outstretched arms.

Daniel reached me first. "Darling, what—?"

Steven and David Kirkland gasped in horror. "She's hurt."

"Dear God," breathed Daniel.

I opened my mouth but a wave of weakness like a black fog invaded my body and I floated away like a speck on a gray horizon.

Chapter Twenty-two

The Brimstone hospital was a four-bed establishment served by a single nurse and old Doc Hardcastle, who had been a horse-and-buggy doctor as long as I could remember. I heard his raspy voice before my eyes fluttered open to the high gray ceiling.

"I'm telling you, she's not answering questions from you or anybody else," the doctor declared. "Good Lord, she's as weak as a kitten from loss of blood. I don't care if you've got a job to do or not, Chief. She's my patient, and she's not talking to anybody until I say so."

"Look, she's coming around now. I saw her blink her eyelids," said the policeman. "Just a question or two."

"No. Now get yourself out of here before I have to grab you by the seat of the pants and lift you out."

I heard Whitney growl.

"Don't you be threatening me, you overgrown bullfrog. The young lady has been through enough, and you'll not be adding to her discomfort. All your sputtering about obstructing justice is just so much hot air as far as I'm concerned."

Whitney said something about putting a guard at the door.

"You can't do that. This isn't any jail."

"I damn well can. She's not going to talk to anyone until she talks to me."

"You're barking up the wrong tree this time, Chief."

The voices faded away and I let myself fall back into a blessed state of unconsciousness. The next time I awoke, I was surprised to discover that the groans I had faintly heard while coming to were my own.

"It's all right, dear," said a soothing voice. "We had to put twenty stitches in that side and fifteen more in your arm. But you're going to be just fine." A round-faced nurse with salted black hair bent over my bed. Her smile was reassuring as her gentle hands smoothed back the hair from my face. "I know it hurts, but you're a lucky girl."

Lucky girl . . . lucky girl. The phrase repeated itself in my brain over and over again until the words turned into mocking laughter. I couldn't keep one thought in my head for more than several moments.

"It's the laudanum," said the nurse, observing my confused expression. "It eases the pain but puts everything at sixes and sevens. Don't fight it, honey. Just close your eyes and sleep. Everything will sort itself out in a day or two."

She was right. Little by little the pain receded and my strength returned. I was grateful for my improvement, but increasingly tortured by the memory of all that had happened.

"Steven . . . I have to talk to my brother," I murmured. I had wanted to be there when he heard the truth about our parents. How had he reacted to the sordid story? And Elizabeth? Had my brother's life blown up in his face with cruel devastation?

"Sorry, Miss Banning," the nurse said, shaking her head. "Chief Whitney has a guard outside your door. No one can get in to see you. There's been quite a ruckus about it. Reverend Norris has threatened to tear the door down several times."

"But I don't understand. Why is Chief Whitney guarding me? I'm not in any danger now. Millie's dead."

The nurse patted my hand but kept her jaws clamped shut. She fussed around my bed and avoided looking me in the eye. She left me staring at the ceiling with a pain in my heart that had nothing to do with my knife wound.

Why was Chief Whitney refusing to let me have visitors? I knew then that the nightmare was not over.

"Well, now, I think there's some color in your cheeks at last," said Dr. Hardcastle on his next visit. "It's about time you sat up, and in a day or two, we'll have you on your feet."

"I want to go home."

"You still need some care."

"Maude can take care of me."

He pushed his gold frame glasses back on his nose. "Well, now, I don't know if those arrangements would be satisfactory with Chief Whitney."

I swallowed. "I don't understand. Why would he object?"

He avoided my eyes just the way the nurse had. "There's still the matter of Millie Dillworthy's death to be straightened out. No one really knows what happened. And he doesn't want anyone talking to you until he hears your story."

Relief brought a weak smile to my lips. "Please ask him to come and see me. I'll be happy to tell him everything I know." I realized then that I was the only one who knew that Millie had killed Walter and that she had been stealing large amounts from the store for a long time. "I have some information that will clear up a lot of things.".

"Are you sure?"

"Certainly. I have nothing to hide. Might as well answer all his questions and then he'll let me go home." There was no doubt in my mind that Chief Whitney would accept the truth of my statements.

He came to see me later that afternoon. His familiar scowl was at odds with his solicitous greeting. "I'm glad to see you are feeling better, Miss Banning." But then he brought his words in line with his expression. "I was beginning to wonder if your invalid state was just another part of your scheme."

"What are you talking about," I said. "Surely, you don't think I find being confined to a hospital bed a pleasant experience? I want to go home. Dr. Hardcastle assures me that as soon as I answer your questions, he will dismiss me." That was not exactly true but I decided not to let the policeman put me on the defensive. "I hardly see the necessity for restricting visitors to my room, in any case. Surely you're not concerned about my welfare? There's no need, now that Millie's dead."

His eyes narrowed. "Tell me how you killed her."

"I . . . I pushed one of the large mirrors over on her. But of course you know that." I closed my eyes, remembering the shattering glass and the warm, still body pinned underneath.

"Why?"

My eyes flew open. "Why?" I answered with disbelief. "Because she was going to kill me. Didn't you find the knife with my blood on it?"

"Yes, it was still in her hand. As if she were trying to protect herself."

An arctic chill crept up the entire length of my body. "Protect herself? She was attacking *me*."

"Why?"

"Because I found out that she was the one who murdered Walter."

"And how did you discover that?" His voice was smooth, even, as if he expected that I was going to say all these things.

"She told me after I found the carnival money in her possession."

"So *you* found the money pouch?"

I nodded. "It was in a silver chest in the desk drawer. Didn't you find it in the business office? I threw it at her when she threatened me with her knife."

"Yes, we found the bag. It's the one that was stolen, all right. And you say that Millie hid it in the silver box?"

"Yes. I accidentally dropped it and the lid opened. Walter had given her the box as a gift. She admitted that they were lovers and that she killed him in a jealous rage."

I could tell from Whitney's steely eyes that he didn't believe a word I was saying.

"I'm telling you the truth."

He gave me a cold smile. "Let me get this straight. Millie stole the carnival money and when you found the bag, she admitted that she killed your brother. Anything else?"

"Yes, she said she'd been taking money from the store."

"But your brother says the books are accurate."

"She fixed them to hide the theft."

He gave his hat a twirl. "Funny thing. Millie

didn't have more than fifty dollars to her name when she died, aside from the pouch containing the carnival money—which someone could have left with her after murdering her. How do you account for that?"

His question was like a blow to the stomach. "But that's not possible. Millie told me she was the one who had bought the organ for the church—she said she had enough money to keep her and Harold in fine married style."

"Then where is it? Where's the money you claim she stole from the store?"

"I don't know."

"Of course, you don't—because Millie was innocent. She was trying to defend herself when she somehow found out that it was you who had hidden the money pouch in that silver box."

"No, that's not true."

"I have to compliment you on devising such an intricate and clever scheme, but I've been on to you for some time. You're not going anywhere, Miss Banning, but to jail. I'm going to see to it that you're charged with the murder of Mildred Dillworthy."

Chapter Twenty-three

The inquest into the death of Mildred Dillworthy was held in Judge Samuel Tucker's chambers, a large, impersonal room furnished with a scattering of hard-backed chairs placed in front of a worn desk. Cabinets filled with leather books lined the walls, and dust motes danced in the slats of sunlight that filtered through the high, arched windows.

My mouth was dry and my heartbeat rapid as I entered through a side door with Dr. Hardcastle on one side of me and Chief Whitney on the other. For nearly two weeks I had remained isolated in my hospital room. My physical condition had been improving but my anxiety had grown with each passing day.

The judge, a portly Theodore Roosevelt look-alike, was already seated at his desk. Seven or eight people occupied chairs near the front of the room. All heads swung in my direction as I entered the room.

Daniel and Steven! I think both men would have rushed to me immediately if a glower from the judge had not discouraged them from doing so. Nina Milburne sat behind them and branded me with her usual acidic stare; Brian refused to meet my eyes.

Elizabeth put a handkerchief to her nose and sniffed. David Kirkland solemnly nodded his gray head, and Harold Haines wore the forlorn expression of the bereaved. He absentmindedly pulled at his thin goatee and kept his head lowered.

Chief Whitney indicated a chair placed to the right of the judge's desk and I gratefully sat down. My legs were less than dependable after so many hours of confinement.

Doc Hardcastle squeezed my shoulder and whispered reassuringly in my ear. "I'll stop the proceedings the moment you feel you've had enough."

I smiled gratefully at the doctor and nodded. Chief Whitney remained standing behind me. His posture indicated he was prepared to intercept me if I attempted to flee the room. He needn't have worried. Even though my condition was much improved, my arm was still in a sling and many sleepless nights had sapped my energy. I doubted if I could have stumbled as far as the door without assistance.

Daniel searched my face anxiously. His forehead was furrowed, his mouth tense, and a taut muscle pulsed visibly in his cheek. I had heard his raised voice several times outside my hospital room door, and once I thought he was going to assault the deputy that Chief Whitney had stationed there.

"I'm her minister!" he had shouted. "You can't prevent me from seeing her."

"Chief's orders!" the guard had snapped. "I don't want to lock you up, preacher, but I will if you keep on threatening me."

He sat in a wooden chair near a window, his hair gleaming red in the muted light. I ached to brush back the wayward strands falling over his forehead. For a moment I felt strengthened by his love. The smile I gave him didn't seem to ease his mind. His back was rigid; he was ready to leap to his feet at the first provocation.

When I saw the way my brother, Steven, sat slumped in a chair, I knew that Nina Milburne's sordid tale had reached his ears. I was sorry I had not been able to comfort him when he'd finally learned the truth. My heart went out to him.

Judge Tucker shuffled papers on his desk, then turned to face me. I found to my surprise that I could meet his eyes unflinchingly. There was no longer anything to hide.

"Miss Deanna Banning?"

I nodded.

The judge's dark eyes scrutinized me. He fingered his black walrus mustache. "I have been going over all the testimony collected by Chief Whitney concerning the death of Mildred Dillworthy. The purpose of this inquiry is to determine whether or not the victim's death was, indeed, a case of self-defense as you have declared, or whether Officer Whitney's suspicions of murder warrant an indictment and trial. Do you understand?"

"Yes." My tongue was dry and thick. *I am innocent. I have nothing to fear.*

"All right, then. I would like to hear in your own words exactly what happened the night Miss Dillworthy was found dead and you were taken to the hospital with severe knife wounds."

I searched for a place to begin. Had Brian told anyone about his visit to my room? No, he wouldn't involve himself even if I were marched to the gallows. I felt a cool draft on my neck and I knew Chief Whitney was waiting, ready to prove my story false. The truth was my only defense. What had I to fear?

"Please begin, Miss Banning," ordered the judge.

"I went to the store to speak with my brother,

Steven," I said. "I knew that he would be working on the books with Millie that night." Words flowed easily as I verbalized the nightmare that had been relived over and over again in my mind: the discovery of the money bag, Millie's confession about her embezzlement as well as Babcock's and Walter's murders, the bloody chase through the store, and finally the desperate scene at the mirror ending in Millie's death.

When I had finished, Judge Tucker picked up several sheets of paper. "Chief Whitney has not been able to substantiate any of your claims. He found no evidence that Mildred Dillworthy was ever involved in a romantic entanglement with her employer, Walter Banning. The victim left no vast sums of money, nothing to indicate she was guilty of theft or embezzlement. And the Banning ledgers show no visible discrepancies. How do you account for these contradictions, Miss Banning?"

He waited. Everyone in the room seemed to hold their breath. Dismay and fear shot through me. For a moment, my mind went blank. I had told the truth, but the judge had silenced me with a few short sentences. What could I do or say now that the truth had been declared an inadequate defense? "Millie fixed the books," I countered evenly, steeling myself for combat. "She told me she had covered her tracks and was ready for Steven to see the ledgers."

"But how could Miss Dillworthy have hidden the disappearance of large amounts over the period of several years? She was only hired help, after all."

"Millie ran the store. My brother turned everything over to her. She had a free hand. She ordered the stock, paid the bills, and kept the books. When it looked as if the store would go under, she needed a plan. That's why she killed Mr. Babcock. She needed time to prepare a proper set of ledgers that would hide the theft."

"And what did she do with the money she supposedly embezzled from Bannings, and stole from the carnival?"

"She donated a new organ to her church, for one, and told me that she intended to live in high style when she got married."

"Your Honor, our investigation has failed to find any bank accounts in which the victim could have deposited the amount of money we're talking about," said Chief Whitney briskly.

The judge massaged his thick chin. "Nothing of value was found in Miss Dillworthy's modest dwelling?"

"No, Your Honor. No jewelry. No expensive paintings or fashionable clothes. Nothing to indicate that the woman was anything but what she seemed. A hard-working, conscientious lady struggling to make ends meet."

"I don't know what she did with the money," I said, desperate. "I only know that Millie had been stealing from Bannings for a long time. And she stole the carnival money."

Chief Whitney gave a derisive snort behind me. What more could I say? The policeman had already made it clear that there was no question in his mind that I had taken the money bag and had killed Millie to keep her silent. From the judge's granite expression, I knew he was thinking the same thing.

"I swear to you I'm telling the truth," I protested as firmly as my palpitating heart would allow.

Suddenly, Daniel was on his feet. "If Your Honor would allow me to speak."

"You are out of order, Reverend Norris!" the judge snapped.

"I know, Your Honor, and I apologize, but I believe I can clear up this matter of the money."

For a moment I thought the judge was going to dismiss his statement as a clever ruse or delaying tactic, but His Honor seemed to think better of it. "And why haven't you offered such information to Chief Whitney?"

"Because it wouldn't have done any good. A jackass can't see either side of the road with blinders on."

The remark brought a ripple of chuckles, a gasp from Nina Milburne, and a glare from the judge. "State your information, Reverend."

"As you know, I am pastor of the First Methodist Church. Harold Haines is one of the deacons. From time to time, Mr. Haines makes a contribution in the form of a sizable check." Daniel turned around and looked at the bereaved man. "Isn't that right, Harold?"

Millie's fiancé swallowed hard. At his nod, Daniel turned back to Judge Tucker. "Since those checks are drawn on a Denver bank, I decided to inquire about the state of Mr. Haines' account. Through a cooperative bank manager, I discovered that a pattern of large deposits has accompanied Harold's two-year engagement to Millie Dillworthy. Also, I learned that payment for an expensive organ was drawn at that account. Since Harold is also a bookkeeper, and was planning on marrying Millie Dillworthy, I suggest that His Honor may want to question Mr. Haines about this substantial savings account."

Judge Tucker sent a withering look at Chief Whitney. Then his gaze returned to Daniel. "Yes, I believe I should." He pointed at Harold Haines. "Please stand up, Mr. Haines."

I couldn't help but feel sorry for the older man as Judge Tucker leveled a volley of questions at him. Harold tried his best to deflect the questions but he was no match for the judge's vigorous, aggressive bombardment.

"I warn you, Mr. Haines, that lying will only bring a charge of conspiracy upon your head. Now, once more, did Mildred Dillworthy give you any money at any time during your courtship?"

Harold's lips trembled. His goatee quivered. He looked at the floor and nodded. The next minute he was blabbering like a child caught red-handed. Yes, Millie had indeed been giving him money to deposit, and yes, he knew it had come from the store. He had helped her find ways to cover the embezzlement. "But Millie felt she was entitlted to it. The Banning family had misused her for years. Especially Walter."

"Was she ever involved with Walter Banning romantically?"

He nodded again. "Millie told me they had been lovers. I don't think she ever forgave him for treating her so badly."

"And did she kill Walter Banning?" demanded the judge.

"I don't know."

"Do you think she was capable of killing someone?"

Harold sighed heavily. "I know Millie liked to get back at people who crossed her. That's why she took the carnival money. It was a way to get even with the whole community for the way they treated her."

"And did she admit to killing Mr. Babcock?"

Harold Haines' face wrinkled up in a pathetic sob. "Yes, she told me she had to! To protect our future." He covered his face with his purple veined hand. "I loved her," he croaked.

"Thank you, Mr. Haines. You may sit down." Judge Tucker looked down at the papers on his desk. There was only a painful silence as Harold choked back his sobs.

Chief Whitney shifted his weight behind my chair. "Your Honor, in light of this new evidence, I submit that Miss Deanna Banning's statement concerning the victim's death should be accepted as valid. It is clear from Harold Haines' testimony that Miss Banning acted in self-defense."

The judge nodded. His walrus mustache flared as he banged his gavel. "So be it. All charges dropped against Miss Banning. This court is adjourned."

Chapter Twenty-four

Daniel picked me up in his arms and carried me from the carriage into the house. "Getting in practice for carrying you over the threshold." He bent his head and kissed my cheek.

He's still ignorant of my parentage, I thought. I couldn't believe it! Had Nina and Brian kept their silence after all? They must have. Daniel wouldn't be talking of marriage so lightly if he knew my mother had been a stage actress, considered only slightly more respectable than a whore, and that my father had been shot by a vengeful husband. I was drained of energy. How was I going to face the man I loved when he knew the truth about me?

Daniel set me down gently on the sofa in the family parlor, which was suddenly full of people. I felt like the prodigal daughter returned, from the way everyone fussed over me.

Steven brought pillows for my back.

Maude clicked her teeth in utter dismay at my peaked face. "Lordy, lordy, what have they done to you, child?"

Elizabeth assumed her Lady-of-the-Manor role and bustled about making certain that David

Kirkland and Daniel would be staying for lunch. She swept out of the room with Steven and Maude in tow.

David Kirkland kissed my hand. I remembered his shocked look when I had stumbled forward to the front door of the store, covered with my own blood. "I've been very concerned about you. What a relief that the truth came out, thanks to Reverend Norris."

Daniel sat down beside me on the sofa.

"How did you know to look at Mr. Haines' bank account, Reverend Norris?" asked Mr. Kirkland.

"Well, I could claim divine inspiration," answered Daniel with a grin, "but I'm afraid the Good Lord depended upon my experience as a Pinkerton detective to provide the answer. I spent one summer tracking down thieves who were stealing from the Baltimore railroad."

"You did what?" I couldn't decide whether to be shocked or amused. I decided on the latter. This barefoot preacher never ceased to amaze me. "Is there anything you haven't done?" I asked, laughing.

He winked at me. "Well, I haven't been married. But I'm about to remedy that. Deanna—?"

My laughter died out. "I told you before—"

"I know what you told me. And remember what I said? When I found out why you rejected my proposal, I would ask you again." His fingers lightly tipped my chin and he looked into my eyes with a steady loving gaze. "Will you marry me, Miss Deanna Banning?"

I didn't understand. If he really knew the truth, he would know how impossible marrying me would be. "You can't know . . . ?"

He gently kissed my forehead. "I know everything."

"Nina Milburne told you?"

"No, Mr. Kirkland did. He came to see me after

300

having lunch with you that day in the hotel."

My eyes flew to the older man and then back to Daniel. "How could he know?"

David Kirkland gently took my hand. "I know this is going to be a shock . . . I can only hope it will be a pleasant one. I'm your natural father, Deanna."

He was trying to make a fool out of me. "I don't believe you. Why are you doing this to me?"

"It's true. I loved your mother." He looked up at my mother's portrait and his voice was tender as he said, "I loved her as deeply as a man can love any woman. We met by accident on my first trip to Colorado and fell hopelessly in love. When her husband returned from his trip back East, he wouldn't let her go, even when he knew she was carrying my child . . . or twins, as it turned out. There was nothing I could do. He kept her like a prisoner. In desperation, we made plans to be together. Your mother was bringing you and Steven to me the night that she was stranded in the snowstorm with Nina Milburne."

"But Nina told Brian that my father had been shot by a jealous husband."

"A lie."

I couldn't speak. My questioning eyes searched Daniel's. "Is he telling the truth?"

He smiled gently. "I know it's hard to believe but, remember, I told you that I had a feeling David wasn't what he seemed. I caught him watching the house several times, and he made too many excuses to be around you."

"After your mother died, I knew that I would only complicate your lives if I made my presence known, so I stayed away. But after I sold my business, I had to come back to Brimstone and see how my son and daughter were doing." He smiled wistfully at me. "I couldn't get enough of looking at you, Deanna. My lovely, beautiful daughter. I'm afraid I wasn't as discreet as I should have been."

"The way he looked at you made me suspect that he was more than casually interested in you," said Daniel. "I must confess I was guilty of thinking the worst. When he told me he was your father, I was filled with foolish relief. We went to the hotel to tell you but you weren't in your room. We were on our way to Hunters Hall when we met Steven in front of the store. You know the rest."

"Your mother was a wonderful person, Deanna. Just like you and Steven. You have every reason to be proud of her. Because she was so pretty, she was persuaded to try the stage, but she never liked it. That's why she agreed to marry Banning—in order to escape from that kind of life."

Mother. Her soft smile in the painting suddenly seemed just for me. Suddenly tears were streaming down my cheeks. "Does Steven know?"

Daniel brushed my moist cheeks with his hands. "Yes, darling. He knows. David has spent a lot of time with him while you were in the hospital. And Elizabeth is happy to accept David as Patty's and Nicky's grandfather. The children have already begun to love him."

"And I love *them*," David Kirkland said in a husky voice. "And I'm going to help Steven get started in his new business. Retirement doesn't agree with me. I've promised Elizabeth that she'll not want for any fineries, the best life has to offer."

I couldn't find my voice. So much joy. So much promise, after so many years of pain. Steven was going to live his dream after all.

"And what about you?" asked Daniel softly. "Are you going to marry me, Deanna?"

A shadow spread across my happiness. Daniel had accepted my parentage but what about others? "What if the church members don't approve?"

"I don't need anyone's permission to marry the woman I choose. And darling, you aren't marrying them—only me. They will accept us as we are, or we'll find our happiness someplace else."

Steven entered the parlor at that moment and handed me a beautiful bouquet of his special crimson roses. He leaned over and kissed my cheek.

Tears welled up in my eyes.

"Have you asked her, Reverend?"

Daniel nodded.

"And what did the lady say?" prodded Steven.

I slipped my hand into Daniel's. "The lady said yes."

"A wise decision," said my father.

For once in my life, I didn't argue.

*"MIND-BOGGLING . . . THE SUSPENSE IS UNBEARABLE . . .
DORIS MILES DISNEY WILL KEEP YOU
ON THE EDGE OF YOUR SEAT . . ."*

THE MYSTERIES OF DORIS MILES DISNEY

THE DAY MISS BESSIE LEWIS DISAPPEARED	(2080-5, $2.95/$4.50)
THE HOSPITALITY OF THE HOUSE	(2738-9, $3.50/$4.50)
THE LAST STRAW	(2286-7, $2.95/$3.95)
THE MAGIC GRANDFATHER	(2584-X, $2.95/$3.95)
MRS. MEEKER'S MONEY	(2212-3, $2.95/$3.95)
NO NEXT OF KIN	(2969-1, $3.50/$4.50)
ONLY COUPLES NEED APPLY	(2438-X, $2.95/$3.95)
SHADOW OF A MAN	(3077-0, $3.50/$4.50)
THAT WHICH IS CROOKED	(2848-2, $3.50/$4.50)
THREE'S A CROWD	(2079-1, $2.95/$3.95)
WHO RIDES A TIGER	(2799-0, $3.50/$4.50)

*Available wherever paperbacks are sold, or order direct from the
Publisher. Send cover price plus 50¢ per copy for mailing and
handling to Zebra Books, Dept. 4164, 475 Park Avenue South,
New York, N.Y. 10016. Residents of New York and Tennessee
must include sales tax. DO NOT SEND CASH. For a free Zebra/
Pinnacle catalog please write to the above address.*